PETER LAST

Out of the Shadows

SHADOW FOR HIRE

BWP
Fantasy

Bluewater Publications
Killen, AL 35645
BWpublications.com

Library of Congress Control Number: 2018962349
ISBN 9781949711028

Published in the United States by Bluewater Publications.
Printed in the United States of America.

This is a work of fiction. Names, characters, businesses, places, events and incidents are either the products of the author's imagination or used in a fictitious manner. Any resemblance to actual persons, living or dead, or actual events is purely coincidental.

Credits
Editor – Sheri Dee
Editor – Rachel Last
Cover Art – Christina Myrvold
Interior Design – Maria Yasaka Beck
Managing Editor – Angela Broyles

Acknowledgements

I would like to express my sincere gratitude to everyone who helped make this book a reality. I would specifically like to thank the following individuals who made this book possible through their constant help, suggestions, and snide comments.

• My wife, for continuing to support me in my endeavors, even when date night gets postponed so I can do 'book stuff'.

• My mom and dad, for raising me to be the man I am today. Also, for not taking me to a mental institution when I mentioned how my characters "told me they didn't want to do that."

• Rachel, an author in her own right, who still gives me advice when I need it and even co-authored a story with me.

• Paul, though not an author by any stretch of the imagination, for fixing the problems with my storylines when I couldn't make the continuity match up.

• Sheri, for continuing to be my biggest fan. Her editorial skills have helped bring my stories to life.

• My publisher, for the continued support and advice which goes far beyond what I would normally expect. Together we can make anything happen!

• All my fans who continue to read my work voraciously. I wouldn't want to write without you.

• Finally, and most importantly, God for giving me the ability and opportunity to do this. My writing is all for You.

PART 1

A Royal Game

Archery

The arrow overshot the target by a good two feet. Raven wasn't sure if this was better or worse than her previous arrow, which had fallen short, but at least it was different, and the only way to improve was to do something different. She nocked another arrow and let it fly, watching as it too overshot the target. With a huff of frustration, she fired the next arrow with little concentration, causing it to fall extremely short.

"Don't worry about it, Raven," Midas said from where he stood behind her. "This is just the practice round."

"I know!" she snapped. "But if I can't hit anything now, what are the chances I'll hit something next round when it counts?"

Her next arrow, purely by chance, hit the target. The next was low again, digging into the dirt a few feet short.

"Even when I manage to hit something, I can't follow it up with another good shot," Raven complained. "I'm as erratic as a rabbit who lost its hole."

"Don't beat yourself up, Raven," Leopold chimed in. "You're doing this because, out of the three of us, you're the best shot. If Midas or I were in your shoes, we'd be failing even more miserably."

"Is that supposed to make me feel better?" Raven retorted. "It might if I was competing against you two, but my opponents are people who have actually trained for this sort of thing."

"He's just saying we aren't going to fault you for not doing well," Midas said. "It's just a competition after all. Anyway, we aren't even in this for ourselves."

"That doesn't make me feel better," Raven said. "I can handle failing you, but Maria's a different story. She's done a lot for us, and I don't like the idea of letting her down."

"You won't be."

The three members of The Shadow turned to face the baroness, Lady Maria, their sponsor in these games. The event was put on every year by the king, and all the nobility were allowed to enter a team. This time, Maria had chosen them.

"Morning, Maria," Midas was the first to speak. "That's a nice dress. You decided to go low key. I like it."

He was referring to her attire, a simple yet elegant gown which stopped several inches shy of reaching the ground. There was no train, frills, fluffs, or other ornamentation, just the simple green of the dress to compliment her natural beauty. Such a comment would have been a recipe for punishment with most nobility, but Maria was of a more down-to-earth stock and forwent most honors and formality. Besides, everyone knew Midas had a crush on her, feelings which did not go unreciprocated.

"Thank you, Midas," Maria acknowledged the compliment. "Raven, don't worry about how the archery turns out. There's more to these games than shooting a few arrows. Besides, my team hasn't ever been victorious, so even if you lose it's not a big deal."

"I just don't understand why you didn't choose someone else to shoot for you," Raven said. She fired and missed the target again. "Wouldn't it have made sense to get someone who has actual experience with a bow?"

"I could have done that, but I didn't want to upset the balance," Maria explained. "You're a team, you three and Daniel, and I didn't want to force anyone else into the mix. To separate or overstuff a team just for the sake of winning a game is a terrible idea."

"Some people certainly don't believe that," Midas commented with a glance down the line of archers still practicing. "There are some teams here with a separate person for each event. Each of us is competing multiple times."

"That's because most of the nobles here are only interested in winning," Maria said. "I have something much better than winning in mind. You trust Daniel and Raven to choose and plan your jobs for you, right? Well, right now you're in my arena. Trust me when I say I know what I'm doing."

"One other thing before I leave." She handed armbands to the members of her team. They were simple in design, a piece of leather with ties to fasten them around either the upper or lower arm. "These arm bands depict my family crest and will identify you as members of my team. You are required to wear them during the competitions."

"Raven, you want me to put yours on?" Midas asked, stuffing his band into his pocket. Raven handed the crest to him and extended her left arm from her chest, allowing him room to work.

Leopold examined the picture on his arm band, Maria's family crest, she had said. It was round in shape, the edges of the circle embellished with loops and curls of silver. The focal point of the crest was an image of the mythical Pegasus, wings extended in a mighty flap as it soared through the sky. It seemed familiar to Leopold, as if he had seen it a long time ago. There were plenty of crests featuring mythical creatures, particularly flying beasts. He had also certainly seen plenty of these crests in Maria's castle. There was no identifying the actual source of his déjà vu.

A bell sounded, and the archers ceased firing. At another tone, they headed down to their targets to collect arrows.

Raven followed suit, and while Midas and Leopold stayed at her shooting post, Maria left to take her seat in the nobility's viewing bench. The guard she had brought with her was minimal, two armed servants, while those of the other barons were often a score or more. The skimpiness of her guard and competing team seemed to be the topic of interest at this event.

"Maria, where's the rest of your soldiers?" one of the barons taunted. "Your lands may be small and your subjects docile, but things are different out here."

"Ah, Baron Jasven, so nice to see you and your sixteen guardsmen," Maria responded as sweetly as possible. "To answer your question, I believe there are only two possibilities. Either one of my men is as good as eight of yours, or I don't constantly have people who are trying to kill me. I suppose that happens when you're nice to people."

"Making friends again, I see," the king said as Maria took her seat beside him. "You know, Maria, I may be on your side, but there's only so much I can do to protect you. It would be wise of you to not poke the hornets' nest."

"Baron Jasven is like a lion who has eaten his fill and is lying in the sun," Maria said. "He is quick to roar at others but slow to pull his full belly from his sunning rock."

"And yet, if he does find cause enough to rouse himself to action, he is just as deadly as any other lion," the king said. He raised a hand to readjust the thin, golden circlet on his greying hair. "I have lived this life many years more than you and have found politics to be an important but strangely fickle game. You would do well to at least try to learn to play it."

"This is true," Maria agreed. "A fact with which I have been wrestling."

"And what of the games?" the king asked. "Jasven has a point. You seem to have brought quite a small team this year. Your three young people do not look promising no matter how talented they might be."

"There are four of them, actually," Maria responded. "The fourth is older and more experienced, though he's a tactician so you won't see much of him."

"You could have at least put someone in archery who can shoot an arrow," the king said. "The girl down there looks like she's never picked up a bow in her life!"

"That's because she hasn't," Maria said calmly. "She's been practicing almost non-stop for the past month, but there's only so much you can learn in that short of a time."

"Seriously, Maria!" the king exclaimed. "If I didn't know better, I would think you were trying to mock the event. You could have just stayed home if you didn't want to win."

"I'm not tossing in the towel yet, uncle," Maria responded. "Archery is certainly not her strong suit, and I don't think she'll even place in the event, but there's a lot more to these games than bow and arrows. It is possible to lose a battle and still win the war."

"Yes, but one doesn't usually plan on losing a battle," the king said.

"Unless it's a strategic retreat," Maria shot back. "Just sit back and watch the whole event. I think you'll understand my choice by the end of the tournament."

Swordplay

The archery had not gone well, though it had turned out as expected. Admittedly, Raven had improved since she had begun training with the bow a month ago. Her showing during the competition even demonstrated improvement over her practice round, but it was still woefully behind many of the other archers. She was eliminated after the first set of shots.

Maria met them after the round, trying to raise their spirits with her "lose a battle and win the war" speech. Raven didn't take it to heart, but it had a positive effect on Leopold and

Midas. They didn't blame Raven for not being good at archery, but they would still have to make up for the loss. Luckily, the competition had just begun and there was plenty of time to recover the lost ground.

"The next event is sword fighting," Maria informed them as she led them across the castle grounds. "It will be held in two hours' time."

Though the games were, as a whole, located all across the royal city of Kraljevi, the initial ones were all situated on the grounds of the king's castle. Only on the second of the two days did the events venture out into the city and surrounding countryside.

"Sword fighting means it's my turn," Midas said. "Call me cocky, but I've got a good feeling about this."

"That's just because you've never met an opponent you couldn't beat in fair combat," Leopold said. "Let's hope that holds true today. I know I signed up as your second, but I don't want to actually have to do anything!"

"Plus, we need a solid performance here to make up for my failure," Raven put in.

"Not your failure," Midas said forcefully. "*Our* failure. If one of us fails, all of us fail. We're all separate, but we're all parts of the same team. None of us has ever been able to survive on our own, and we're not about to change tactics now. We all succeed or we all fail. It's that simple."

"That's easy for you to say when you haven't let everyone down," Raven said.

"You think you let us down by doing your best at something you're not very good at?" Maria asked, turning about. "You will never let me nor either of your friends here down as long as you do the very best you can. Let's get one thing straight: I chose this team for a reason. You may not understand it, but I promise you I know what I'm doing. Have some faith."

"Bemoaning the past won't help us now," Leopold said. "We can still pull this out, but only if we keep looking forward."

"Fine," Raven said unconvincingly. She would try to put this in the past, but losing never came easy for her.

"I never expected this to be easy for you," Maria said. "The games are not like real life. They will put you out of your element, even in events at which you normally excel, but I expect you to adapt and overcome. I expect you to give your best effort, and if you do that, you will make an impression."

"A good one, I hope," Midas said. They entered the sword fighting arena where the ring was still being constructed. Four posts had been driven into the ground as the corners of the combat area, and thick cords were being stretched around the perimeter. Other than the workers carrying out the assembly, the area was deserted.

"This is what you'll be fighting in," Maria said. "It is well known by most soldiers and guardsmen as it is commonly found in castles. Though you've visited mine often enough, I don't take you for people who frequent castles, and I wanted Midas to become familiar with the layout before the competition began."

"Good thinking, Maria," Midas said as he approached the ring curiously. "I've seen these things set up before but never had the occasion to use one. I always thought anyone who fought in such a small square was pretty stupid. After all, you're rarely confined to such a small area in real battle. On the other hand, this ring seems pretty large compared to those I've seen in the past."

"It is," Maria agreed. "Besides sword play, it will also be used during the total war event where larger groups of combatants will fight each other. It has been expanded to make room for the larger numbers of people."

"After the sword fighting competition is the wildcard," Midas said. "Have you found out what it's going to be yet?"

"I have," Maria replied with a grimace. "I was hoping it would be something in your wheelhouse, but today's activities will be concluded with juggling." She pantomimed the motion.

"But none of us know how to juggle," Raven said. Her voice was even, but Leopold could tell she was irritated. Ever the strategist and planner, not knowing what one of the events was going to be had rankled her nerves. Finding out none of them would be effective competitors couldn't be easy for her.

"The logical decision is me, of course," Leopold said quickly. "It shouldn't be Midas since he'll be tired from fighting, and you've already competed today, Raven. It's only fair that I do something to carry my own weight around here."

"You don't know anything about juggling," Raven said.

"Neither do either of you," Leopold said. With a wink, he added, "Besides, I think it's my turn to mess something up today."

"If you're sure," Raven said uncertainly.

"I insist," Leopold said. "This way Midas can focus on fighting, and you can study his opponents and give him some strategy tips. All I have to do is figure out how to keep eight stupid balls in the air at one time!"

"This seems like as good a plan as any," Maria said. "But, Leopold, don't wander too far. You're Midas's second and need to be on hand in case anything happens."

"Okay, now if everyone knows what they're going to be doing, I'm going to need a rundown on the competition," Midas said. "It's one-on-one sword play so I'm assuming a bracket system of some sort."

"Well, Midas has Maria to help him," Raven said as she watched them stroll around the sword fighting ring, the baroness talking all the while and occasionally pointing to things. "Do you want me to help you with your juggling? Otherwise I'll have nothing to do for a while."

"That sounds great," Leopold answered. Any excuse to spend time with Raven was good for him, though he would never admit as much. Instead he said, "I can use all the help I can get! Hopefully juggling isn't as hard as it looks, but somehow I doubt it."

Midas was fast, but his opponent was faster. He took the brunt of the force on his shield, stopping the sword cold and jarring Midas's arms and shoulders painfully. A fraction of a second later, he struck back at Midas, extending his left arm in a lightning fast, shield-fisted punch. The middle of the round metal implement smashed into Midas's chest and threw him backwards while the edge caught his jaw, causing lightning to explode across his vision. He staggered backwards, trying to maintain his balance even as his legs turned to jelly. His opponent waited for a few long seconds to laugh, and the gesture of derision saved the round. Before he had a chance to charge Midas, the bell sounded, signaling that the match was two-thirds completed. A single round to go.

Midas staggered toward his corner, using his sword as a cane to keep him on his feet. He made it exactly six steps before he collapsed to the dirt, and Maria's men rushed out to help him to his stool. Leopold took one look into his brother's eyes as he was helped along, his feet trailing uselessly behind him, and saw something he had never seen before: a glazed, incoherently vacant stare. The blow Midas had taken had shaken him to his core. Without thinking, his gestures automatic, Leopold undid the clasp of his cloak and allowed it to fall in a pile behind him.

"What are you doing?" Raven asked. She was so shocked at his actions she hadn't had time yet to be concerned.

"Midas isn't going to be back up for the final round," Leopold answered. "Which means I have to take his place. That's what a second does in a sword fight."

"You can't go out there, not against that giant!" Raven said. The concern had finally caught up with her, and her words bordered on frantic. She gestured to where Maria's men were trying to bring Midas around and added, "They'll get him up and he'll fight until the final bell. You won't have to."

"Midas has fought through every prior round of this competition and two bells of this one," Leopold said. "He deserves a rest even if it weren't for the beating he just took."

"He'll find a way to win," Raven argued. "He plowed through every other opponent with no problems. He's had fewer than a dozen points against him all told. He's good. He'll make it work somehow."

Leopold stopped and turned to face Raven.

"Raven, listen to me," he said. "Everyone needs help sometimes, even my big, bad brother. Look at him. He isn't getting back up for a while, which means it's my turn to help him. Trust me; I can do this."

Leopold gave a smile meant to reassure her and started walking toward the fighting ring. The referee was back in the center, looking to both combatants. The final battle was about to begin.

"Don't go," Raven pleaded. "He'll tear you apart."

"This is what a second does," Leopold said. "I knew what I was getting into when I signed up for it. Have a little faith in me, alright?"

"Faith?" Raven asked as he ducked through the ropes and into the ring.

Leopold turned to face her and took her hands in his.

"I promise you I will walk out of this ring on my own two feet," he said, holding her gaze for a brief moment before releasing her hands and walking out to the middle of the ring where the referee and other combatant waited.

"Will you be taking over as second?" the referee asked.

"What he means to ask is if I busted your friend in the face so hard he won't be coming back out to let me finish kicking his butt," the opponent taunted.

"Yes, I will be taking over as second," Leopold answered the referee.

"Are you ready to begin the round?" the referee asked, eyeing Leopold's knife and short sword still in their sheaths.

"I'm ready whenever he is," Leopold said with a nod toward his opponent.

"If you are both ready, the round begins now!" the referee called and backed away quickly.

"You may want to draw your weapons, little boy!" Leopold's opponent taunted and clanged his sword loudly against his shield.

"In response to your previous taunt, my brother could tear you apart with his bare hands if you hadn't gotten in a lucky hit," Leopold said. His arms still hung at his sides, motionless. "As it stands, I will have to finish the job for him."

"Finish the job?" the opponent asked in a mocking tone. "Have you forgotten that I'm leading?"

Almost before he finished speaking, he swung his sword in an overhanded power stroke at Leopold's neck, giving a guttural roar as he did. Leopold retreated a single step and tilted his head up and back, allowing the blade to sing past him harmlessly. He watched silently as his opponent was spun sideways by the momentum of his own sword, waiting until he had turned to face Leopold again before speaking.

"You lead by a single point," Leopold said. "A cheap blow to the chest, but a point nonetheless. A single point can easily be made back."

"Not if you never even take out your weapons!" the opponent yelled. He thrust his weapon forward twice in quick succession, but Leopold easily dodged both attacks.

"When we leave this ring at the end of the round, I will be leading by at least half a dozen points," Leopold said calmly, almost as if he was having a quiet conversation over lunch. "And do you know what the funny part about it is?"

"What?" the opponent growled.

"There's not a thing you can do about it," Leopold answered.

"What if I just kill you and gut your carcass!" the opponent shouted, faking a right-handed strike but switching to an over and left-handed blow at the last moment. Leopold dropped forward into a fighter's stance and, faster than the eye could see, drew his knife and deflected the sword's blade away. As his opponent continued forward from the momentum, he leaned in, slashing across his breastplate from right shoulder to left hip. The sound of metal on metal shrieked across the crowd, making the scoring of the point obvious to all. The opponent righted himself quickly and turned to face Leopold who was now standing nonchalantly behind him.

"Now we're tied," Leopold said simply.

His opponent was furious. The passive taunting coupled with his inability to hit Leopold, and now this? What was the world coming to if he couldn't best a small boy at sword fighting? He was just bumbling around because he'd fallen for the oldest trick in the book. He'd let this little twerp, this upstart, get inside his head and had become sloppy as a result. Enough was enough. He took a moment to center himself, then went on the offensive once again. The combination double strike attack he used was tricky enough and fast enough to catch anyone off guard. Anyone but Leopold. The boy deflected the first strike with his knife while drawing his short sword with his left hand. The second strike he trapped between his two blades, instantly regretting the action as he felt his whole body jolt with the impact. He couldn't let on, though, lest the whole persona he had been building fall apart.

His opponent was silent now. His lack of taunting seemed to improve his form, and the next attack was a sneaky one. The opponent's sword swung upward from the ground, the tip just near enough to hit Leopold's breastplate. It was a cheap move, one which wouldn't cause damage in a real battle but which would net a single point in this competition. In theory, most swordsmen wouldn't see the attack as a viable threat and fail to block it, giving an easy point to the person who struck. The strategy might have caught Leopold off guard if he hadn't already given thought to using it. As it was, he played the loopholes enough to anticipate how to perform the attack as well as how to guard against it. Using crossed blades once again, he shoved the attacking sword left just enough to clear his shoulder. Spinning inward, he delivered a double-bladed strike to his opponent, etching two scratches in his breastplate. It wasn't a two-point strike as he would have liked but instead a point and a half. It was good enough to put him in the lead.

Leopold didn't wait for his opponent to recover but struck again at the chest, hoping for an easy score. His blades met a shield before they could reach their target, and he had to spin sideways and use his short sword to deflect a blow coming at him. He tried to back up only to feel the ropes which made up the ring press into his back. He had nowhere to run, nowhere to dance away this time. Swords and shield flashed, accompanied by the raucous clanging of metal on metal as each combatant tried to gain an advantage over the other. Leopold was buffeted by the shield twice and each time barely escaped from the accompanying sword strike. Dodging was incredibly difficult in these close quarters, a type of fighting he was not used to. Normally he would slide a knife between the enemy's ribs and be done with it, but when an opponent couldn't be killed and just kept coming…

Leopold moved in even closer, ignoring his opponent's attempts to rebuff him with the shield. Slashing with his knife forced the rival to back away and bought enough room for Leopold to circle away from the edge of the ring. He was almost away when the foe, seeing his quarry escaping from the trap, swung with his shield. Leopold tried to block the blow, but his weapons were crushed up against his chest as the shield knocked him backwards. The world spun as he hit the ground and rolled. Somehow he saw his adversary dashing forward swinging his sword, and he was barely able to deflect the blow as he continued to tumble.

Leopold forced himself to his knees as he slid, jumping to his feet when he finally came to a stop. The opponent was fifteen feet away, his back no more than three feet from a corner post of the ring. The positioning was finally correct. It was time to finish this match. Leopold rushed forward, his soundless charge eerie when compared to the extremely loud attacks of his opponent. He raised both weapons, baiting the enemy into guarding himself, then went to his knees when he was only a yard out. He slid past the other combatant. A slash over his shoulder with his short sword was rewarded with a ringing as it contacted back armor. Another point.

By this time, Leopold had finally found his stride. The key, he determined, was to fight like he was up against a whole squad, but instead of moving from person to person, stay focused on the single opponent. He jumped to his feet out of the slide, scaled the corner post of the ring in two steps, and launched himself backwards over the head of his opponent who was not prepared for the sudden display of acrobatics. Leopold landed immediately before him, slashing with both weapons across his breastplate. A point and a half.

But Leopold was far from done. Tucking his body in as close to his opponent as possible, he trapped the shield with his left arm, preventing escape, and beat away at the breastplate in front of him with his knife. A dozen points later, he released the shield and shoved his opponent away, kicking him backwards into the post. The opponent gathered himself and rushed forward for one last attempt at redemption. Leopold ducked and hit him in the legs, toppling him forwards like a felled tree. The boy rolled sideways, avoiding the girth of the man, climbed to his feet, and headed back toward the corner where Midas was now fully cognizant and coordinated. Leopold let the tip of his sword drag along the back plate of his opponent's armor as he passed, just before the bell rang indicating the end of the match.

Leopold sheathed his weapons, then looked up to see his brother, cheering as loudly as anyone else. The older brother had carried them all the way to the final match and Leopold had finished the job. This was teamwork at its best. Raven stood beside the large boy, cheering her heart out as well. She cupped her hands around her mouth, trying to make her words heard, but they were drowned out in the cacophony of victorious celebrations of the spectators. Leopold smiled and gave a partial wave. It was sharing moments like this, winning sword play when they had expected to lose every event, which drew them closer together. This was what made them a family.

Leopold stopped to give an exaggerated wave and bow to the crowd. When he stood back up, he looked to his family again, but the exaltation from moments before was now replaced with horror as they stared and pointed towards him. Midas made a gesture, one Leopold had never seen before, and yet somehow he knew exactly what it meant. Jerking his knife out of its sheath with his right hand, he passed it over his left shoulder just in time to be crushed beneath the force of a blow descending towards his neck. Rotating the blade to point at the sky and protect his neck, he spun his head around to see his opponent glaring two holes through him, furious that his attempted assassination had failed. Already, two royal guards pulled him away from Leopold, forcing him to drop his weapon and binding his hands behind his back.

Leopold returned his knife to its sheath and, as calmly as possible, headed back toward his friends. Had he just been a hot-headed combatant or had it been a premeditated attempt on Leopold's life? Being in The Shadow had taught him to be paranoid, but this was a gathering of royalty. Many of those present would no doubt love to see him dead had they known who he was, but they couldn't, could they? At least some of them had probably contracted The Shadow in the past, but the only face they would have seen would have been Daniel's, hence the reason he wasn't present. There was no way anyone would recognize Leopold.

No one, except for Baron Jasven, the one who had tried to start a war with Maria over the horse. The realization was instantaneous and so groundbreaking, it caused Leopold to pause. He and Raven had negotiated the contract opposite Jasven, and a few days later, Leopold had threatened the baron. He looked up to the stands and almost instantly spotted the baron watching him with a glower. There was no proving if Jasven had actually hired the sword fighter to kill him, but there was no doubt in Leopold's mind that he recognized the young upstarts who had foiled his plans at war.

"Let's get you out of here," Midas said as he helped Leopold through the ropes of the ring. Even with his weapon sheathed, the boy was large enough and imposing enough to easily forge a path through the crowd which had quickly developed. Raven brought up the rear, her hand tightly gripping the handle of the knife on her belt. She scanned the crowd for any signs of danger, but with this many people in the crush, it was hard to see anything.

It took them several minutes to get away from the sword fighting ring, and when they did, things were far from over. The next logical step was to head back to where Maria's tents were pitched on the south side of the castle grounds, but before Midas could get his bearings, a group of guards came out of nowhere and surrounded them. The Shadow pulled their weapons from their scabbards, determined not to go down without a fight, but the commander of the soldiers stepped forward with sword sheathed and empty hands extended.

"We're not here to hurt you," he said, taking off his helmet. "I am Captain Payne. The king sent me and my men to escort you to the castle for your own safety."

"What of our sponsor, the Lady Maria?" Raven asked.

"She'll meet you there," Captain Payne answered. "We should move now. The king does not like to be kept waiting in matters such as these."

"Sounds good, Captain," Midas spoke. "We're willing to go with you. I'm going to trust you, but if you have any thoughts of funny business, just remember I've still got my sword. I promise I'm a lot better against groups than one-on-one."

"A bit paranoid, are we?" Captain Payne asked, bemused by Midas's blustering.

"Some would say so, but at least I'm still alive," Midas said.

"As intimidating as you are, the one I'm really afraid of is your young companion," Captain Payne said. The guards formed up around the Captain and his three charges, and together the group made their way toward the castle.

"You're intimidated by my little brother, Captain?" Midas asked with a sidelong glance at the younger boy. "You should be. Sometimes he scares even me."

Juggling

"After what happened, you still want to participate in the juggling competition?"

To say the king was irate would have been an understatement. He had been pacing the length of Maria's assigned living chamber when Captain Payne had arrived with his charges and hadn't stopped since. In contrast, Maria was quite composed, rising to greet her team when they entered but remaining seated since then.

"I don't just want to, I need to," Leopold said, standing his ground before the king who suddenly stopped his pacing to loom over the boy.

"Why do you *need* to?" the king exploded.

"First place in the sword fight didn't make up for our flop in the archery competition," Leopold said calmly. "If we don't even show up for juggling, we might as well forfeit the whole tournament."

"You're worried about the competition?" the king asked incredulously. "What about your life?"

"I seriously doubt my life is in danger, your majesty," Leopold said. The king dismissed him with a wave of his hand, but the boy continued, "The man from earlier was nothing more than a hot-headed combatant. I don't think I'm in danger of a jester pegging me to death with his juggling balls!"

"He was not just a hot-headed combatant!" the king bellowed.

"Shouting won't do anything to strengthen your argument, uncle," Maria finally spoke. "I have put my full trust in these three in the past, and it has always paid off. Leopold knows

17

better than to take foolish chances. If he thinks it's safe enough to attend the juggling, I am inclined to agree with him."

"What about a pass?" the king asked. His tone had changed from anger to desperation at the realization everyone in the room disagreed with him. "Your team will be exempt from the juggling without penalty."

"That wouldn't be fair, your majesty," Leopold said. Again the king waved him off, but he persisted. "We will play by the same rules as everyone else. To do otherwise would be to allow you to show favoritism."

"And if someone makes an attempt on your life?" the king asked. "What then?"

"Pardon my asking, but why do you care so much?" Leopold asked brazenly. "You've never met me before and from what little I know about kings, it seems like you should have more important things to worry about than the safety of a single competitor."

"For twenty-three years these games have been held," the king said. "In that time, never once has a guest under the protection of the crown been harmed. You will not be the first casualty, not on my watch."

"With all due respect, your majesty," Leopold began, "I stopped the last man who tried to kill me without even looking at him. That was after I utterly humiliated him in the sword fighting ring. Do you still think I'm in danger of a few assassins, if someone really does want me dead?"

"Trust him, uncle," Maria put in. "Leopold can protect himself."

"So be it," the king said in a resigned tone. "I hope you know what you're doing, boy, because if you go down this road, the best I can do is have Captain Payne assign you a guard detail."

"Thank you, your highness, but I'd appreciate it if they would keep their distance," Leopold said. The king grimaced noticeably. "I don't want anyone who makes an attempt on my life to know there are other people watching over me. The less they know, the cockier they'll be and the more likely it is that they'll overplay their hand."

"So be it," the king said. "Captain Payne, see to it." He swept out of the room, Captain Payne close behind. The door clicked shut behind them, and no one said anything for several seconds. Then, Maria started laughing.

"What's so funny?" Raven asked.

"I don't think the king likes me too much," Leopold commented. "As many times as he grimaced at me and waved me off, I think he'd rather I weren't here at all."

"I agree," Midas said. "I got the distinct impression the only reason he wasn't saying anything outright was because Maria was present."

"You're right," Maria said and wiped her eyes. "He hates terms of office as much as I do. Every time you said 'your majesty' or 'your highness,' he died a little inside, I think. He would have warned you off immediately if I weren't here."

"Well, I wish he would have," Leopold said crossly. "It could have saved a whole lot of trouble."

"Enough," Raven said. "That doesn't matter right now. We need to decide what to do about the juggling."

"I wish Daniel were here," Midas said. "He'd have an idea if nothing else."

Moments later there was a knock at the door, and Midas went to answer it.

"Speak of the devil," he said and opened the door wide to allow Daniel into the room.

"I can tell you're here to discuss strategy," Maria said as she rose from her chair. "Did you see what happened this morning at the swordplay competition?"

"Indeed," Daniel answered. "I'd like to speak to my associates about what comes next."

"I'll leave you to it," Maria said, motioning for her guards to follow and heading to the door. "I have other things to attend to."

"Excellent, we'll see you at the competition," Daniel said. He shut the door behind Maria's guards and turned the lock. "So, what have we gotten ourselves into this time?"

"Baron Jasven is sore about us shirking his job," Leopold answered.

"So what?" Daniel asked. "I'm the one who always meets with the clients, and I've been staying out of sight."

"Jasven was the one who hired us to kill his own horse in Maria's castle," Leopold explained. "If you'll recall, Raven and I were the ones who met with him. My guess is he saw we were here and wants to kill us."

"If that's the case, why doesn't he just tell the king?" Midas asked. "He'd take care of us no problem, and the baron would be free of everything."

"Simple," Raven replied. "If he rats us out, we can accuse him of hiring us to start a war. It wouldn't end well for any of us."

"Then we're safe from his accusation, but not from his men," Daniel said. "The combatant who attacked Leopold wasn't sponsored by Jasven, but he does belong to the team of one of his close allies."

"Great," Leopold said. "I definitely didn't want to worry the king, but it turns out we actually *do* have people after our heads. What's the play?"

"You go to the juggling competition," Daniel answered. "The rest of us will keep an eye on you and try to catch any more assassins before they can do anything. Don't take prisoners; kill on sight."

"Unnecessary killing doesn't sit well with me," Midas said hotly. "Besides, if we capture anyone who comes, their testimony could incriminate Baron Jasven."

"A valid point, but that is exactly why we can't allow them to be caught," Daniel pointed out. "The moment Jasven is accused of attempted murder, he has no reason to keep our identities a secret. Whether you like them or not, our only two options are to keep him out of this or to kill him before he can talk."

"Understood," Raven agreed. "I don't like it any more than you do, Midas, but Daniel's right. The king already has men tasked with watching over Leo, but they'll be looking to capture if possible. You stay with Leo and keep him safe. Daniel and I will hide among the crowd and take out the assassins if necessary."

"And what do I do?" Leopold asked.

"You need to practice your juggling," Raven said. "You've got a lot to learn and only a few hours to learn it in."

"So, do you have any idea what you're going to do?" Midas asked Leopold. "For your act, I mean."

"I was thinking about juggling," Leopold said. "It's something I've always been good at."

"Okay wise guy, don't tell me," Midas said. He led the way toward the juggling stage, eyes on the move, searching for danger. Behind them but out of sight, Raven and Daniel blended into the already forming crowd. Midas wore a cloak with a hood while Leopold had on a large, floppy hat to hide his features.

"Fine," Leopold said, deciding to humor his brother. "I figured I'd juggle a chicken. It might earn me some bonus points."

"A chicken?" Midas asked. "Why don't you throw in a few eggs and call it a day?"

"Great minds think alike," Leopold said. "I figure if I can pull off a chicken and three eggs, I'll be a crowd favorite!"

Midas couldn't tell if Leopold was being serious or not. If his younger brother wasn't serious, his comment wasn't one to be dignified with a response. If it was serious, well, Midas didn't want to think about that.

"I think the competitors are gathering behind the stage," he said instead, ignoring the whole chicken business. "Do you think they'll let me back there with you?"

"We can just say you're my assistant," Leopold suggested. "As a matter of fact, I'll need someone to chase down the chicken if I drop it."

"You're not actually going! to juggle a chicken, are you?" Midas asked, turning to look at his brother for the first time since leaving the castle.

"Well, it'd be pretty boring if I just did three eggs!"

The jugglers were indeed around the rear of the stage in an area blocked off for them by two dozen guards. Whether they had been briefed on the situation previously or just assumed Midas was a competitor was unclear, but he had no trouble entering with Leopold. As soon as they passed the guards, the press of the crowd disappeared, and they were able to breathe easier.

"You do your thing and I'll keep my eyes open for danger," Midas said.

"Do my thing?" Leopold asked. "What exactly is it that you think I'm going to do?"

"I don't know, practice I guess," Midas answered.

"Practice. That's cute," Leopold said. "Look around. Do you see anyone else practicing?"

"No, I guess not," his brother admitted.

"That's because jugglers don't practice while waiting for an event," Leopold said. It seemed that though he hadn't been juggling for more than a few hours, he already felt akin to this crowd. "The practice I've managed to tuck under my belt will have to be enough."

"It doesn't seem like it would be a good idea to start cold," Midas commented.

"That's why you warm up before going on," Leopold said, somewhat condescendingly. "Practicing while waiting is frowned upon, but you can warm up when you're the next one on. See that man over there? You can tell he's next because he's juggling."

"That's a lot of mighty specific talk for someone who doesn't know anything about juggling!" Midas said with a smile. "If I didn't know better, I'd think you were actually well informed on the subject!"

"Of course not, Midas," Leopold laughed. "I just keep my eyes open and learn as I go. But if you didn't know me I could have passed for a juggler, right? Especially one so good he sees it as an actual vocation instead of just a brainless pastime?"

"You nailed it," Midas agreed, sincerity in his voice.

"Good," Leopold said. "Appearance is half the battle. If I look and act like I know what I'm doing, the judges will receive my performance much better than otherwise."

"You do realize the other half of the battle is actually providing a performance worthy of a good score, right?" Midas asked. "You can't fake your way through juggling and expect to do well."

"I'm not an idiot," Leopold shot back. "I know a little bit about juggling, but if I combine what I've learned with a little panache, who knows."

"And I suppose it doesn't matter how well you do in this event," Midas said. "The main thing is we aren't cowering after the attack in the sword ring."

"We may not be cowering, but they don't seem to have been put off by our bravado," Leopold commented. He motioned with his head, "Look in the crowd over there."

Midas turned in the direction Leopold had indicated, scanning the hundreds of people in the crowd. Sure enough, a group of men stood in plain sight, scanning the jugglers, clearly looking for someone. They didn't stick out like a sore thumb per se, but to Midas it was clear as day.

"Take this bag," Leopold said, and Midas felt the mouth of a sack being thrust into his hand.

"Why? Do you need to use the bathroom?" Midas asked, but when he turned to his brother, the younger boy was gone. "I hate it when he does that!"

Midas quickly scanned the crowd for his brother but didn't expect to see anything. When Leopold wanted to stay hidden, it was nearly impossible to find him. Curious, Midas opened the bag in his hand and peered inside. It contained what appeared to be juggling paraphernalia: balls, batons, even handkerchiefs. A small basket of eggs was visible on top as well as a live chicken. It squawked angrily at Midas who snapped the mouth of the bag shut.

Was his brother mental? Midas had thought he was only joking about the chicken, but here it was in the bag of tricks. Leo had done strange things in the past, but this had to take the cake! Carefully, Midas eased the mouth of the bag open again for a second look. The chicken didn't squawk this time, but it eyed him angrily.

"You, from Lady Maria's team."

Midas looked up from the sack and pointed to himself, mouthing a question.

"Yes, you," the game official responded. "You're up next. Take your place over by the steps to the stage."

"Are you sure it's my turn already?" Midas asked. "See, my brother is the juggler and he had to go relieve himself. I'm sure he'll be back soon."

"Look, mister, I don't care who goes on stage," the official said tartly. She was at least a foot shorter than Midas, and, in other circumstances, he might have found it humorous how she had to crane her neck to look up at him. Right now, all he felt was intimidation from the short, stocky woman before him.

"Then I can just wait for him to come back?" Midas asked.

"I don't care who goes on stage," the official reiterated. "But, if no one goes on when it's your team's turn, you'll forfeit the round."

"When is our turn?" Midas asked.

"Whenever the guy before you finishes," the woman said unhelpfully. "He's on now, so I'd go start practicing if I were you."

"Jugglers don't practice. We warm up!" Midas told the official's back. Snatching Leopold's sack of juggling stuff from the ground, he stomped off to the stairs which led to the stage, grumbling to himself all the while. If his brother wasn't back soon, they wouldn't be talking for at least a week. And that was if the chicken didn't kill Midas.

Applause erupted from the other side of the stage and a few moments later, a juggler came down the stairs. It was Midas's turn. Slowly, as if marching to the gallows, he scaled the steps and poked his head through the curtain of the stage.

Leopold shoved his sack into Midas's hand and ducked low, scurrying to the edge of the crowd. The guard he slipped past never knew what happened nor did the people whose feet he stepped on as he navigated the sea of legs around him. This was one of the advantages of being small, one his recent growth spurt was quickly rendering obsolete, but he was glad to take advantage of it while he still could.

When he had spotted the men previously, they had been congregated in a single area, but now they were beginning to spread out. Like a lion choosing its prey, Leopold spotted one of them leaning against a wall at the mouth of an alley. He was separated enough from his comrades to make an easy target and hanging out near an alley was just asking for trouble.

With a burst of speed, Leopold rose to his full height and ran headlong into the man, hitting him in the stomach with his shoulder. The two forms tumbled into the alley unnoticed by anyone who cared. Leopold clamped a hand over the man's mouth before he could cry out and dragged him further into the shadows. The man struggled the whole time. He lashed out with his hands and feet and even bit at the hand covering his mouth but to no avail. Leopold propped his prisoner up against the wall and laid a knife to his throat. The struggling stopped immediately.

"I have little time to waste and little patience for people who waste it," Leopold growled. He kept his head tilted slightly forward so his hat hid his face from the man before him.

"Do you want my money?" the man asked. "It's yours. Take it!"

"I just said I don't have patience for people who waste my time!" Leopold snarled, pressing his knife harder against the man's throat. "I don't expect you to tell me who you're working for, which is fine since I already know. What I want to know is where your compatriots are stationed."

"What compatriots?" the man whimpered.

"Wasting time again," Leopold said. "Let me spell it out for you. When Lady Maria's juggler gets on stage, some of the men you are working with will try to kill him. One last chance to tell me where they're stationed."

The knife was pressed so hard against the man's throat now that blood was beginning to run down his neck.

"Okay!" he said. Leopold decreased the pressure slightly. "There are two crossbowmen in balconies overlooking the stage."

"Only two?" Leopold asked, pressing the knife harder. "I don't believe you!"

"Please don't kill me!" the man begged. "I swear I'm telling the truth."

"I still don't believe you, but I have need of you for something else," Leopold said. "I need you to give Baron Jasven a message for me, can you do that?"

The man nodded, terrified of the shadowy figure in front of him.

"Tell him Baroness Maria and her people are under the protection of The Shadow," Leopold said. "Can you remember that?"

"Yes," the man whimpered.

"Good," Leopold said. "Also tell him he needs to back off and relinquish his feud with Lady Maria lest The Shadow fall over him as it has fallen over so many before him."

Leopold didn't wait for a response before wrapping his arms around the man's throat and sliding behind him for more purchase. The man struggled uselessly, but Leopold held on tightly. The choke he was using only took a handful of seconds to work, and soon the man was out cold. Leopold let him slump to the ground.

The crowd was thinnest at the edges, and though this was the long way around, it was also the fastest. Leopold skirted the juggling stage area and headed for the buildings on the far side. The man had said there were two crossbowmen on balconies waiting to kill Lady Maria's juggler, and Leopold had a good idea of where the best vantage points would be.

Slipping in the back door of a shop, he headed for the stairs, taking them two at a time as he climbed the floors. The third floor was an apartment of some sort, and he knocked on the door, tapping his foot impatiently as he waited. After several long moments, the door cracked open revealing the face of an older man.

"What do you want?" the man asked.

Leopold didn't have time for this. He forced his way through the door, pushing the old man back roughly.

"I say, what's the big idea?" the man exclaimed, reaching for a cudgel leaning against the wall.

"I don't want to hurt you or take any of your possessions," Leopold said even as he searched the rooms of the small apartment. "My brother is in danger and time is of the essence."

His short search of the apartment had not turned up doors to a balcony.

"There is a balcony on this building," he said, turning to the old man. The only thing he saw was a swinging cudgel which he dodged easily. "Where's the balcony? Tell me and I'll get out of your home.

"Or I can throw you out myself!" the man exclaimed.

The cudgel swung again, and Leopold slipped around it, heading for a shuttered window. The next blow of the club smashed into the shutters, flinging them open and affording Leopold his first view of the balcony. It was a story above him. Without hesitation, he hopped onto the window sill and out, clinging to the notched, wooden planks composing the building's siding. It was quick work to scale the wall to the next level and step onto the balcony behind the unsuspecting assassin.

His crossbow was leaning up against the balcony railing, loaded but unthreatening.

Leopold knew he could easily dispatch the man in front of him. A knife blade between the ribs would be simple, but something stopped him. This man certainly appeared in a bad light, but what if he was the wrong person? What if he was simply in the wrong place, with the wrong crossbow, at the wrong time? Leopold had killed people in cold blood before, but this time was different.

"Hey," Leopold said. The words startled the assassin so much he actually jumped as he spun around. "You're here to kill someone, aren't you?"

The assassin stared stupidly at Leopold for a second before fumbling frantically for the sword at his hip. Leopold shook his head and drew his knife. Dashing forward, he easily blocked the swipe from the assassin's blade and slashed offensively, dropping the man in an instant.

"Next up is the juggler representing Baroness Maria," an announcer from below said.

Leopold spotted movement from the corner of his eye and jerked his head toward it. One building over and one floor up, another man, dressed as the one he had just killed, was shouldering a crossbow. There was no time to make it to the balcony, Leopold knew. His eyes landed on the still-loaded weapon leaned against the railing in front of him. He had never shot a bow of any sort, and this lack of experience caused a moment of hesitation. There was no other option, he knew, so he shouldered the weapon and pointed it at the archer above him. He aimed down the length of the arrow and squeezed the trigger when he saw the assassin's head. Not waiting to see if he had hit anything, he scaled the balcony railing in a single step and vaulted to the adjoining building, barely finding purchase with his fingers on the rough stone. It took him only seconds to climb to the balcony.

The bolt he had fired had buried itself in the wooden stock of the assassin's crossbow and knocked it from his hands.

Leopold pounced on the man who was still struggling to re-acquire his weapon and slew him with a single slash. Just like that, the threat was obliterated, but Leopold wasn't finished. He vaulted over the balcony railing, aiming for a rope suspending a line of triangular pendants over the juggling area. He slashed the rope as he grabbed it, riding it like a swing down toward the stage. He let go of the rope and rolled across the stage.

Jumping to his feet, he faced the crowd and raised his hands to an enormous applause. But this wasn't an acrobatics competition, it was all about juggling. Looking toward the stairs, he saw Midas poking his head through the curtains at the back of the stage.

"Toss me the eggs," Leopold mouthed to his brother, indicating with his hands the size and shape of what he wanted. "Then toss me the chicken."

"What's your assessment of the threat, Raven?" Daniel retained his calm as he usually did in circumstances such as this. He rubbed his hands together, but otherwise there was no indication of his nerves.

"They tried to kill me!" Midas shouted, slamming both fists down on the table behind which Daniel was seated. It was a very nice table, as nice as the rest of the furniture in the room. They had the king to thank for their accommodations. After the attack on Leopold in the sword fighting ring, he had insisted that Maria and her people stay in the castle. Now, The Shadow was congregated in Midas and Leopold's room.

"If it makes you feel any better, I think they were trying to kill me," Leopold said.

"I don't think any single one of us was the target," Raven pointed out. "Unless I miss my mark, they want us all dead. I don't believe they care in what order we die."

"Then the threat is high for all of us," Daniel concluded.

"Now hold on, boss," Leopold said. "They've tried to kill me twice, but to no avail. The score stands at us two, bad guys zero."

29

"What's your point?" Midas asked.

"They aren't very good," Leopold said. "I mean, they might be in normal circumstances, but compared to us, they might as well be amateurs. We're not in any real danger."

"Not in any real danger?!" Midas turned on his brother. "They've made two attempts already. The way I see it, they may fail a hundred times, but they only need to succeed once. No doubt, Jasven has enough men to see this thing through to the end."

"I sent the baron an intimidating message through one of his men," Leopold said. "It may be enough to make him back off."

"That's an optimistic viewpoint to say the least," Raven countered. "With what we know, we can take him down, and he knows it. He won't stop until we're all dead."

"Or until he is," Midas said. "If we kill him, this is all over. We're good enough to do it, too."

"That's a bit cold-blooded for you, Midas," Leopold commented.

"He's already trying to kill *us*," Midas said. "Besides that, I don't know if he means harm just to us or to Maria as well. I won't stand by and see her hurt."

"We will not kill Baron Jasven," Daniel ended the argument. "At least, not here at the king's games. He takes the security of his guests very seriously and would not rest until he found the baron's killers. We're good, but I have little doubt his men would follow the clues back to us."

"Do you think we should make a tactical retreat?" Raven asked. "Should we run away?"

"We can't," Leopold said. "Even if Jasven isn't crazy enough to go after Maria while he's here, we'd be hanging her out to dry."

"What do you mean?" Raven asked.

"He means that we're Lady Maria's team at a competition put on by the king," Daniel answered. "What kind of a position do you think she would be in if we just left after the first day of events?"

"Well, if we have to stay and we can't kill the baron, we're in a very sticky situation," Raven said. "We'll want to stay out of sight as much as possible, and we'll need to be incredibly vigilant during the competitions."

"What about Maria?" Midas asked.

"I don't think Jasven is crazy enough to kill her while we're here at the tournament," Leopold said. "Even if he is, the king has enough guards protecting her to take care of any threat. Raven's right. We should look to our own well-being."

"Well, if that's settled, I'm going to go and get some sleep, and I'd suggest the same for the rest of you," Daniel said, rising from his seat. "I've been keeping a low profile this whole time, so it's likely my face isn't associated with you or Maria. I'll keep my ears open and let you know what I find out."

"Thanks, Daniel," Raven said. "Be safe."

Raven locked the room's door behind the wizard and turned back to the brothers. Midas had taken Daniel's place and was slouching in the chair with his feet propped up on the table in front of him. Leopold flopped onto the bed with a satisfied groan. Raven suspected the activities of the day had drained the brothers more than they had her.

"Not ready for bed yet?" Midas asked.

"Of course I am," Leopold answered. "That's why I got into one."

"I wasn't talking to you," Midas said. "Raven is still here."

"Oh," Leopold said. He pulled a pillow over his face, continuing to speak into it but all that came out was a mumbling sound.

"So," Midas said to Raven. "Not sleepy yet or is there another reason for your lingering here?"

"Well, since you ask," Raven said, pulling a chair to the table and sitting down opposite Midas. "Daniel thinks he's safe because no one should affiliate him with us or with Maria, but obviously we're a different story. Anyone who was at the tournament today knows the three of us are Maria's team and has made it clear they won't hesitate to kill us."

"Even though we're in a castle, you still don't feel safe," Midas said.

"Correct," Raven admitted. "I don't think I'm going to get any sleep in a room by myself."

"So you want to sleep in here with us?" Midas asked.

"And take turns at watch," Raven added. "I know we need sleep, but it would make me feel a lot better if I knew we were responsible for our own safety."

"Fine with me," Midas said. "What about you, Leo?"

There was a muffled sound from the bed.

"Leo says he's fine with it as well," Midas liberally translated his brother's unintelligible mumbling.

"There are three of us and only two beds," Leopold withdrew the pillow from his face to say. "I vote Midas has to sleep on the floor."

"There're two beds in here and only two of us will be sleeping at a time, genius," Midas said. "No one has to sleep on the floor."

"In that case, I don't care as long as I don't have to take the first watch," Leopold said. He pulled the pillow over his face again.

"Real night-owl that one is," Raven said.

"Oh yeah," Midas agreed sarcastically. "That's why he always takes the first shift. Likes to stay up late."

"I guess he's more of an 'early to bed, early to rise' kind of person," Raven said.

"Yup," Midas agreed.

A silence fell between the two friends. It wasn't uncomfortable, separating the two as silence sometimes does, but simply existed. Neither had much to say, nor were they tired enough to go to sleep. After several minutes of this, Raven finally broke the stillness.

"It was a good job you did today," she said, looking up at Midas. "I always knew you could get first place in the sword fighting, but even so it was a bit of a surprise."

"I wasn't able to do it by myself," Midas said. "My little brother had to swing in and rescue my butt at the last second."

"You carried us single handedly until the final bell of the final round," Raven said. "That's nothing to be ashamed of."

"I'm not ashamed," Midas said quickly. "I said this morning that we're a team. A failure for one of us is a failure for all of us, and, conversely, a success for one is a success for all. Leo is old enough to handle himself, and I'm very glad he was able to finish what I couldn't."

"And after all that, he still managed to foil his own assassination," Raven said. "And *then* he juggled three eggs and a chicken. Even though it was only for a short time, it was still impressive. Where did he even learn to juggle?"

"I asked him the same question as soon as he came off stage, and you know what he said?" Midas asked. "He said, and I quote, 'Juggling is like pickpocketing. They both require fast hands.'"

"That's the most ridiculous thing I've ever heard!" Raven exclaimed. "Sure, they both require fast hands, but so does sword fighting."

"And while I'm great with a sword, I'd be terrible at juggling," Midas said. "I think we can chalk this up to yet another hidden talent of my little brother."

"Yes, he does have a habit of surprising you when you least expect it, doesn't he?" Raven said. Her eyes drifted to Leopold who, admittedly, didn't look like a hero at the moment. His limbs were flopped unceremoniously across his bed, and where the pillow had slid off his face, she could see his mouth hanging open slightly.

"Right," Midas said with a laugh.

"What?" Raven asked, jerking her gaze from Leopold to Midas. "What are you laughing about?"

"You," Midas said. "If the way you talk about him wasn't enough, the way you look at him would be. Have you talked to him yet?"

"I talk to him all the time," Raven evaded the question.

"Come on, you know what I'm talking about," Midas said. "Have you told him how you feel?"

"It's complicated," Raven said vaguely.

"How complicated can it be?" Midas asked. He stopped short at the sound of Leopold snorting and rolling over in his bed. After the younger boy had settled again, Midas continued in a softer voice. "You like him, right? Why is this so complicated?"

"Have you told Maria how you feel?" Raven asked.

"How I feel about what?" Midas asked.

"Don't be stupid," Raven said. "Everybody knows you have feelings for her. Have you told her about them?"

"Maria is a baroness," Midas said. "Even if I did feel affection for her, nothing would ever come of it. I may be good enough for now, but she's royalty and I'm nobody. Our relationship can't ever go anywhere."

"You like her, and I know she likes you," Raven said.

"How can you know what she thinks?" Midas shot back.

"Because I can see!" Raven exclaimed, gesturing to her eyes. At Midas's puzzled expression, she threw her hands in the air, exasperated at his cluelessness. "She definitely likes you even if you're too dense to realize it. Maria is the most laid-back noble I've ever met. If there was ever a chance for a commoner to marry royalty, you have the best shot. All you have to do is be honest with yourself and with her."

"Aren't you doing the exact same thing I am?" Midas asked, turning the tables back on Raven. "There's only one way you can settle your feelings for Leo and that's by talking to him."

"I've been easing into it," Raven admitted. "Testing the waters by doing things to see if I can get him to tell me how he feels. So far my luck hasn't been great."

"Boys are stupid and don't take hints very well," Midas said. "Take my word when I say my brother has strong feelings for you."

"How do you know?" Raven asked.

"You're not the only one with eyes," Midas answered with an exaggerated gesture to his eyes, clearly mocking Raven's previous action. "If you just ask him, you'll see I'm right. For both your sakes, I wouldn't put it off for too long."

"Same to you," Raven said. Midas had no response.

"So," he finally broke the silence. "Should I take first watch?"

"Sure," Raven said, heading for the vacant bed. She had pushed far enough for one night.

Baron Jasven was eating a late dinner in his tent when his guard ducked in to inform him of the arrival of a Lord Sauvage.

"Let him in," Baron Jasven said, dabbing his mouth with the silk napkin in his lap. The guard disappeared to return moments later with a cloaked and hooded figure. Baron Jasven stood and motioned his guest to a chair which he took, throwing back his hood as he sat.

"To what do I owe the pleasure of your visit, Lord Sauvage?" Baron Jasven asked.

"You owe it to your stupidity," Lord Sauvage said viciously. "You've been meddling with things you shouldn't be meddling with."

"I do not know to what you are referring," Baron Jasven said as he continued to eat his meal. "Can I get you anything to eat or drink?"

"You know exactly to what I refer," Lord Sauvage snarled, ignoring the offer of sustenance. "It was sloppy what you did in the sword fighting competition. I told you there were to be no attempts made on the Baroness while we are here at the games!"

"You mean the idiot who attacked her champion in the final match?" Jasven asked, looking up from the meat he had been cutting. "That wasn't even my man."

"Don't play me for a fool," Lord Sauvage snapped. "He was the champion of one of your allies, but I know you were behind it."

"Even if it were me, that wasn't an attempt on the Baroness," Baron Jasven said hotly. He was getting angry at the way Lord Sauvage was treating him.

"This is the king's tournament, you buffoon," Lord Sauvage said. "He will investigate any fatal crime against those here. Besides that, with the blood relationship between the King and the Baroness, an attack on her team might as well be against her."

"Fine, you caught me," Baron Jasven said, raising his hands in mock surrender. "I ordered the strike against her team, but that will never find its way back to me."

"You're right, it won't," Lord Sauvage said. "I bribed the jailer to poison your would-be assassin."

"There was no need!" Baron Jasven said. "He would never have talked."

"The king's men have many ways of getting confessions out of people," Lord Sauvage said. "This man would have led them to your ally who in turn would have led them to you. But now the threat is gone."

"There was no threat to begin with," Baron Jasven said, but Lord Sauvage cut him off.

"You listen to me," the cloaked man said, rising to his feet. "You disobeyed my orders, and it almost cost you your life. The only reason I chose to save you is because you could implicate me and, as I said before, the king's men have ways of getting information from even the toughest characters. I saved you this time, but I have little patience for people who cannot follow simple orders. You are not to make a move against Maria or her team while they are at this tournament. If you do, I will silence you like I silenced your assassin."

Lord Sauvage didn't wait for a response but swept out of the tent in a flurry. Baron Jasven dropped his utensils on the table and folded his hands, squeezing them so hard his knuckles turned white. At his station in life, there were few people he was afraid of, but Lord Sauvage was one of them.

After a few moments, he rang a small silver bell, and a page appeared. Quickly the baron scribbled out a message and gave it to the lad along with the name of the message's recipient. The young boy left quickly, leaving Baron Jasven alone again. He slowly retrieved his knife and fork and continued to eat. He still thought there was no concern of his assassination plans getting to the king, but Lord Sauvage knew of them already. For his sake, there would be no more foul play at this tournament.

Obstacle Course

"I hope this obstacle course is better than the last event," Midas grumbled.

"Agreed," Leopold said. "I mean, I understand why long-distance running is part of the competition, but boy was it boring."

"If you thought running it was bad, you should have been in the stands," Maria said. "After you left the city, there was literally nothing to do for close to two hours. Then you came back into the city, finished, and that was it. No excitement whatsoever."

"Sitting in the stands, under your sunshade must be so taxing, your ladyship," Midas said sarcastically. "I see your boredom and raise you the pain in my side which persisted for most of the race."

"You might have a point, but I can't hear you make it over the sound of your whining," Raven shot back. "I was right beside you for the whole race, and you don't hear me complaining, do you?"

"The obstacle course will certainly be more eventful than the cross-country race," Maria promised. "It's much shorter for one thing, just over a quarter of a mile long. As the name implies, it also has a series of obstacles you will have to face, which should make things more interesting."

"What kind of obstacles are we talking about?" Midas asked. "Mud pit? Walls? Ice cold water?"

"Yes, yes, and yes," Maria answered. "If you can dream it up, there's a good chance you'll see it today. The course is new every year so veteran teams don't have an advantage over new ones. You'll just have to stay ready for whatever comes your way."

"Excellent," Midas said. He flexed his fingers, his knuckles cracking in response.

"As to the rules," Raven said. "You mentioned earlier that they were a bit different than what we've seen so far."

"Correct," Maria agreed. "The goal is to get your team members across the finish line first. It is permitted to use any and all means available, shy of killing someone of course, to prevent other teams from finishing. All members of each team are required to compete."

"So all three of us will be out there," Leopold said. "But doesn't that mean there'll be teams with dozens or even scores of people?"

"Yes," Maria said. "It'll be difficult for you, though not as much as you may think. A team only completes this event after fully half of their members have crossed the finish line. With three on our team, only two of you must cross to finish."

"Interesting," Midas said thoughtfully. "In that case, how do we want to play this thing?"

"I'm fast, Raven's pretty fast, and you're big," Leopold said. "How about you run interference for us while we book it to the finish as fast as we can?"

"I like it," Raven said. A bell rang indicating the teams should begin to take their places. "Any advice for us before we go, Maria?"

"This competition may seem short and that it will be over in no time, but beware," the baroness warned. "You can count on the fact that things will not go according to plan. The whole competition has dragged out for hours in the past. Watch your-selves. If there is to be another attempt on any of your lives, this would be the perfect setting for it."

"Good to know," Raven said. "Anything else?"

"Nothing," Maria said. "I know you will do your best."

"What, no hug for luck?" Midas asked, his arms out.

"Not with you being that sweaty," Maria said in mock dis-gust. "My lucky hugs are reserved only for my clean, bathed champions."

With a dramatic twirl of her dress, she headed to the stands, a row of seats for the nobility set well up in the air to afford them a perfect view of the course. The Shadow headed the opposite direction toward the starting line. At Maria's sug-gestion, they had donned pants, long sleeves, and boots for this event, and as the course obstacles came into view, they under-stood why. Many of them would have been uncomfortable in the clothes they had run the cross-country race in while others would have been downright painful.

"Good luck hug?" Raven asked Midas with a raised eyebrow.

"Shut up," Midas said.

"What?" Leopold asked, confused by the exchange.

"Last night Midas was trying to convince me there could never be anything between him and Maria since she's nobility and he's a commoner," Raven explained. "I told him otherwise."

"Come on, Leo, back me up on this," Midas said.

"I'm with Raven on this one," Leopold said. "Personally, I think you're too scared to ask her. Never knew I had a chicken for a brother!"

"You're supposed to be on my side," Midas grumbled. "Whatever happened to you and me against the world?"

"Hey, I just call it like I see it," Leopold answered, raising his hands defensively.

"Midas, I like giving you a hard time as much as anyone, but that's enough of this for now," Raven said. "We need to talk strategy. What are we going to do for this race?"

"I say we make a bust for it up the right side of the course," Leopold suggested. "We'll probably make better time if all three of us stick together."

"But if anyone falls behind, leave them and keep going," Midas added. "I can say that because if anyone is the weak link here, it'll be me. Since only two of us need to finish for us to win, there's no sense in throwing the whole race because I get held up."

"Agreed, but we only leave you if there's a bad hang-up," Raven said. "For instance, if you take on a group of ten opponents to give us a chance to get away, I'll see you after the race."

"Sounds good," Leopold agreed. He put his hand in front of his friends. "'Go team' on three?"

Raven and Midas gave him withering looks and continued for the starting line. Leopold followed them, taking his place to the far left of his friends. There was nothing left to say so they simply waited for the call to start. They didn't have to wait long.

———†———

"You may be my niece, Maria, but I have to agree with the barons on this one," the king told Maria in a low voice. "Only having three people on your team might have worked in the events up to this point, but it won't end well for these last two."

"You don't think so?" Maria asked coyly. "Why not? With three teammates, only two of them have to cross the finish line to win. The second smallest team needs ten people to cross. I think that puts me at an advantage."

"Only two may need to cross, but they'll never get anywhere close," the king returned. "With so many people trying to stop them and fewer people to protect them, they'll barely make it out of the gate."

"Midas will make sure the others have the space they need," Maria pointed out. "That may not even be necessary since all three are fast enough to get ahead of the pack."

"Well, the best of luck to your team, but in the past a lot of people have banked on getting in front of the pack," the king said. "It has yet to turn out well."

"Agreed," Maria said. "All those teams had one major flaw, though."

"Pray tell."

"They weren't my team."

"You think you have some sort of good luck spell floating over you?" the king asked. "How does being your team make a difference?"

"How many did I bring to the games last year?" Maria asked.

"Twenty-seven, I believe," the king answered.

"And the year before?" Maria asked.

"Fifteen," the king responded. "I still don't see your point."

"I didn't arrive at the number of three arbitrarily," Maria said. "I've tried teams of many sizes and constructions and know the strengths and weaknesses of each."

"And yet in all that, you have yet to win the games a single year," the king said.

"I know. A fact which will change this year," Maria said.

"I'll concede the fact that you're in contention for the top prize, but you certainly don't have a solid lead," the king said. "The games up to this point were all designed for either one person or three. Your team hasn't been at a numerical disadvantage yet. They'll be crushed in these last events."

"This team is my super team," Maria said. "You don't have to take my word for it. Just watch this next event."

The call for the competitors to get ready sounded across the grounds, and the king leaned forward in his seat.

"Okay, let's watch this together," he said.

A trumpet blared signaling the race had begun, and The Shadow rushed forward into the obstacles. Midas took the lead followed closely by Raven and trailed by Leopold. This only lasted for a short dash to the first obstacle. A wall about six feet tall blocked their path. It was laughably easy to scale, and even Midas had no trouble getting over it. He was the last one over, and as he climbed, an opponent grabbed at his ankles, trying to slow him down but to no avail.

A few people were at the next obstacle already, but Leopold wasn't worried. They were sparse and scattered, a few from one team and a few from another. Being the weakest but fastest members of the teams, their goal was to cross the finish line as quickly as possible. They would likely reach the end without any reasonable opposition, but they also couldn't win the game by themselves. The Shadow was together and in front of the pack, exactly where they needed to be.

"Come on!" Midas encouraged the others toward the next obstacle. A large mud pit was carved out of the ground, bridged only by logs hung from ropes.

"Raven, you go first, then you Midas. I'll bring up the rear," Leopold ordered.

Raven climbed up onto the log and crossed it in a low crouch. Worried by the number of opponents already over the wall, Midas mounted the bridge too early. He was two steps on when Raven climbed off, shaking the whole construction enough to set him off balance. For a tense moment it looked like he might fall, but miraculously he maintained his balance and crossed the mud pit safely.

From the noise, Leopold knew some of the other teams were close, but he forced himself not to look back as he scrambled up onto the log and scurried across it. He was almost halfway across when Midas yelled something while Raven motioned frantically. A jolt shook the log, threatening to send him toppling into the mud. His knees folded even further than before, bringing his body closer to the log while his arms shot out, balancing his body on the rocking bridge beneath his feet. All this time, he never stopped moving forward.

He had almost reached the rope suspending the log by the time the second jolt shook him. Using the movement to his advantage, he leaped for the rope, grabbing it with both fists momentarily before climbing it as quickly as a monkey. He hauled himself onto the framework from which the log was suspended and quickly walked it to the edge of the mud pit. He took the ten-foot drop in stride, adding a roll to help with the landing.

"Midas, do your thing," Leopold said as he rose to his feet and dusted himself off. His brother grabbed the near side of the log bridge and lifted it several feet above where it naturally hung. The three men on the log threw out their arms for balance.

"Have a nice trip, gentlemen," Midas grunted and dropped his end of the log. It freefell momentarily before snapping to a sudden stop against the rope to which it was attached. The men toppled off the log and fell the five feet to the mud, slopping into it with a nasty sucking sound.

"We need to keep moving!" Raven called. Midas gave one last look at his fallen opponents before turning to meet the next stage of the course.

"I'm impressed," the king told Maria without taking his eyes off the action below. "Your team is doing quite well despite my earlier misgivings."

"I told you as much," Maria said proudly. "I wasn't exaggerating when I said this was a super team."

"After what I've seen, I hesitate to mention it because I feel I will have to eat my words again," the king said, "but the obstacles get successively harder as the course continues. They have to wade through that mud pit there and climb a steep slope immediately after."

"Difficult, but not impossible," Maria said.

"True," the king conceded. "I half expect them to blaze through it without a problem."

"And then they'll be home free," Maria said smugly.

"Not exactly." The comment was from the baron sitting next to Maria. He had clearly been eavesdropping on the conversation and deemed this moment to be the perfect one to interject. "It's a twenty-foot wall with no handholds on the face and no way to climb it. With only three team members, there's no way they can get even the required two over the top."

"It appears that way, doesn't it?" Maria agreed.

"I'm not one to take sides in such things, but I have to agree with Baron Jasven," the baron beside Maria said. "There's no way you can win this year's tournament."

"That's a sentiment he expressed from the very beginning, yet we're still in the running," Maria said. "He speaks more from spite than logical reasoning."

"Yesterday I would have agreed with you, but it appears as though you have forgotten to factor in the long run," the baron said. "Your team will never place in this event."

"And what if they do, Baron Godfrey?" the king asked, leaning across Maria to look into the baron's eyes. "Suppose they manage to find a way to conquer the wall at the end and, for the sake of argument, come in first? What will you say then?"

"It'll be a miracle," Baron Godfrey answered. "I haven't looked at the standings recently; however, with their showing, or lack thereof, in the archery and the cross-country competitions, I believe they'll still have to survive for quite a spell during total combat to have a chance."

"Then you wouldn't be opposed to making a bet?" the king asked. "Because I'll lay money on Maria's team taking first place in the whole games."

"If they pull off a miracle on the obstacle course, my confidence in them will grow considerably," Baron Godfrey said. "At the current time, however, I don't think they have a chance."

"Then I expect good odds on the bet," the king said. "How does twenty to one sound?"

"Given their current standings, those odds are a bit high, don't you think?" Baron Godfrey said.

"I'm betting on the underdog, Godfrey," the king said with hands extended palms up in a small shrug. "You've got to give me some reason to put money on them."

"Even so, twenty to one seems a little high," Baron Godfrey said. "How about seven to one?"

"Ten to one or no deal," the king said.

"Done," Baron Godfrey agreed, extending his hand. He named an amount which the king appeared to consider for a moment. After a short pause, he took the baron's hand and shook it, sealing the bet.

All through the king and Baron Godfrey's conversation, whispers had been running up and down the line of nobility. Upon reaching Baron Jasven, he stood up and worked his way toward the king. He finally blundered past Godfrey and Maria to a spot directly in front of the monarch.

"What's this I hear about betting on the games, your majesty?" he asked the king.

"Come on, Jasven, you know I hate the term 'your majesty'," the king said. "Please just call me 'sir'."

"As you wish, sir," Baron Jasven said. "But back to my original question. Did I hear you were betting on Maria's team? Because I'll take you up on that bet no matter the odds."

"Well, I just made a bet with Godfrey here, and normally I have a strict one-bet-per-event rule," the king said hesitantly.

"Your majesty," Baron Jasven began.

The king visibly flinched and raised his hand for silence.

"On the other hand," he said, "I think I can make an exception for you. The next event is total combat. You know the rules: eight men to a team and the last one standing wins. Maria's team only has three members, but I will still bet you they win that event."

"With pleasure, your...sir," Baron Jasven caught himself at the last moment.

"Given the situation, I had better get some good odds," the king said.

"Of course, sir," Baron Jasven agreed. "How does twenty to one sound?"

"That sounds brilliant," the king answered. "How much should we wager on it?"

"It's just this mud pit and then the wall at the end!" Leopold shouted over his shoulder.

"I can't believe you used the word 'just'," Midas said as he staggered abreast of his brother. He leaned forward, bracing his palms on his knees and gasping for breath. The last obstacle had been a killer.

"Do you see the size of the wall?" Raven asked. She also sounded out of breath, and her appearance showed how exhausted she was. She pointed to where teams were already creating pyramids of people, trying to get over the final obstacle and the finish line. "It has to be at least twenty feet tall. How are we supposed to get over it?"

"You leave that to me," Leopold said more confidently than he felt. He was actually very tired, probably at least as tired as his companions, but knew he couldn't show it. His skill set made him the de facto leader for this race, and showing weakness on his part could undermine his companions' resolve.

"Well, the mud pit is one thing I can handle," Midas said. "Come on, Raven, let's get this over with."

Midas picked Raven up in one arm and waded into the mud, slogging through the sticky, brown, mess. Leopold turned away from the pit, facing the oncoming opponents, looking for a few in particular. The rules of the game dictated that to win, half of the members of a team had to cross the finish line. This meant at least half of the people on the course were not interested in anything but finishing, but the minority were the ones who made this game so difficult. They were not looking to finish quickly but to interfere with other teams and prevent them from reaching the end.

A few of these opponents, often referred to as strikers, seemed to have it out for Maria's team specifically. Though this was very annoying, it was not unexpected. Being the only ruling baroness in the realm, Maria was not popular among many of her male peers. Then there was Baron Jasven, a man with a personal grudge against Maria. From the identifying badges each team wore, it seemed to Leopold that an inordinate number of the strikers coming after Maria's team were employed by him. As always, he kept a sharp eye out for the weapons of would-be assassins, but it seemed after the attempt in the sword fighting ring, none were eager to try their luck.

As if on cue, two men wearing Jasven's crest converged on Leopold, splitting up to approach from opposite sides. Leopold knew he could take them, at least he could do so easily when he wasn't tired, but this wasn't the time to engage. With two teams already working on scaling the final wall, a drawn-out confrontation could very well be game changing, even if he were victorious. A quick glance over his shoulder confirmed Midas was not having a problem with the mud. He was at the halfway point now, his progress even and unchecked. Whenever he overtook someone, he would push them under with his free hand and pass them.

Leopold retreated along the edge of the mud pit, moving perpendicular to the many contestants who had no thoughts but to reach the finish line. His two assailants ignored all these targets, confirming his suspicion that he and his team were the primary target for Jasven's men. He continued to retreat, drawing the men further away from Midas and Raven, all the while looking for a way through the mud. If his teammates could both cross the finish line, it would be enough to win; however, the chances of them scaling the wall without his help were small.

"Give it up, boy!" one of the men chasing him called. "No matter how far you run, we're going to catch you and throw you in the mud. There's nothing you can do to stop us!"

"Just like there was nothing I could do to stop you last time?" Leopold taunted. "You'll have to catch me first if you want to dunk me."

He considered dashing into the mud and making for the other side, but he wasn't as strong as his brother. The mud would pose a real threat for him, and the men would give chase into the mud. They would catch him before he made it half way.

"It's inevitable," the other man said. "You can't keep running forever. You're running out of room."

"I like to think I *can* run forever," Leopold shouted back. He had come up with an idea, one which had as much of a chance of failing as succeeding, but it was worth a shot. Without hesitation, he sprinted to the edge of the mud pit and leaped from the solid land to the shoulders of a man not two feet out. The man shouted in surprise and shook his shoulders to dislodge the boy, but he was already gone, jumping to the next person.

The trail of shoulders he had picked out began to develop holes as the people moved at different speeds and some stopped to catch their breath. The longest jump landed him in the mud with a nasty slop, but he was close enough to his target to grab their shoulders and climb onto them, despite the frantic slapping from below. He jumped from the last pair of shoulders to the slope he had to scale, a steep bank almost too slick to climb. Leopold tried to dig his fingers into the packed dirt, but they just scratched through the top layer of sludge, sending him sliding back down toward the mud. He caught hold of an exposed root stopping his rapid descent and giving him time to rest and think.

As he caught his breath, he could feel the root slowly pulling out of the soil. His boots slid on the muck beneath them, slowly inching his heels toward the mud. To his right, a thin, almost dry path carved its way to the top, unused because it was largely a sheer climb. At the top, a bulge of earth and rock blocked the path, so anyone who took it would find themselves suspended out over the mud again before they made it to the top. It was an impossible option, which was Leopold's favorite.

The root in his hand came loose, and he maintained his grip on it as he leaped for the dry path. He caught hold of a small crevice in the bank with his free hand and used the end of the root as a spike to pull himself upward. Releasing the crevice, he used each end of the root in opposite hands to drag himself forward. This path wasn't as sheer as it had first seemed, and the going was easier than he expected. Soon, he abandoned the root and began to use the handholds of the dirt and rock.

The bulge at the top was difficult. Leopold's feet swung uselessly beneath him as he inched away from the wall, clinging tightly to the overhang above him. One hand at a time, he inched his way backward. The five feet seemed to take forever as his heart beat wildly from the adrenaline and sweat dripped into his eyes. His arms were shaking with fatigue when he finally reached the outermost point of the bulge and resumed his upward struggle. Three feet later, a hand grabbed his wrist. He tried weakly to struggle before realizing the hand was pulling him upward, not pushing him back down.

"Hello again, Leo," Midas said, setting his brother on the ground.

"Can I have just a moment to rest?" Leopold asked.

"We're almost to the end," Midas said and pulled Leopold to his feet.

"Yeah, don't quit on us now," Raven chimed in. "We're almost there. Just a twenty-foot wall."

"I'm not quitting, just taking a breather," Leopold said. "I need enough air to tell you how we're going to finish this out."

"No time for that," Midas said as he dragged his brother toward the wall. "I've been knocking people back down into the mud pit since we got up here, but there's only so much I can do. I think one of the teams may have already finished and there are a few more hot on their heels."

"Okay," Leopold said, finally able to stand up straight. The cramp in his side was bearable now, though not by much. "We only need to get two of us over the top, so here's the plan. We make a stack, Midas on the bottom, then me, and Raven on top."

"That'll never work," Raven said immediately. "Even on each other's shoulders, we'll never make it up twenty feet."

"Then we do it on each other's hands," Leopold said.

A few long moments of stunned silence met his statement.

"I think we can do it," Midas said.

"Are you crazy?" Raven said.

"Raven, you're on top," Leopold said. "I know I can lift you on my hands, so if Midas thinks he can do the same for both of us…"

"Let's do it," Midas said. "I certainly hope I'm strong enough to lift both of you shrimps."

"I'm going to get dropped and break every bone in my body," Raven said in a defeated voice and followed the brothers to the wall.

Midas braced his shoulder against the wall, and Leopold clambered onto his shoulders. Raven didn't like the plan, but she knew when it was time to shut up and be a team player. As soon as Leopold was situated, she scaled the brothers and crouched atop the human ladder. Ever so slowly, Midas rotated toward the wall. For a moment they came completely away from it, rocking slightly as they tried desperately to maintain their balance. After a tense moment, they tipped into the wall, finally facing it.

The next part was the trickiest by far. Midas raised his hands palms up next to his shoulders, and Leopold inched his feet forward onto them. Midas grunted with the effort of lifting his hands above his head but managed to do it smoothly enough to prevent anyone from falling. Now it was Leopold's turn. He did the same thing, lifting his palms even with his shoulders. Raven sloppily but quickly transferred her weight to them, and Leopold strained as hard as he could to lift her.

"Hurry up," Midas called from below, his voice a groan from the strain on his body.

"What? Too weak?" Leopold grunted back as he continued to push Raven upward.

"No, but strikers are coming," Midas answered. "I don't want to get hit and do nothing about it."

"Raven?" Leopold groaned.

"I heard him," Raven said. "I just need a few more inches."

Leopold stretched as high as he could and stood on his toes.

"Is that high enough?" he gasped.

In response, the weight on his hands disappeared so suddenly that he toppled backward. He could feel Midas's hands beneath his feet, struggling to balance the tower but to no avail. Leopold landed painfully on his back, the breath knocked out of his lungs. He looked up to see several figures approaching but was unable to move to do anything about it. Suddenly Midas was standing above him, raising his fists at the approaching strikers.

"Get your butt off the ground, Leo!" he shouted to his little brother.

The first of the strikers closed in, and Midas laid him on the ground with a single blow. Leopold forced himself into an upright position and struggled to his feet. Midas was in the thick of it now, fending off two or three of his attackers at a time. They were faring poorly at the moment, but he was just one man.

"Get to the finish line!" Midas shouted. With a roar, he grabbed a striker in each arm and pushed several more toward the mud pit. They struggled to get away from the charging giant, but in his anger, he managed to keep them flying before him until the whole group tumbled down the bank and into the mud.

Leopold ignored the strikers coming after him and rushed toward the largest pyramid of people trying to scale the wall. He ascended the backs of the outside of the pyramid until he ran out of flesh to climb. Another five feet stood between him and the top when he took things into his own hands. The wall was constructed of planks laid edge to edge, but two of them hadn't been snugged up properly. A gap existed, just large enough for three of Leopold's fingers. In an incredible display of acrobatics which used the last reserves of his energy, he rotated himself until his head was pointing at the ground and extended his feet into the air as high as he could.

There was no way he could reach the top alone, but he trusted his team. Just as his arm was about to give out, he felt Raven grab his ankles and pull him up. She was by no means as strong as Midas, and Leopold helped her as best he could. It took a bit of wiggling and struggling, but eventually Leopold flopped over the top of the wall and collapsed onto the walkway behind it.

"Lady Maria's team takes second place," the official nearby shouted down the wall. The message was relayed up to the nobility, and if Leopold had looked, he would have seen Maria stand and applaud. As it was, he was too exhausted to do anything but sit and recover his strength.

Total War

"Did we really decide this was a good idea?" Leopold asked. "Because right now, it seems like a very bad one."

The three youngest members of The Shadow stood back-to-back in the same arena in which the sword fighting competition had taken place yesterday. Now, eight-man teams representing each of the barons were congregated in the ring, facing each other, ready for the final competition of the games: Total War. The regularly steel weapons of all combatants had been replaced with wooden ones which were considerably less lethal but would hurt all the same.

"I don't know about you, but I like the challenge," Midas said lightly. A wooden buckler was bound to his left arm, and he had forsaken the sword, his preferred weapon, for a club.

In his own words, "A sword without an edge is nothing more than a club anyway." There was no armor in this competition. A touch of any weapon to the head or chest was enough to eliminate an opponent.

"This isn't about good or bad ideas," Raven said. "Honestly, I don't even think it's about winning. Maria wants to make a point, and this is her way of doing it."

"She's trying to make a point?" Leopold asked incredulously. "With what she's put us through already, what could it possibly be?"

"I don't know," Raven answered. "But she's paying us well to do this for her, so we've got nothing to complain about. Anything for the money, right?"

"Even broken bones and a lot of pain?" Midas asked. "I have a feeling we're all going to be in a lot of pain before we finish here."

"Sissy," Leopold taunted. "You've lived a cushy life up until now, apparently. I'll take broken bones and pain as long as I don't have to swim through a moat and shimmy up a toilet chute again."

"Those are some pretty low standards," Midas said.

"Agreed," Leopold said. He added sarcastically, "It's a sad, sad life I lead."

"Look alive, you two," Raven said. "The match is about to begin."

A bell sounded, and the eight-person armies were at each other's throats almost instantly. The Shadow stayed where they were, backs together and weapons pointing out. They were safe for now since no one was interested in trying to take them on at the moment.

"So, do we have any plans?" Leopold asked as he watched the fighting happen around him. Soldiers swung their wooden weapons at each other, simulating attacks to various parts of the body or just beating an enemy down with the weight of their clubs and swords. Competition officials wearing brightly colored shirts dashed in and out of the violence, declaring people dead and sending them from the ring in a steady flow.

"I vote we don't get fake-killed," Raven offered.

"Not the extremely thorough and well-thought-out plan I'm used to from you, but okay," Leopold agreed. He twirled the two short, wooden swords in his hands.

"Or you could listen to the resident expert on fighting," Midas interjected. "We should stay in this knot until they decide it's time to attack. Their numbers should be thinner by then, and we'll form a short line with our backs to one side of the arena. We don't split up under any circumstances, do you understand?"

"No offense, Leo, but I think I'm going to go with Midas on this one," Raven shouted above the din of battle.

"Why should I be offended?" Leopold called back. "It's your plan we're ditching, not mine. I don't care what we do, just tell me so I can do it."

"We wait," Midas said firmly. "Let our enemies take each other out as long as they want to."

The melee continued to rage for at least a quarter of an hour before there was any sort of reprieve. More than half of the original combatants were gone though not equally from all teams. Some had been defeated in their entirety while others had only lost one or two members. Now they formed back into teams, panting with the exertion and eyeing each other up.

"If we want to have the advantage, we need to attack now while everyone is tired," Midas said. "That team only has two members left. We take them first."

"Or we go talk to them," Raven offered. "We could ask them to help us."

"We're on different teams so why would they help us?" Midas asked.

"Just leave the talking to me," Raven said. "If I can't convince them, we'll go with your plan."

"So long as I get to hit something with my club, I'm good," Midas said.

"You'll get to, I promise," Raven said. "Just follow my lead for now."

She led Midas and Leopold across the ring toward the two-person team. The other, larger teams allowed them to pass unhindered, no doubt assuming they were going to knock out the smallest team left in the arena. And why not let someone else do the dirty work for a change? The two-person team raised their weapons as The Shadow approached, readying themselves for the inevitable battle, but Raven handed her sword to Leopold and stepped forward, holding her hands out to show the right one was empty and her shield was the only thing in her left.

"We haven't come to attack, but to talk," Raven said.

"We don't have anything to talk about!" one member of the two-man team growled.

"Don't we?" Raven asked. "I think there's an agreement we can come to which will benefit both of our teams."

"I don't see how. We both want to win this competition, something which isn't possible for us both to do."

"Consider this," Raven said. "We have three people on our team and you have only two. Neither of our teams can stand up to the larger ones."

"We'll go down fighting."

"I'm sure you will, but you won't win," Raven countered.

"Does this conversation have a point?" the apparent spokesman for the other team asked testily.

"We can't contend with the larger teams, and neither can you, but we might stand a chance together," Raven said.

"You want us to work with you? Why?"

"As you said, our teams cannot both claim victory," Raven explained quickly. She had been keeping an eye on the rest of the battle ground, and it appeared she was running out of time. "Right now, we both have close to no chance of winning, but if we team up, at least for long enough to eliminate some of the larger teams, we each might have a chance at taking first place."

"She makes sense," the second member of the other team said. "At least for the moment our interests lie in the same direction."

"And what if at the end, we're the only two teams left standing?" the spokesman for the other team asked.

"That's a bridge we may never have to cross," Raven said. "If, however, we are the last two teams standing, we retreat to one end of the ring and you to the other. Then we duke it out. Your worst match up then would be one against three which is better than the two against seven you face now."

The two-man team turned slightly to converse in low voices, apparently turning the idea over between them. Raven threw a glance over her shoulder and noticed her conversation with the other team had drawn the attention and ire of some of the other armies.

"I'd decide quickly, if I were you," Raven said, turning back to the two people in front of her. "Your time is running out."

"We accept your offer," the spokesman said. "So, how do you want to do this?"

"It's up to you," Raven answered. "Either you can take one flank while my team takes the other, or we can intersperse you two between the three of us. And if you're worried about a double cross, remember we're in nearly as much of a hard place as you are. We will not attack you until the very end."

"We'll take the left flank," the spokesman said, headed to take his place next to Midas who would hold the center of the formation.

"Good choice," Raven said as she turned and headed back to the line. "Leo, my sword."

She caught the wooden weapon in her hand and twirled it once to get used to the weight. Moving to the right flank, she stood beside Leopold and prepared for the coming onslaught.

"Any last words of encouragement or advice?" she called down the line, never taking her eyes off the enemy. Out of the corner of her eye, she could see an official take his place, ready to call casualties as they occurred. Two more were running from across the field.

"Hold the line and don't fake-die," Midas answered sarcastically. There was no time to respond as the enemy was already upon them.

The first wave was an army of seven. They crashed into the smaller army, in a line abreast, trying to flood around the edges. Raven and the soldier on the other flank slashed and stabbed, keeping the outer enemies at bay while Midas clubbed those in the middle aside with his weapon. The officials skirted the fierce combat, pulling out contestants as they were touched in the chest or head, and in half a minute the skirmish was over. None of The Shadow nor their allies had been touched, but had massacred the entirety of the attacking army.

"You're really good at this," Midas told the two strangers beside him. Though short, the skirmish had been incredibly physically taxing, and he was out of breath.

"I should be," one of the other soldiers said. "I've been training since I was a child."

"Same here," Midas responded. To say as much was to take extreme liberty with the words 'training' and 'child', but he figured it didn't matter given the circumstance. "Whose team are you on?"

"Baron Godfrey," the spokesman answered. "And you?"

"Baroness Maria," Raven answered, remembering just in time to insert her title.

"You're the famous three-person team?" one of Godfrey's soldiers asked. "The baron speaks quite highly of you after the last competition. He seemed duly impressed by your performance."

"And I'm impressed by yours," Raven said. "With seven against five, I thought for sure some of us wouldn't be here right now, but we all are."

"Same here," the spokesman from Godfrey's team said. "So, what's the plan now? Choose a target and attack?"

"We wait," Midas answered. "With any luck, some of these nit-wits will dispatch each other without our having to lift a finger."

"I think one of these so-called nit-wits are coming to meet us," Leopold said, pointing with his swords to a single figure approaching their small line.

"Attacking all alone?" Midas hailed the man as he drew near. "Has the sun addled your brain?"

"No, though to take on all five of you alone would certainly be against my senses," the man responded with a small chuckle. "I recognize you from a time you came to my lord's castle."

"Baron Dietrich?" Midas asked.

"Correct," the man answered, displaying the crest on his sleeve. "My team has been destroyed and I am the only one to escape. I was hoping to attach myself to your squad, at least for a time."

"The more the merrier, though you'll have to stand in front of me," Midas said. "The last thing I need is for you to dispatch me from behind."

"I will, of course, do as much if you insist," the man said, "but there is no reason for such precautions. I know I cannot win this contest alone and only hope to survive a bit longer than what I have already."

"Then welcome to our ranks," Midas said. "You'll stand beside me, to my left. What is your name?"

"Dustin," the new ally replied immediately. "I thought I was to stand in front of you."

"I changed my mind," Midas returned. "You'll post beside me or not at all. The choice is yours."

"Beside you it is," Dustin agreed and moved to take his place in the line-up.

"We have six now, we can take any of the teams out there," one of Godfrey's men said after a few moments of silence.

"And still we wait," Midas responded. "Every time we initiate contact, we stand the chance of losing someone. The more fighting the other armies do with each other, the better."

"Um, boss, I don't think that's going to happen," Dustin said. "Look."

The other teams, seeing what was happening, had started to converse and combine. Negotiations were clearly still ongoing and there were a few hold out teams, but the army opposing that of Maria, Godfrey, and Dietrich was already close to forty strong. Midas hoped the armies not aligning themselves to a side would come to him, but they didn't. As the larger, combined team formed ranks and advanced toward The Shadow and their allies, it swept aside these small pockets of resistance until there was no one left. The large army had sustained a few losses in the skirmishes bringing their numbers down to around thirty, but they still outnumbered their opponents five to one.

"If they charge, we won't hold up under it," Midas told his friends. "We attack first. Form an arrowhead to break their ranks. If our charge doesn't take us all the way through them, circle up wherever we stop. It will be our last stand."

He took the silence as agreement.

"Well, then, it's time to fight!" he shouted, swinging his club above his head and giving a battle cry.

The small army took off across the ring, building speed as it went and sweeping backwards to assume an arrowhead formation with Midas at the tip. He hit the enemy with a roar, using his club to smash them aside like wheat. The eliminations he and his allies inflicted were large as seen by the constant stream of contestants exiting the battle area, but there was no hope of crashing straight through the enemy. As the momentum of the charge dissipated, the smaller army closed into a circle with weapons bristling outward. The larger army backed away from the small group of survivors, leery of what they could do, but just when it seemed the immediate danger was gone, Midas felt a sword slap into his chest.

"Disqualified!" an official shouted, ending the game for him.

Leopold looked around to take stock of the situation. The larger army had been cut in half but so had his as Midas and Godfrey's two soldiers left the arena. Now he had but two companions to go back-to-back with, and they faced fifteen angry looking opponents. Well, the odds were better than when he had begun the event. He turned to Raven and Dustin, the only two left in his army.

"Go back-to-back and don't give an inch," he commanded.

"What are you going to do?" Raven shouted.

Leopold didn't hear the question as he dashed from the safety of his team and hurled himself headlong into the enemy. He crouched low and spun, using his leg to trip one man. He touched his sword to the man's chest while using the other weapon to block an attack. He was beset by two men now, so he pounced on one, bearing him to the ground and eliminating him. Leopold dropped a sword and jerked the shield from the fallen soldier's hand, standing and turning to the crowd of enemies coming toward him. It was much smaller than he expected, which meant Raven and Dustin were doing their jobs.

Leopold hurled himself back into the fray, dispatching four men as they backpedaled from his frenzied charge. Blows cascaded on his shield as the opponents tried desperately to break his guard, but he held it strong, absorbing every stroke they dealt. By now there were six enemies left, but Raven was leaving the arena, disqualified by a blow to the forehead. Even from where he was, Leopold could tell it was a nasty bruise and was probably starting to welt up.

Dustin was barely holding his own against two of the opponents, and Leopold rushed to his rescue. He hit one of the men in the back as he passed, then took a place beside his single remaining ally. Dustin smashed the other soldier in the head with his sword, bringing the number of enemies down by one more.

"Two of us and four of them," Leopold said. "What do you think of those odds?"

"They're a sight better than just a minute ago," Dustin answered as he panted for breath.

"I'm tired of this circus. Let's finish it," Leopold said.

Moving together, he and Dustin advanced slowly, but mutiny was on their side today. Two of the enemies were on the same team, but the other two were not. A short scuffle broke out among them resulting in only one soldier remaining at the end.

"Two on one," I like this even better," Leopold said. "Would you like to do the honors or should I?"

"Two swords are better than one," Dustin said. Leopold nodded and together they converged on the man, splitting to come at him from opposite sides. The battle was over quickly. Dustin attacked first, and the opponent moved to defend himself. Leopold saw an opening and struck out with his sword, ending the fight.

"So, now it's down to you and me," Leopold said.

"No, it's just you," Dustin said. "I saw you in the sword fighting competition. In no world could I ever beat you."

He raised his sword in salute, then tapped himself on the head with it and walked out of the ring. For the second time in two days, Leopold found himself victorious in the sword fighting ring with the crowd cheering wildly for him.

"All in all, I'd call this a success," Maria told Leopold, Midas, and Raven. Once again, they were meeting in the castle behind closed doors. Though the games were over, and many of the barons had already left with their entourages, the king still feared for his niece's safety.

"A success except for the part where we didn't win," Midas said. He was looking at the floor, and disappointment was heavy in his voice.

"As I said before, leave the strategy to me," Maria responded. "This was never about the games but something much more important. I wanted to make sure you were given the credit you are due, and these games were the way to do it."

"What are you getting at?" Raven asked.

"You'll find out before we leave," Maria answered. "Suffice it to say, the king was pleased with your performance. Though he had to pay out to Baron Godfrey because you didn't win, he received a substantially larger bet from Baron Jasven because you won Total War."

"It's always a good day when we get to stick it to Jasven," Midas said.

"Yes," Maria agreed. "Baron Dietrich also sends his regards. Your performance in the tournament has certainly been noted."

"He wasn't angry with Dustin for letting me win, was he?" Leopold asked.

"On the contrary," Maria said. "He told me it was what he would expect from his team."

"Good," Leopold sighed with relief. "I wouldn't have wanted him in trouble for what he did."

"I also need to thank you for what you've done to help relations between Baron Godfrey and myself," Maria said. "Your actions toward his team have been a great help in the way he sees me. I am hopeful this may turn into an alliance."

"Glad we could help," Midas said.

The conversation turned to other things and lasted for quite some time. It was no surprise it ended with Midas and Maria leaving together. She offered to take him on a tour of the castle, an offer he quickly accepted. Shortly after they left, Daniel entered the room.

"Well, as nice as this has been, it's time to get back to work," he said. "Where's Midas?"

"Out with Maria, of course," Raven said. "With most of the barons gone, they figured it was safe to go on a walk alone."

"Well, find him and tell him the vacation is over," Daniel said. "We're leaving early tomorrow morning."

"You mean to tell me this was a vacation?" Leopold asked incredulously.

"Of course," Daniel said. "And it worked. I feel refreshed and ready to get back out there."

"In that case, remind me never to go on a vacation with you again," Leopold flopped into a bed and pulled the pillow over his eyes. "With you, they're just too exhausting."

PART 2

The King's Contract

"Hurry up, you two," Raven said.

Leopold and Midas were still packing their things, even taking their time about it. She had been ready to leave an hour previous and was reaching the end of her patience with the brothers. The sun was just beginning to shine through the opaque windows of the castle, but Daniel had wanted to leave with the sunrise. They were already behind schedule.

"I don't see what the big hurry to get out of here is," Midas said grumpily as he stuffed extra clothes into a pack. "The king seems more than happy to put us up, Maria being his niece and all. We could stay here for another day or two and actually get the vacation Daniel promised this would be."

"I'm with Midas on this one," Leopold spoke up. "In what way is it a vacation to do what we always do but for the amusement of nobility? We even got paid for it, so it doesn't really qualify at all."

"Well, it's a good thing neither of you are paid to decide when we take a break and when we get to work," Raven responded. "This isn't a democracy, you know. Daniel said we leave with the sun, and that's what we're going to do."

"What's his deal with rushing out of here anyway?" Midas asked. "At first I thought he would be nervous about being in Kraljevi since it's the royal city, but he seemed fine with the idea. But now that the games are over and the nobility has left, he seems set on getting out of here as soon as possible."

"It may surprise you to learn that most of our clients are nobility," Raven said.

"Yes, that does surprise me," Midas said, pausing in his packing. "I thought we were the outlaws."

"Well, most people in positions of authority find themselves in awkward situations from time to time," Raven explained. "Then they find it easier to deal with things either in an illegal or unethical way, or perhaps they would just rather not be tied to a specific activity. No doubt Daniel was using the tournament as a way to get some contracts. Now it's over, and he has no reason to stick around."

"Working even on vacation," Leopold snorted. He pulled the straps on his pack and tightly tied them off. "Typical Daniel."

"So nobility use us whenever they want to do something people won't like," Midas said thoughtfully. "Doesn't that make us the bad guys?"

"Just now you said we were outlaws," Raven responded. "Some people would say we're the bad guys, but we're just doing what other people tell us to do."

"That doesn't really make us any better, does it?" Leopold asked.

"You wouldn't blame a shovel if it were used to club an innocent person to death, would you?" Raven asked. "Nor would you give it credit if it were used to plant food for an entire village. We're the shovel, just doing what we're told."

"I don't think you actually believe what you're saying," Leopold said. "If we're just a tool in the hands of others, why did we back out on the contract the first time we were at Maria's castle?"

"Because it would have meant the destruction of an entire city and the people in it," Midas answered.

"That's my point," Leopold said, pointing a finger at Raven. "We refused to take part in something which would bring harm to countless innocent people. A shovel doesn't stop someone from using it for evil purposes because it has no heart, mind, or soul, but we do. We're not just a tool. We *are* responsible for what we do, whether good or evil."

"If we didn't do it," Raven said, "someone else would. We can't stop anything from happening. The rich and the powerful decide the course of history, not pawns like us."

"Maria doesn't believe that," Midas interjected. "She would never hire someone else to skirt the law on her behalf. She doesn't believe the rich and powerful have the right to decide the fate of others."

"That's precisely what makes her the bravest noble I have ever seen," Raven said. "She has the courage to release control and give it back to others. She refuses to back down from an unpleasant issue or a tough decision, no matter how much it may test her mettle. She takes responsibility for her actions regardless of the consequences."

"That's all I'm saying we should do," Leopold said.

"It's not our decision to make," Raven said. "Remember our motto?"

"Of course I do. 'Anything for the money,'" Leopold answered. "But do we believe that anymore?"

"It's Daniel's guiding light," Raven said simply.

"I know Daniel believes it, but do we?" Leopold asked again. "We aren't a shovel to be used by some noble, nor are we one to be used by Daniel."

"What if we have to do evil so we can do good?" Midas asked suddenly. "If it weren't for us, Benny would still be a prisoner at Rajikline, but we wouldn't have gotten the job were it not for our reputation. Let me remind you, our reputation is not very pleasant."

"Do evil to do good, huh?" Leopold said. "I don't know. What I do know is wealth is no longer a good enough reason for me to do anything. Some things aren't worth the money."

"What of our debts to Daniel?" Raven asked. "We owe him for what he did for us. Is that not a good enough reason to follow him?"

"He took us in, sheltered us, fed us," Midas agreed. "But we've more than paid our debt to him."

Maybe you have, but not me, Raven thought. *A life for a life. He saved mine and now he owns it.* With a huff she addressed the boys. "Enough of the philosophical discussion. Daniel wants to leave, so get ready to move out."

"Ready," Midas responded and fastened his pack.

Shouldering their packs, The Shadow blazed through the halls of the castle. Daniel was waiting for them in the courtyard, and, though he gave a quizzical look, he didn't say anything. Silently he led the way toward the castle gates, but before they had gone a score of steps, a voice of great authority sounded across the grounds.

"Wait," the king boomed.

"Oh great," Daniel grimaced. As he turned around to face the monarch, however, his visage changed to one of a willing subject. "Your majesty, what can we do for you?"

"I would request your attendance in my throne room in half an hour," the king answered. "I simply need time to bathe and dress."

The king was close enough now to block the sun shining behind him, and The Shadow saw he was not dressed in his royal clothes but a simple bath robe. He wore nothing to indicate his station except a signet ring on his left hand.

"Simply our audience, your majesty?" Daniel asked. "It must be something of great importance for you to be seen in such a state this early in the morning."

"You will see of what importance it is in half an hour," the king said. "Until that time, feel free to go to the kitchens. They will see to your breakfast."

"Too bad," Midas commented as the king left. "I was really looking forward to dried meat and hard bread for my first meal of the day."

"The bread wouldn't have been hard," Daniel said with a scathing look at Midas. He glanced at the gate guards before turning back toward the castle. "Well, let's go get some food and see what the king has to say."

———————

"I saw you in the tournament and was duly impressed with your performance," the king said from his throne. Maria was seated to his right while The Shadow was arrayed in a semi-circle before him.

"Thank you for your notice, your majesty," Daniel said, bowing slightly.

"I was actually talking to the other three, but I see you speak as the leader," the king said. "Please forgo the titles. You may refer to me simply as 'sir'."

"Yes sir," Daniel said, bowing slightly again. "It is always an honor to know we have caught the eye of the king."

"I say, sir, you sure don't look like a king to me," Midas said brazenly. "When you were watching the games, you at least had a crown and some robes."

Indeed, the king had traded his bed clothes for more appropriate attire, but there was still a remarkable lack of nobility in his look. He wore no crown, extravagant clothes, or excessive jewelry. His signet was the only adornment he wore. Though his clothes looked expensive, they were nothing more than a wealthy merchant could have afforded.

"Midas," Daniel said in a low voice, but the warning was drowned out by the king's response.

"Young man, you have a remarkable lack of self-control in what you say. I know people who would have you beheaded for less."

"Your Majesty, I'm sure you have countless subjects who would be happy to tell you that day is dark and night is light,"

Midas said, quoting a local proverb concerning folly. "Would you prefer I be one of the mindless sheep?"

"I would not," the king replied. "As to my lack of kingliness, you could say it's contagious. I caught it from my niece."

"You couldn't tell it from looking at him now, but he used to be somewhat of a pompous blowhard," Maria agreed with a smile. "I've been working on him, though, and he's almost bearable."

"Almost," the king repeated. "A word my niece refuses to eliminate from her description of me. But I didn't call you here to learn about me. I have a proposition for you."

"A proposition?" Raven finally spoke up. "Are you referring to a job?"

"Yes," the king agreed. "Even in my position, sometimes I find myself in situations I cannot easily resolve. I have a problem I think people of your particular skill set could take care of."

"What kind of job, sir?" Daniel asked.

"For the past six months, a rash of thefts and robberies have plagued my city," the king explained. "I have made several investigations into them, but none have turned up anything substantial. I would like you to take on the next investigation."

"You want us to bring down a few robbers?" Raven asked. "Sir, if you don't mind my asking, what makes you think our performance in a physical tournament qualifies us to do this?"

"You are all certainly physically impressive," the king agreed. "My favorite performance was from the young boy, Leopold is your name, correct? I understand you hadn't juggled before this competition. But I did not simply choose you for your physical abilities. There was intelligence to the way you acted, an intelligence I think would be well suited to doing this task I am asking."

"Far be it from me to deny the request of the king," Daniel said with a bow.

"Do not accept this job simply for the fact I am asking you to do it," the king said. "I do not wish to use my position to gain your help; however, if you do this for me, the crown will owe you a great debt of gratitude." There was a pause and he added, "I will also pay you."

"We would be more than happy to take on this task for you, sir," Daniel said. "We can hash out the details of payment later."

"I would rather do it now," the king cut the wizard off. "I do not like the idea of you working without understanding the compensation."

"Very well, sir. Would you like to talk here in front of everyone else or retire to another location?" Daniel asked.

"We could also leave," Leopold offered.

"You may stay if you wish," the king informed the others, "Daniel and I shall be staying in here to discuss business."

"Thanks for the offer, sir," Leopold said. "Don't take this the wrong way but I think I'd rather get stretched on the rack than have to sit through the boredom which is money matters."

"Stretched on the rack, you say?" the king asked with a smile. "I can arrange it if you wish."

"I don't want to put you to all the trouble, but thanks all the same, sir," Leopold said and quickly headed for the door. The laughter of the others followed him out of the throne room.

"Leopold, wait."

Leopold turned around to see the king heading down the hall toward him. He turned to face the king and straightened his posture. He didn't know what was on the king's mind, but he certainly wanted to make a good impression.

"I just wanted to congratulate you on your performance in the games," the king said when he reached Leopold. "Your team was certainly one to watch. You, in particular, were a surprise. For starters, the way you handled yourself in the swordplay competition was impressive."

"I was just doing my part, sir," Leopold said. "We worked together as a team, and the team was what earned our ultimate place in the standings."

"Modesty is a good trait to have," the king said. He gazed at Leopold for a few moments before continuing. "You remind me of someone I once knew."

"Who is that, if you don't mind my asking?" Leopold said.

"My son," the king answered somewhat sadly. "He would be about your age now if he were still here."

"I'm sorry to hear that, sir," Leopold said, his words sounding incredibly inadequate given the gravity of the situation. "What happened to him?"

"He was taken from me and my wife when he was still quite young," the king answered. "Kidnappers who never made their demands known. I would have given them whatever they wanted in order to get my son back, but they simply disappeared after they took him."

Silence fell between the king and Leopold. The boy didn't dare break it and allowed it to continue until the king gave an absent smile.

"You look a lot like I imagine he would, you know. He even had a birthmark on his shoulder where you have yours," he said. "In fact, when I first saw you, I thought you might be him, though upon closer examination, it's clear you are not."

"Was your son's name Benny?" Leopold asked before he knew what he was saying. His heart skipped a beat, and his mouth became instantly dry as he mentally berated himself for the mistake. The last thing he wanted to do was get into a discussion with the king about Benny when the very topic would almost certainly lead back to his criminal occupation.

"Benjamin was his given name, but Benny to his friends," the king answered in a startled fashion. "How did you know?"

"I knew him once," Leopold answered vaguely. Though his face remained calm, even stoic, he was frantically racking his brain for a feasible reason he knew the crown prince. "A long time ago."

"Then you are originally from Kraljevi," the king surmised, understanding crossing his face. "Benny was always interested in sneaking away to mingle with the common folk, much to the chagrin of his nurse and caretaker. He thought, and I now believe he was correct, that the only way to rule a people was to get to know them. He had wisdom far beyond his years."

"Yes indeed, born in Kraljevi," Leopold latched onto the king's first statement, relieved to have a ready-made excuse for his knowledge of Benny. To add believability to his story, he embellished, "I remember climbing the trees in the public garden with him."

"Yes," the king said sadly. "He did enjoy his romps through the city."

An uneasy silence fell between them which Leopold was hesitant to break. Eventually, his desire to remove himself from this awkward situation destroyed his reservations and he spoke.

"I'm sorry for your loss, sir. Perhaps," he paused, choosing his next words carefully. "Perhaps he will be found again. There is always hope."

"I fear your optimism is ill placed," the king said in a sorrowful tone. "Some things are simply too good to come true in real life. Well, I should get back to Daniel. I just wanted to give you my regards before I forgot."

"Thank you, sir," Leopold said and bowed slightly.

He waited until the king was gone before turning to head back down the hall the way he had started some minutes ago. From what the king said, something was badly amiss. The Shadow had rescued Benny from castle Rajikline and sent him home, but he clearly never made it. Was it possible the king's son and the Benny he knew were two different people? It would be an incredible coincidence if this were the case. No, Leopold finally decided. Benny was certainly the king's son, though what had happened to him after Rajikline was a mystery. One which Leopold would check into eventually, but he didn't have the time right now. The king was loading The Shadow up with another job even now, and besides, he was famished. He took a left and headed for the kitchen. The breakfast he had consumed previously hadn't been near enough to satiate the growling in his stomach.

As he sat eating, Raven stuck her head into the room and looked about. Her eyes settled on him, and she moved in his direction, sitting down opposite him. She regarded his full plate with a quizzical look, which he answered with a shrug of his shoulders. He was a growing young man and had the right to eat a lot.

"So how does this job suit you?" Raven finally asked.

"Working for the king?" Leopold responded. "Taking down a ring of thieves? Yes, as long as it doesn't involve assassinating anyone or doing anything else illicit, it suits me."

"Daniel chose this job," Raven said. "I know you don't have the highest opinion of him, but he's not evil like you seem to think."

"I don't think he's evil," Leopold said. "I think he's driven by money, which can cause him to do evil things. To him a job is nothing more than the commission it carries, for better or for worse."

"So you don't have a problem working with him as long as the jobs are what you consider to be good?" Raven asked.

"I don't have a problem working with Daniel," Leopold said. "He's a smart guy and he looks out for us. As long as the jobs are legal, I'm perfectly fine staying on his payroll, but we both know the illegal jobs pay more. One day he's going to take one I can't stomach doing, and then we'll part company."

"You would turn your back on your family for your own peace of mind?" Raven asked in a slightly wavering voice.

"For my conscience, I *would* turn my back on Daniel," Leopold answered.

"What if I threw in my lot with him?" Raven asked. "Would you turn your back on me too? And what about Midas?"

"I have a duty to you, Midas, and Daniel, but my primary duty is to myself," Leopold said. "If I can't live with myself, what good would I be to the people I care about? If I can't stand the sight of my own reflection, how could I expect you to do the same?"

"So what's going to be the breaking point?" Raven asked. "From what you've said, killing is out, but what about thieving?"

"I don't even know myself what the point will be," Leopold answered. "Whether it's stealing something, killing a person, or killing a horse, all I know is when the time comes, I'll part company with Daniel. I have a feeling I'll never see him again afterwards, but I don't want that to be the case with you."

"What do you mean?" Raven asked. She knew exactly what he meant but wanted to hear him say it.

"I'm not afraid of losing Midas," Leopold began. "He and I have been together for a long time, and I have no doubt whatever I do, he will be right behind me. On the other hand, I have no idea what you will do. I like you and don't like the prospect of never seeing you again."

"You like me?" Raven repeated his words, suddenly very interested in the woodgrain of the table.

"Yeah," Leopold said. "You and Midas are some of the only friends I've ever had or at least the only ones I can remember. Friendship is a rare enough commodity as it is. I don't want to lose one of my only friends over something so stupid."

"Friends," Raven said in a disappointed voice. "Is that all you see me as?"

Leopold looked up from his food suddenly, shocked by the question. Raven and his relationship had been defined by tiptoeing around the issue and constantly avoiding their true feelings. Though the words of her question weren't quite specific enough to directly point to the real issue, they were far more direct than anything she had said previously or what he had said, for that matter. He'd always been careful to avoid saying the words as if somehow it would make things easier. If there was a time to tell her how he felt, it was now, or he could chicken out like he always had in the past. What the heck! What was life worth living if he didn't take a few risks and put himself out there?

"No," Leopold said, swallowing the food in his mouth. He put down his fork and reached across the table. He looked about to take Raven's hand in his, but hesitated, finally settling in awkwardly covering her fingers with his own. "The truth is, Raven, I…" He stumbled over his words as sweat began to bead on his forehead. After a few moments, he found his voice again, and now it had strength. He was so committed to getting out what was on his mind that his words were rushed as they tumbled out from between his lips. "I love you. Now, I know I haven't even been friends with a lot of girls, but everyone says love is unmistakable. If that's true, there's no doubt in my mind of my love for you. I've seen people as young as us happily married and if things were different, I would have already asked you to marry me. I'd do it right now except…" He trailed off.

"Except what?" Raven asked, her voice catching slightly in her throat.

"You know I disagree with Daniel on some things," Leopold said. "I also know you owe him a lot more than either Midas or I do. I don't know what it is he did for you, but you still feel a debt to him. What happens when Daniel and I disagree and I leave? Would you stay with him or go with me?"

"I don't know," Raven answered. "If there was a reason for me to go with you…" She stopped, unable to complete the sentence around the knot in her throat.

"You wouldn't, Raven, and I think we both know it," Leopold said. "No matter what feelings you may have for me, you feel an obligation to Daniel. I know you're a good person and that you will continue to pay your debt of obligation until it's paid in full. You may not want to, but you would end up going with Daniel."

"You're right, I would," Raven confessed, tears running down her cheeks now. "But I also love you. Isn't that enough?"

"No," Leopold answered, removing his hand from Raven's. "I'm sorry, but it's not. If I get married, I want it to be to someone who will take me over everyone else in the world as I would them. So long as you have an obligation to anyone who you put above your love for me, we can never be more than friends."

Raven put her head in her hands, tears running everywhere now. Leopold had never been good at dealing with crying people. *Especially ones to whom I just professed my love,* he moaned to himself. Somehow he didn't think she would appreciate him patting her shoulder. On the other hand, not doing anything would probably be a fatal error as well. Cursed if he did and cursed if he didn't. Silently he reached across the table to take her hand in his. If this was to be a no-win situation, he'd rather lose trying to comfort her. His gesture did seem to calm her down, and her tears began to subside.

With his free hand, Leopold retrieved his fork from the table where he had placed it and resumed eating. Winning or losing, tears or no, he was still hungry. No matter how this turned out, he could at least start the day with a full stomach.

"In a nutshell, here's the situation," Daniel said. The Shadow was congregated in a large, private room of the castle. A circular table took up a good chunk of the middle of the room, but enough space was left around it for smaller tables, chairs, and other furniture against the walls. Two intricate wall hangings gave the room some color, while maps of Kraljevi, the surrounding areas, and the entire kingdom offered a more practical touch to the décor. Midas was holding his hand high in the air, so Daniel pointed to him.

"What is it, Midas?" the wizard asked with a sigh.

"How did you manage to get us into this room?" the young man asked. "It looks pretty fancy. Everything in here probably costs more than the grand total of what I'm worth."

"The king has kindly offered this room as a staging point for our operations," Daniel explained. "He has also given us access to many of the services the castle has to offer."

"So, to be clear, this room is kind of like our headquarters? We've never had a headquarters before!" Midas said with a meaningful look at Leopold. This was normally the time when his younger brother would interject and they would go on a back-and-forth long enough to drive Daniel crazy, but today Leopold was distracted and withdrawn. From past experience, when he was like this, Raven was usually furious with him over something, but today she didn't appear angry. Instead, there was a sadness on her face which Midas couldn't quite pin down.

"Yes, Midas, this room is our headquarters for the duration of our contract with the king," Daniel agreed amiably. He seemed oblivious to the emotional state of his team, and with as happy as he looked, the king must have agreed to quite a large payment for the job.

"So what have we gotten ourselves into this time?" Leopold asked.

"Well, as the king mentioned earlier, the job is to investigate and take down a ring of thieves," Daniel said. "They've been plaguing the city for several months now, and the four investigations the king has ordered all turned up nothing. They were all led by Captain Payne, leader of the king's guards."

"So, do we think he's dirty?" Midas asked. "He could be part of the ring or just taking bribes to make sure it isn't discovered."

"Perhaps he's incompetent or simply out of his depth," Daniel said. "Captain Payne's innocence or guilt is one of the things the king wants determined by our investigation."

"What are the marks on this map?" Leopold asked, examining a hanging on the wall. In all, twenty-seven pins stuck out of it.

"Those are all the places in the city which have been struck by the thieves," Daniel answered. "As you can see, the crimes have been committed all over the city and the most recent even occurred in the castle itself. Something of extreme sentimental value was taken, and the king very much wants it back."

"So, our three tasks are to determine the innocence or guilt of Captain Payne, determine who is behind the ring, and reclaim the king's possession," Raven spoke up. "Does that pretty much sum it up?"

"Well, yes," Daniel answered.

"It should be pretty easy," Raven said. It was evident her brain was working, but her voice indicated she just couldn't summon the willpower to care about any of this.

"Pretty easy to solve a rash of crimes?" Midas asked. "Please tell me you know something I don't, because from where I'm standing, we don't even know where to begin."

"We're a group of criminals," Raven said. "We have connections. If we can't get to the bottom of this in a matter of hours, we're much worse at our job than I ever imagined."

"And since we're the best at what we do, we'll have it wrapped up by sunset tomorrow," Daniel said. "Of course, I told the king the end of the week, so he'll be impressed when we finish early. Who knows? We might get a bonus!"

"When do we start?" Leopold asked.

"Now," Daniel answered. "We'll split into two groups."

"I'll go with Midas," Leopold said at the same time Raven said, "I'll go with you, Daniel."

The wizard looked from one to the other several times before continuing.

"Raven and I will go to the criminal haunts of the city and see what we can turn up," he said. "Midas and Leopold, you go and interview each of the people who were robbed. See if you can get any useful information out of them."

"Sure thing, boss," Midas said. "Do you have a list of people and places?"

"Here," Daniel answered, extending a rolled-up sheet of paper. Leopold took it.

"Sounds good," the younger boy said. "Is there anything else we need to know?"

"Just get what information you can and meet us back here in two hours," Daniel answered.

"Good," Leopold said. "Come on, Midas, let's get out of here."

Midas followed Leopold out of the room and through the corridors of the castle. The younger brother was moving quickly as if trying to outrun something, and Midas had to jog to catch up, something he was unaccustomed to having to do. As soon as they were out the gates of the castle, Leopold unrolled the paper and looked it over as he continued to walk.

"This place should be our first stop," he said.

"No, the first order of business is for you to tell me what's going on," Midas said.

"We're going to interview people who have been robbed," Leopold answered evenly.

"I never treat you like an idiot, so please don't treat me like one," Midas said. "I can tell something is wrong, and I have a feeling it involves Raven."

"Ding ding ding! You win the grand prize!" Leopold said snidely. The look on his brother's face made him immediately regret the words. "Sorry, I didn't mean that. Yes, something's wrong, but I don't want to talk about it."

Midas nodded and made a small noise in his throat.

"I get it," he said as he walked past Leopold. "Let me know when you do want to talk about it."

"What?" Leopold asked, chasing after his brother.

"What you're having right now is girl problems," Midas said. "You're going to try to figure them out for yourself for a while, but once you realize you don't have the answer, you'll want to talk to someone else."

"How do you know?" Leopold demanded.

"Because I'm going through the same thing," Midas said. "I'm all the way up to the talking to someone else stage."

"You're having girl problems?" Leopold asked. "Right. What kind of problems could you possibly be having?"

"Well, obviously they're between me and Maria," Midas began.

"There's no problem," Leopold cut in. "You like her, and she obviously likes you."

"Yes," Midas nodded. "Which makes the issue even more painful. She's nobility and I'm not."

"She doesn't care about stuff like that," Leopold said. "Raven's right, you're lucky. Maria is probably the only noble in the whole kingdom who would even entertain a relationship with a commoner such as yourself."

"And what about a relationship with a criminal?" Midas asked. He stopped and turned so suddenly, Leopold almost ran into him. "What do you think the Lady Maria, baroness of this kingdom, is going to think of me when she finds out I'm a member of the infamous group known as The Shadow?"

Leopold stared at his brother for several long moments, trying to formulate a suitable answer. This was a complication he had never thought of before, and one with no easy answer.

"What if she never finds out?" he finally asked.

"Impossible," Midas answered. "I could never move past whatever it is Maria and I have without telling her myself. She may be able to see past the nobility issue, but our relationship up to this point is based on a lie. It can't continue unless I tell her, but then I don't know what she'll think of me. She could end up being my ticket straight to prison."

A moment of silence passed as Midas allowed the gravity of the situation to settle on his brother. He could almost see Leopold's brain working, trying to figure out a loophole or a way through the problem. He expected him to throw out a condolence, a solution, or even an argument, but he never expected what happened. Leopold threw back his head and laughed out loud. He started walking again, heading down the street toward their first interview, still chuckling as he went.

"What's so funny?" Midas asked, genuinely puzzled by the reaction.

"You said you could tell I was having girl problems because you were in the same spot," Leopold explained. "Well, we are, but we're looking in opposite directions. You're afraid of what Maria will do if she finds out you're a criminal, and I don't know what Raven will do if I straighten out my act and *stop* committing crimes! It'd be a little bit ironic for me to ask you for advice, wouldn't it?"

"That is pretty funny," Midas agree with a smile.

"On a serious note," Leopold said. "The last few jobs we've done have had good pay and, more importantly, not illegal. No assassinations, kidnappings, or even stealing. But we both know it's only a matter of time before Daniel finds a high paying job which would put us back on the wrong side of the law."

"We're already on the wrong side of the law, brother," Midas said. "We're just pretending not to be for the moment."

"That's my point," Leopold said. "The thing is, I don't know if I can stomach our line of work anymore. The next illicit job Daniel turns up, I may be parting company with him. Raven has said herself she would stay with Daniel. What about you?"

Midas didn't say anything for a while. After a heavy sigh, he finally spoke.

"We're criminals, brother," he said. "It may not be who we are, but it's what we've done and it's what we do."

"I see," was all Leopold could get out while keeping his voice even. Despite his best efforts, a lump formed in his throat while tears formed in the corners of his eyes.

"That being said," Midas continued, raising a finger to indicate he hadn't finished. "You're my brother, my first real friend. No matter what I think of the decisions you make, I'll go wherever you go and do whatever it is you want to do. I've tried a life of crime already so why not a life apart from it?"

"Thank you, Midas, I'm glad to hear you say that," Leopold said. He looked down at the paper in his hands to hide the motion of wiping a tear from his eye. "I think the tailor shop we're looking for is right down there."

"Seriously?" Midas asked. "Who in their right mind would rob a tailor shop?"

"I don't know," Leopold answered. "But it's our job to find out."

"I know the criminal element in any city has to be careful and doubly so in Kraljevi, but aren't the sewers a bit cliché?" Raven asked as she followed Daniel under the low, dripping ceilings of the pipes running beneath the city. If Leopold had been with her, he would have pointed out that this was relatively clean compared to some sewers he had been in. Storm water as well as waste traveled through it, keeping the vast majority of the filth moving downstream and not festering and breeding disease as it did in other places. But Raven didn't know, and to her, this was every bit as bad as Leopold swimming through the moat and climbing up the latrine pipe at Rajikline.

"The sewers are a cliché because they work so well," Daniel said. "They have access to almost every part of the city and they're practically a labyrinth in and of themselves. Only problem is, the city guard knows who hangs out down here, so the doors in have to be camouflaged pretty well."

"Labyrinth and camouflage don't sound promising unless we know what we're doing," Raven said. "We do know what we're doing, don't we?"

"You know me, Raven," Daniel said in mock offense. "Am I the type of person who would foray into the sewers if I didn't know what I was doing?"

"No," Raven admitted. "You always have a plan."

"Exactly," Daniel said. "Right now, the plan is to follow this tunnel until it dead ends, take a right, then the first left. There's a hidden door shortly after marked by a vent-hole to the surface."

"Marked by a vent-hole," Raven repeated. She was silent for about a hundred feet before speaking again. "Daniel, have you ever had to choose between the work we do and something else you cared about?"

"Where is this coming from?" Daniel asked, not looking back at Raven but continuing his forward trek, torch held high to illuminate the tunnel.

"Nowhere specifically," Raven lied. "It's just that the work we do is bad, isn't it? Why do we do what is evil?"

"Simple," Daniel answered. "We do it for the money."

"And what if the money is ever not enough to justify what we do?" Raven asked. "What if it doesn't ward off the ache I get in the pit of my stomach every time we cause someone pain when we kill or steal?"

"You've been talking to Leopold and Midas, haven't you?" Daniel asked. "You can't trust the brothers to know what's best."

Raven didn't hear him speaking, lost as she was in her own internal turmoil. Ignoring what the wizard had said, she continued.

"On the other hand, the people who are supposed to make and carry out the laws also do things like we do. They're supposed to be the ones people trust and look up to. If they do it, why shouldn't we, especially when we make a decent wage doing it?"

"And don't forget the very people you speak of who make and carry out the laws are the ones who hire us a lot of the time," Daniel said. "By offering our services to everyone, all we're really doing is leveling the playing field to take the advantage away from the nobility."

"But then money becomes the defining factor," Raven said. "The poor never have a chance, never have someone to stand up for them. We aren't leveling the field, we're just making it about money instead of nobility."

"The poor have never been a driving force in the world, nor will they ever be," Daniel said dismissively. "Don't waste too much time pitying them. It's a cutthroat world out there. The poor can't help us, so we don't help them."

"Leopold, Midas, and I were poor when you found us," Raven said. "Why did you help us?"

"You may have been poor in money, but certainly not in your abilities," Daniel said. "I did for you because you could return the favor and help me. That's how the world works. Only fools waste their time on charity, and it ruins them eventually."

"Lady Maria helps the poor," Raven countered.

"I understand the soft spot you have for the baroness," Daniel said. "But the fact of the matter is, she helps the poor and only fools do that. What has she ever gotten in return for her labor?"

"Our pity," Raven answered.

"And what did we get for our trouble?" Daniel asked. "An inability to get decent contracts, and two associates whose newly discovered consciences prevent us from taking any of the really good jobs we may find. It may take a bit of searching, but somewhere down the line, someone ends up standing out in the cold. That's the way it always is with do-gooders."

"I understand everything you're saying, but Leo definitely disagrees, and I think Midas might agree with his brother," Raven said. "I feel so torn. My feelings for Leo are so strong, yet the direction he pulls me…sometimes I don't know what to do."

"I told you your feelings for the brothers, particularly the younger one, would be a problem," Daniel said. "It has become abundantly clear to me they lack the will to always do what is necessary."

"You misunderstand," Raven said. "It's not that I disagree with them but that I agree with them more than I would like. I agree with them, but I also owe my life to you. Sometimes I wonder if 'anything for the money' is what I believe, but it's what you believe in."

"Raven, listen to me," Daniel said. His mind was racing, and he put a hand on her shoulder to give himself more time to think. So the brothers weren't allured by the glitter of gold anymore? This was unfortunate though not unforeseen. "You are still quite young and don't know all the ways of the world. Right and wrong, good and evil are not as obvious as you and the brothers seem to think. There are no such things as good or evil, just what is best for you and what isn't.

"In all the time you've been with me, I've done nothing but look out for your best interests. While the others may have done the same, they're confused right now. They're in the beginning stages of a crusade for good, and what they don't know is that their path will end in nothing except disappointment and tears. I'm just trying to be a good friend and look out for what's best for you."

"I trust you, Daniel, but what about Midas and Leo?" Raven asked. "They seem pretty set in their way of thinking. Leo even said he would leave if it came to that."

"They aren't against us, just deluded by what they've recently experienced," Daniel said. "After a few lucrative contracts with the rulers of the land, they think being legal is the way to go, but I've been there. The nobility will play them, use them as pawns in their scheming, and throw them out when they are finished. What we need is a way to show them the truth before it hurts them irreparably."

"Couldn't you just tell them?" Raven asked. "They still respect you."

"Their respect for and faith in me has degraded recently," Daniel said. "They wouldn't believe me because to them I'm just a greedy, self-centered miser who will do anything to make money. The thing is, since I actually am greedy and self-centered, they feel justified in ignoring what I say. They just don't have the experience yet to see I'm right."

"Then what do we do?" Raven asked.

"I don't know," Daniel confessed. "Give me some time to come up with a plan. Of course, you can't let the brothers know about this."

"I don't like keeping secrets from them, but if it's for their own good…" Raven trailed off.

"I promise, it is," Daniel said. "You know everything I do is for your best interests, and it's the same for them. The four of us have a symbiotic relationship; if one of us leaves, the rest suffer. Why would I want to do anything but help them?"

"I trust you," Raven finally said.

"Good," Daniel said. "If you follow my lead, I'm sure we can figure something out. We won't lose the brothers, do you understand?" Raven nodded. Daniel pointed up to a spot of light coming down through the ceiling and said, "I'm glad that's settled because we're here, and I'm going to need you focused when we go into this den of thieves."

"They're our people," Raven pointed out. "We should fit right in."

"Yeah, which shockingly doesn't make me feel any better," Daniel said as he reached for the hidden door catch. "Be on the lookout for anything or anyone dangerous."

"Sure thing, boss," Raven said, touching the pommel of the short sword at her waist. "This isn't my first trip to a criminal hideout."

Without a reply, Daniel pulled the catch, and the door opened from the side of the sewer tunnel. The new passageway was every bit as dark as the sewer tunnels, but it wasn't of the same construction. The stone floor, walls, and ceiling of the sewer were replaced with dirt when Daniel and Raven stepped into the burrow behind the secret door. The portal clicked shut behind them, cutting off all light except what was cast by the torch.

Daniel led the way forward through the darkness. Though the trip was short, the element of the unknown made it seem much longer. The pool of light cast by the torch illuminated just what was around them. Periodically it fell on ceiling supports, posts set into the ground holding up boards designed to keep the roof from caving in. The shadows cast by them shortened and lengthened eerily as they passed. They were the only obstructions in the whole tunnel.

The darkness crowded around the light of the torch giving Raven the feeling of a hand of blackness trying to crush the air from her lungs. She started to panic as, for a moment, she was transported back in time several years. She was in the cold and damp cargo hold of a ship out at sea, curled up on the rags which composed her bed. She longed to stand up and stretch her tight muscles or even to lie flat and fully extended, but the bars around her wouldn't allow for it. The cage she was in had been built for something half her size, probably a dog instead of a human. The only light in the whole place was cast by evenly spaced lanterns hanging down the centerline of the hold which did more to cast shadows than illuminate. The light was scarce, but it was something for which she longed and waited patiently. The lanterns were only lit when the crew was below, and though she hated them, she loved the light.

Raven reached for the bars of her cage, but they were no longer in front of her. She was back in the tunnel, Daniel already far enough ahead to have left her in the darkness. She hurried to catch up to him, and before she had taken two steps, he threw open a door and soft light flooded through it accompanied by the sounds of laughter, loud voices, and raucous music. She hurried to step through the door and took in her surroundings. So this was where the criminal underground congregated in the royal city. She immediately located a bar, a group of people playing a variety of musical instruments, and even a fighting pit, empty at the moment though she could imagine what kind of events took place inside. She glanced around the place a second time and smiled. As far as hideouts went, this could have been much worse.

———————+———————

"I can appreciate how scared you were," Midas said kindly. "However, I was hoping to get some different information from you before I left."

"I already told the royal guards when they came through," the blacksmith said.

"I'm sure you did, but we aren't the royal guard," Midas said.

"But you work for the king, right?" the blacksmith demanded. "Can't you just ask the guard to tell you what I told them?"

"We could, but written words don't go a long way in an investigation like this," Midas said. He didn't know if the words coming out of his mouth were true or not since he'd never before been involved in anything of this sort. "I prefer to hear you tell it and see the area which was broken into. I need to see where the items which were stolen were located." He thought of something and hoped it sounded good even as he said it. "I need to be at the scene of the crime to get inside the thief's head."

"The royal guards have already been through here twice with no results to show for it," the blacksmith said. "Do you think you can do better than them?"

"I'm positive we can as long as you cooperate and help us help you," Midas answered.

"Well, I'll remain skeptical until you succeed, but any hope is better than what I've got now," the blacksmith said. "Ever since I was robbed, I've barely been scraping by. I used to be able to keep items in stock for customers, but now I can only do special order jobs which are paid for upfront. Then there's the matter of my tools. The thieves took a lot of them and now I can't do much of anything except for the simplest jobs. Most of my business has gone to my competitors by now."

"Okay, I have a list here of what was taken," Midas said, pulling a sheet of paper from the sheaf in his hands. "Why don't you walk me around and show me where each item was when it was stolen."

As the blacksmith showed Midas around his shop, Leopold did a search of his own, checking the building for ways to get inside. The only two doors on the first floor were stout, built of solid oak, each with strong locks and bolts. Both doors were also equipped with heavy locking bars which the blacksmith claimed to always use at night, the time when the theft occurred. The walls also appeared to be strong, even in the workshop. There were no signs of forced entry anywhere, which interested Leopold.

"What's upstairs?" he interrupted whatever the blacksmith had been telling Midas.

"Upstairs?" the blacksmith asked in confusion. "Nothing was taken from there."

"I know, but I'd still like to know what's up there," Leopold said.

"As you wish," the blacksmith acquiesced. "The stairs are this way if you'll just follow me."

"These are the sleeping quarters for myself and my family," the blacksmith said once they had gained the second floor. The building's floorplan had been divided into three large rooms, each with bedroom furniture in them. Though the rooms were sparsely furnished, what was present was of considerable quality. From a single touch, Leopold could tell the mattresses of the beds were stuffed with feathers instead of the straw typical of non-nobility. The dressers, though simple in appearance, were sturdily constructed of cut lumber and finished to be smooth to the touch, and the wash basins were made of porcelain instead of iron.

"You've done well for yourself, I see," Leopold told the blacksmith.

"Well, yes," the man admitted. "It was well known that I was the best blacksmith around. I had more business than I could handle."

"Could this have been the work of one of your rivals?" Midas asked as Leopold examined each of the bedroom windows in turn. They were of a slightly unusual construction with the heavy shutters on the inside. They were open to allow in the fresh air, exposing the chicken wire stretched between the window panes to prevent birds from entering. The edges of the wire were fastened to the wood, and it appeared the barrier had been present for some time.

"You have a family," Leopold told the blacksmith. "Where are they at the moment?"

"I had them stay at my father's house after the break-in," the blacksmith answered.

"But they were here the night of the theft?" Leopold asked.

"Yes, we all were," the blacksmith answered. "Some of my tools were quite large, and the thieves made enough noise to wake me as they worked. I went down to see what was going on, but one of them must have intercepted me on the stairs and hit me over the head. I woke up on the stairs with a splitting headache and a lump the size of an egg. I rushed downstairs, but they were gone by then."

"And you have no idea how they got in or out?" Leopold asked.

"None," the blacksmith said. "Like I said before, the doors were locked and barred before I went to sleep, and they were exactly the same when I woke up."

"Well, that's about all I need unless you have some more questions, Midas," Leopold said.

"I think I'm good," Midas said. To the blacksmith, "Thank you for your time. We'll do our very best to see the men responsible put behind bars."

"Thank you," the man said. "As I said before, the royal guard has already been through here twice and never turned up anything. Just between you and me, I think they might be part of the whole thing."

"We'll do what we can," Midas said again as he and Leopold left the house. They walked down the street for a few blocks before turning in at a small bakery. Midas bought some sandwich rolls while Leopold chose a table in the small eating area outside. The older brother arrived with the food and they started eating.

"So, do you think we're actually dealing with corrupt guards?" Leopold asked after a few bites.

"Hard to say," Midas answered. "From the people we talked to, I don't even know if all the thefts are related."

"Why do you say that?" Leopold asked and took another bite of his sandwich.

"There aren't any similarities between the robberies," Midas said. "To begin with, the targets are about as different as you can get. A tailor, a blacksmith, and a bakery? The only hits which really made sense were the jewelry shop and the bank. Money spends anywhere and jewels fence relatively easily, but large equipment from a blacksmith would require a black market I've never heard of."

"I agree," Leopold said.

"And the operations of the thieves at the various locations are so different, I'm not even sure they're all the same people," Midas continued. "Some are loud, some are quiet, some are so concerned with being seen they knocked out the blacksmith on his way down the stairs, but at the bakery, the owner saw several hooded figures who fled out the front door when he caught them."

"They certainly sound like different people," Leopold concurred. "Do you think it's all different individuals in some sort of a thieves' society?"

"Maybe," Midas said. "But the thing which bothers me the most is the blacksmith's house. How did the thieves get inside?"

"I had the same question," Leopold said. "The doors were solid oak and the locks and bars were strong. Besides, there was no sign of the doors being forced open."

"Well, if you were going to rob the place, what would you do?" Midas asked.

"I'd use the windows on the second floor," Leopold said, "but there are two problems with that idea. First, most people can't utilize upper story openings like I can. Besides, you remember the wire stretched across the window openings? I checked all of it for signs of entry, but there were none. However the thieves got in, it wasn't through the windows."

"What does that leave?" Midas asked. "Perhaps an inside job? Someone already in the house could have gone and opened the door."

"That doesn't make any sense," Leopold said. "Why would you help someone rob your own house?"

"One of the kids is angry with his father," Midas offered.

"Ruining your family financially because you're mad at your dad seems a bit drastic," Leopold said. "It's possible, of course, since kids can do stupid things but—wait a second!"

"What is it?" Midas asked, scanning the surrounding buildings and streets.

"We need to go," Leopold said, standing up and stuffing what remained of his lunch into his mouth. "I want to take a second look inside all the places which have been robbed."

"And then?" Midas asked.

"Then I want to look inside some of the places which *haven't* been robbed."

"What's a pretty girl like you doing in a place like this?" Raven heard the words at the same time she felt a hand fall on her shoulder.

"I don't know what you're thinking right now, but you need to forget it and just walk away," Raven said, never turning from the bar.

"I'm just thinking you're looking pretty good to be a thief," the voice said as the owner moved around Raven to lean backwards against the bar beside her. "Can I get you something to drink?"

"No, I'm just fine by myself," was what Raven intended to say. Then again, she also expected her admirer to by a creepy old man or unattractive at the very least. His blond hair was dirty as though it hadn't been washed for some time, but somehow it combined with the ragged cut and the stubble on the young man's face to cause an effect of rugged handsomeness. She was caught off guard by his appearance, and the only sounds her mouth made were a series of grunts and squeaks.

"That sounds tasty, but I don't think they serve it here!" the young man said. "My name's Filch, by the way."

"Filch," Raven repeated. She was coming back around, almost in complete control of her faculties again. "Really? You couldn't come up with anything more interesting than Filch?"

"What's wrong with it?" he asked. Raven couldn't tell if the offense in his voice was feigned or real. She guessed the former, not that it changed her reply at all.

"You might as well call yourself thief or pickpocket," she said. "It's a bit of a giveaway and completely devoid of creativity."

"You're right," the young man agreed. "If it were up to me, I would have gone with something different, but unfortunately it was given to me by someone else and it stuck. My real name is Douglas."

"Can I call you Doug?" Raven asked.

"You may," Douglas answered. He waited for a moment before saying, "What's your name, if you don't mind my asking?"

"Raven, and before you say anything, it's my given name," Raven answered. "It was also given to me by someone else. Not sure I would have gone with it had it been my choice, but I'm used to it now."

"Raven," Douglas said thoughtfully. "I like it. A beautiful name for a beautiful girl. It makes sense to me."

"Beautiful, huh?" Raven asked and took a swig of her drink. She pointed to her scar-torn face. "You *are* looking up here, right?"

"Yes," Douglas answered. "I find it's the best way to get to know someone. Plus, I get slapped a lot less than if I looked a bit lower."

"Probably true," Raven agreed. So her scars didn't send him running for the hills. Even if he weren't attractive and refreshingly awkward, this would have been enough for her to give him a second look.

"I've never seen you before," Douglas said. "We don't often see new faces down here. Takes a certain amount of infamy to get invited to this place, if you know what I mean."

"Or, as with the rest of life, if you just know the right person, you can make anything happen," Raven responded. "I came with someone else, but clearly you earned your place here. So what'd you do? Kill a baron? Steal the crown jewels?"

"Oh no, nothing that exciting," Douglas evaded with a smile, turning his eyes away from Raven and scanning the room.

"Oh, come on, it must be some story," Raven persisted.

"Tell you what," Douglas said, returning his attention to her. "You let me buy you a drink, we sit down at that little table over there, and I'll tell you as much of my history as you want to know."

"Sounds good," Raven conceded. "I'll go claim the table. You surprise me with the drink."

"I like your plan, little lady!" Douglas said. Raven headed to the table he had indicated and planned her next move. He might have some information on the recent robberies which meant she needed to know what he knew. Leading people on wasn't necessarily her idea of a good time, but if it had to be done it might as well be someone as handsome and interesting as Doug.

———†———

"This is the sixth house we've been in right *next* to one which was robbed," Midas said as he followed his brother outside. "What do you expect to find, Leo? Do you think the thieves are using the house next door as a staging area?"

"I didn't expect to find anything, which verifies my hunch," Leopold answered. "Besides, the house next door angle wouldn't make sense for the castle robbery."

"Well, then what were we looking for?" Midas asked. He followed his brother back up the road toward the castle.

"Something to tie all these crimes together," Leopold answered. "These break-ins are very different and not, I think, done by the same people. In fact, if they hadn't happened during such a short period of time, they probably wouldn't have been thrown into the same basket."

"Okay, I'm with you so far," Midas said, but his tone indicated the exact opposite.

"Think about it," Leopold said. "Some of these robberies make sense. Expensive loot was stolen and lots of it while others…who in their right mind steals sacks of flour from a bakery? Where's the money in it? Then there's the mode of operation. Some of the thieves are so quiet no one wakes up while others were so loud they woke the whole family and neighbors."

"If it's a lot of different thieves, what's with the sudden crime spree?" Midas asked. "Are they competing for a contract, everyone trying to prove they're the best one for the job?"

"That's a theory to consider," Leopold agreed. "I was thinking more of a conspiracy. There are a lot of thieves, perhaps all of them, working together on this. I think we might be looking at a ring of people instead of individuals all working alone."

"An interesting idea, but where's your proof?" Midas interjected. "You said yourself we need something to tie all these robberies together, but we don't have anything of the sort."

"Actually," Leopold corrected, raising a finger to punctuate the objection, "the last six buildings we were just in gave me all the proof I need. These robberies are as different as you can possibly get, but because of the proximity of their occurrences, we assumed they were linked. I was looking for something common to all of them, but it wasn't until the blacksmith that I realized the link I needed had been in front of me the whole time."

"The blacksmith?" Midas asked incredulously. "He had all his equipment stolen. How does that tie everything else together?"

"It doesn't," Leopold answered. "The link we're looking for isn't in what was taken but *how* it was stolen, or, more correctly, how each place was broken into. See, every place we looked at before the blacksmith had plenty of security risks and lots of ways to break in. In some cases, there was even blatant proof of forced entry, but it was all just to put investigators off the scent. The blacksmith shop was where they went wrong. The place is impenetrable in a common sense, and the only sensible mode of entry wasn't used."

"The windows on the second floor," Midas said. "You mentioned they hadn't been tampered with. But we decided it might have been an inside job."

"That seems unlikely," Leopold said. "Besides, we no longer have to depend on the theory because the thieves didn't enter these buildings from the street or from above. They broke in from below."

"You think they tunneled in?" Midas asked.

"In a manner of speaking," Leopold answered. "They used pre-made tunnels: the sewer system. I thought it was stupid to break into a bakery and steal bags of flour, especially with a fine clothing store right next to it. But the bakery has a bathroom complete with toilets which empty directly into the sewer while the clothing shop doesn't."

"A bit behind the times of the clothing shop, isn't it?" Midas asked.

"Come on, Midas," Leopold chided. "You know as well as anyone how most toilets have to be emptied."

"Yeah, in other cities, but this is Kraljevi," Midas said. "Every indoor toilet I've used here has run straight to the sewer."

"Because we've been put up there the whole time we've stayed in the city," Leopold pointed to the castle towers as they passed through the open gates. "The sewers were designed for castle use without thought of the citizens. It's not expensive to have a hole dug which empties into the sewer, but only some of the houses in the city are located over the pipes."

"And all of the places which were robbed have direct access to the sewer," Midas said. "Okay, I get all that, but my original question remains. Why steal bags of flour, even if you have a convenient way to break into a bakery?"

"I don't believe these break-ins were about what was taken during them," Leopold said. "I think they were practice to see how easy it would be and how much loot could be taken out."

"If you're actually correct and not just on some wild goose chase, then all the robberies were just practice for the job at the castle," Midas concluded. "What was taken from here?"

"I don't know," Leopold said as he flipped through the papers in his hands. "These reports left out all mention of what was actually stolen from the castle."

"If we can figure out what was stolen, we might be able to track down the thieves when they try to sell it," Midas said.

"You came up with that idea all by yourself?" Leopold asked in a surprised voice.

"Cut it out," Midas responded. "I may not be the smartest person in The Shadow, but I've hung around with the rest of you long enough to pick up some things."

"Well, I like the way you think, brother," Leopold said, tucking the folder under his arm. "Now we finally have something to report back to Daniel and Raven. After that, I think it's time we paid Captain Payne a visit."

———+———

"It's quite the story you have, Doug," Raven said. "You certainly earned your place among the notable criminals of history, haven't you?"

"Well, I don't like to brag, but I *am* pretty awesome," Douglas said. He leaned back in his chair and took a long draught of the drink in his mug.

"Doug, I'd like you to meet someone," Raven said, waving Daniel over to her table. "He's the leader of my organization, and he's always looking for more talent."

"I actually prefer to work alone," Douglas said, but Raven pretended not to hear him as she continued to try to get Daniel's attention.

"I'm sorry, what was that?" she asked when Daniel finally started toward the table. She didn't give Douglas time to answer. "Daniel, I'd like you to meet my new friend, Filch."

"Filch," Daniel said, looking thoughtfully at the young man. He finally extended a hand. "Your reputation precedes you and I've heard a lot of it. Nice to meet you."

"The pleasure's all mine, sir," Douglas said, rising to shake Daniel's hand. "Would you care to join us?"

"I would, thank you," Daniel said and pulled another chair up to the small table. "I appreciate the invitation. If I were you and had the sole attention of a beautiful lady such as Raven, I don't think I would invite someone else to interrupt."

"You're too kind, Daniel," Raven said. "Filch was just telling me about his life. Every story seems to be a résumé of sorts."

"They would be," Daniel said. "Right now, Raven, you're in the presence of one of the most influential criminals of our time. And at his age too!"

"A bit of an exaggeration," Douglas said modestly, turning red at the ears. He took another drink to hide his embarrassment, but it was evident he appreciated the compliment.

"I think not," Daniel said. "You are a very talented and determined individual from what I hear. I could use someone with your skills and knowledge."

"As I told the lady, I prefer to work alone," Douglas said. "I never went in for working with others."

"You misunderstand me," Daniel said quickly. "I would never suggest you coming to work for me. For one thing, I'm positive I couldn't offer you enough to tantalize you. No, what I'm interested in is your help with a single job. It would be minimal effort on your part and the payout has the potential to be quite large."

"Go on, I'm listening," Douglas said. From what Daniel had heard about the young man before him, he was swayed by women, good liquor, and easy money. Right now, Daniel was playing to two of these vices. The easy money may have been enough by itself, but with Raven listening, there was also the need to impress her. Douglas had bit and was caught, hook, line, and sinker.

"The job I have lined up is pretty simple," Daniel said. "We're looking to lift some things from a secure location. They're one-of-a-kind and quite expensive."

"Things like you're talking about are difficult to get rid of," Douglas said. "The money might be good when you get around to fencing what you steal, but it will be some time before you can."

"The money won't be an issue," Daniel responded. "I have a buyer lined up already. He's the only reason I took this job. Like you said, without him it would be very nearly impossible to fence the objects. As I mentioned before, the items are also located in a secure location, but for what he's paying, I'd sell him my own mother!"

"It seems like you've got this pretty well worked out," Douglas said. "What do you need me for?"

It was a classic move. The more Douglas was needed by Daniel, the more power he would have when negotiating a fee. The key was to figure out how much Daniel wanted him before the subject of money came up.

"The job is simple, but the location isn't," Daniel explained. "Let's say my client has some very 'royal' tastes when it comes to his art collection. We need to get into the castle."

"Why are you coming to me?" Douglas asked. "Don't get me wrong, I'm good, but this is the castle we're talking about. No one can get in there without getting caught."

"I would have agreed with you a week ago, but my sources tell me a different story," Daniel said. "I understand the king was just ripped off by somebody, and from what I hear, you were the somebody who masterminded the whole thing."

"I think your sources need to keep their mouths shut more often," Douglas said tightly. "Loose lips can get you killed if you're not careful."

"I couldn't agree with you more, but the fact of the matter at hand is, I need to get into the castle, and I know you can help me," Daniel said. "I'll give you ten percent of my contract fee for the knowledge of how to get into the castle. My team and I will do all the heavy lifting while you just sit back and collect your money."

"How do I know you're not setting me up?" Douglas asked. "The money you're offering seems too easy to be on the level."

"It's not easy at all," Daniel countered. "You've done all the legwork already and have information I would like. Basically, I'll pay you handsomely for the information."

"Let me think about it," Douglas said, rising from the table.

"Where can I get in touch with you?" Daniel asked.

"I'll find you *if* I decide I'm interested," Douglas said. "It was nice to meet you, Raven. Good day to the both of you."

"Well, that could have gone worse," Daniel said once Douglas was out of earshot.

"Do you think he can really help us?" Raven asked. "He doesn't seem like the mastermind type."

"Oh, he's not," Daniel agreed. "He's probably a two-bit thief who loiters around this place, waiting for other people to hire him to help with their plans."

"Then why him?" Raven asked.

"A criminal mastermind, particularly a successful one, will most likely be wealthy to a certain degree," Daniel answered. "The promise of money doesn't hold the same allure for them as for a thief like Filch who is probably practically living in poverty. We promise him a large payout for easy work, and he's more likely to take us up on it."

"That doesn't help if he doesn't know the information we need," Raven pointed out.

"The string of robberies taken as a whole constitutes the largest crime spree I have ever heard of," Daniel said. "Filch may be nothing more than a petty criminal, but you can be sure he's privy to some information we aren't. I would guess he was either directly involved in it, or he knows someone who was. The promise of money and the ego stroking we did will send him digging, and he won't give up until he has the information we need."

"Well, you've got a lot more experience in the field, so I'll take your word for it," Raven said.

"Trust me," Daniel said. "The only people more predictable than money-grubbing thieves are money-grubbing lawmen."

"Then do we have anything left to do here?" Raven asked. She drained the last of her drink.

"Go back and meet up with Midas and Leopold," Daniel answered. "I somehow doubt they've turned up something we haven't, but they've surprised me before."

"Back to the brothers, huh?" Raven said. In her mind it was a toss-up. Though she certainly wanted space away from Leopold at the moment, she also wanted to get out of this hole in the ground and feel the sun on her skin again. "Okay," she agreed. "Let's go."

———————

"We're working an angle with someone we met in the criminal underground," Daniel said. He laughed as he realized the humor in the statement. "The funny part is, the criminal underground is actually underground."

"Don't tell me, let me guess, you accessed it through the sewers, didn't you?" Leopold asked.

Daniel looked with surprise across the table at the two brothers sitting opposite him.

"Yes," he finally answered. "How did you know?"

"Simple deduction from what we learned during the course of our investigation," Midas said loftily.

"Something like that," Leopold agreed while simultaneously shooting his brother a glare. "We also have a theory on what links the robberies. We think they all used the same method of entry."

"Makes sense," Raven said more to herself than anyone else. She rose from her chair and began to pace around the room as she spoke. "The thieves must have all used the sewers to gain entrance to the buildings they robbed."

"Wait, what?" Daniel asked. "Why do you think so?"

"Leo just said so," Raven answered, waving off the question with her hand. "But why use the sewer when most of the marks would be just as easily compromised using typical methods?"

"We think it's…" Midas began, but Raven continued to speak.

"The castle, of course!" she said. "The castle was where the final robbery took place, which means the other times were just trial runs for the real heist. It's just a theory, but there's one way to find out. Leo, what was stolen in each case?"

"In some cases it was jewelry, money, or other things of significant value," Leopold answered, "however, in other cases what was taken didn't make any sense. Like twenty bags of flour from a bakery."

"It makes sense if you consider all the thieves were doing was figuring out the maximum size of items they could take out through the sewer," Raven said.

"Exactly," Leopold agreed. "Midas, how come she can figure this out in thirty seconds when it took us all morning to reason through the same thing?"

"Because she's smarter than we are," Midas offered. "Although, to be fair, you did give her the most important piece of information right up front."

"It's more than we had, though still not enough," Daniel said. "All it tells us is that everything we're investigating was in preparation for the castle job. We're supposed to figure out who did this, return what was stolen to the king, and determine if Captain Payne is involved in any way. What we know doesn't put us any closer to accomplishing any of these things."

"On the contrary," Leopold said. "While Midas and I were looking through the files and interviewing the witnesses, it occurred to us how different each crime was from the others. Particularly, we believe they were not all performed by the same people but many different individuals or groups."

"Then we're looking for a guild or ring," Daniel said.

"A theory which is supported by what we just learned was stolen from the castle," Midas cut in. "Many of the items taken were large pieces of art, wall hangings, statues and the like. They'll fetch a good price to be sure, but only to the right buyer.

Most of the pieces are unique enough they couldn't be sold in the surrounding areas because they would be recognized as belonging to the king."

"Then this isn't just a ring of thieves but of smugglers as well," Daniel concluded.

"Exactly," Leopold said. "They'll have to move the loot, but with as expensive as it is, it'll still take a while to find a buyer."

"Is that good or bad?" Midas asked.

"It's pretty much all good news," Raven said. "Groups of people are always easier to find than individuals. It'll also take some time to smuggle the stolen items out of the area which means they might still be here. If we're lucky, we may still be able to recover them for the king."

"Two out of three isn't bad, but what about Captain Payne?" Leopold asked. "We still have no idea if he's involved or not."

"We don't know which side he's on, but it doesn't really matter," Daniel said. "We can tell the king Payne is on the thieves' payroll. If he is, all the better, but either way we'll never know if we were right or wrong."

"We are not selling out a man just because it makes the job easier for us," Leopold said. "If we condemn him, it'll be with proof of his treachery."

"We'll never find it," Daniel said. "He'll have covered his tracks."

"Then we tell the king we didn't find anything to incriminate Captain Payne," Leopold responded. "Better to let a guilty man go free than to betray an innocent one. Besides, what's the worst that could happen if we say he had nothing to do with it and we're wrong?"

"Let me paint you a picture of the worst thing which could happen," Daniel said. "We let him go and he actually has ties to the criminal underground. It gets out to the underground that The Shadow has apparently turned a new leaf because now they help the king track down thief and smuggling rings. We'll never be able to get a dishonest job again!"

"Which doesn't sound so bad to me," Leopold said. "Why don't we talk about this later? It could be we find out he is involved with the thieves, in which case the choice will be easy for us."

"Leopold, I know you're on a path of willful self-destruction, but I won't let you take The Shadow with you," Daniel said forcefully. He stood, leaning forward on the table and glaring at the young boy. "One way or the other, I'll deal with the Captain, and I would advise you not to get in my way."

"And I would advise you to think twice before disregarding what I'm telling you," Leopold said, rising to match Daniel. "I will not be party to the incrimination of an innocent man, and I will do whatever is necessary to keep you from the same."

"Are you threatening me?" Daniel asked.

"Boys, boys, calm down," Raven said. "Just sit back down and keep your mouths shut for a little bit so I can think."

Daniel and Leopold continued to glare at each other, but slowly first one, then the other took their seats again.

"Thank you," Raven said. "Now let's all work on something we can agree on. After all, like Leo said, maybe we'll find the Captain has been a bad boy, and then we won't be at odds."

"I like your plan, Raven," Midas spoke up. "Do you have an idea of where we should start?"

"Daniel and I met a person today," Raven answered. "We were working him to get him to tell us how the robbers got into the castle, but since you and Leo already answered that question, we'll take a different tack. Daniel, this is up your alley. What would you suggest?"

"Well, he thinks we've been commissioned to steal some large, hard to fence items from the castle," Daniel said, still eyeing Leopold and looking for a reaction from the boy. "When we meet with him again, we'll claim to have already pulled the job, but our patron backed out on us. We'll need someone to help us sell our loot."

"Good plan," Raven said. "If we work it properly, we may be able to get some information about the smuggling ring."

"If you know what you're going to do, what about me and Midas?" Leopold asked as he diligently avoided looking at Daniel.

"You get the fun job," Raven answered. "If we want to be convincing, we'll need to steal something from the castle."

"Shouldn't be hard," Leopold said. "We can just ask the king for some items."

"No," Raven said. "If Captain Payne is involved, we don't want him tipping off the smugglers. You'll have to actually break in and steal the stuff if we want to make sure this will work."

"Oh great, I get all the best jobs," Leopold said sarcastically.

"If it's too hard for you," Raven began, but Leopold interrupted.

"I broke into Rajikline, and I can do the same thing here," he said. "What time do you need the stuff?"

"How does tomorrow morning sound?" Raven asked.

Leopold looked at his brother who gave a slight thumbs-up motion.

"Tomorrow morning it is," he said. "Just tell us where."

"I've decided to help you out," Douglas magnanimously told Daniel and Raven. They were sitting on a bench in one of the several mini town squares of Kraljevi, their backs to a fountain which graced the open area.

"I'm glad you're willing to help, Filch," Daniel said, lifting a hand to block the rising sun from his eyes as he looked at Douglas. "See, we've run into a bit of a snag."

"What's that?" Douglas asked. His voice was laced with worry, as he saw the promise of easy money slipping away before his very eyes.

"You were taking too long getting back to us, so we decided to go ahead with the job," Raven said. "It was easy too.

I can't believe how much we were going to offer you for the information!"

"If you've already lifted what you want, what do you need me for?" Douglas asked.

"Our client seems to have gotten cold feet on the whole thing," Daniel explained. "We have a small fortune's worth of art and nothing to do with it, which doesn't help us out at all. We need you to help us get rid of it."

"I'm not really the guy for this," Douglas said and tried to get up to leave. Daniel planted a hand firmly on his shoulder and pushed him back into his seat.

"I know you aren't," the wizard said. "I did some checking up on you and found out you're nothing more than a common thief, muscle for hire."

"He's pretty angry about how you lied to us," Raven commented.

"I didn't lie!" Douglas insisted. "You may have assumed something which wasn't entirely true but…"

"And you let us believe it," Daniel finished. "I don't like it when people waste my time." As an afterthought, he added, "Do you even know who you're dealing with?"

"No, I promise I don't," Douglas pleaded. "You have to believe me. I was just trying to make some money helping you get into the castle."

"I don't really care who you are or why you did what you did," Daniel said coldly. "What I do care about is the fact I have merchandise which needs to be moved. I would very much like for you to prove you aren't as pathetic of an excuse for a thief as I think you are."

"I'll do what I can," Douglas said. "I'll go talk to someone."

"I have a better idea," Daniel said. "How about you get up and lead us to this man you think can help. I'm tired of dealing with peons who can't get done what I need to be done."

"I can't do it," Douglas said, his eyes widening in fear at Daniel's suggestion. He looked around the square for assistance, but the only other people were two young men sitting on the adjacent bench, seemingly oblivious to what was occurring just a few yards away.

"He doesn't like unannounced visitors, especially ones he doesn't know," Douglas pleaded. "He could kill me if I take you to him."

"Or I could kill you myself right here and now," Daniel growled as he drew a dagger and pressed it into Douglass' ribs. "I believe I already made it abundantly clear how much I detest you wasting my time. I am at the end of my patience so either take me to the man who can help me or die. The choice is yours."

"I'll take you!" Douglas was almost bawling now. "Please don't hurt me."

"Stop your whining," Daniel commanded. "Right now you're drawing more attention than a purple unicorn."

"Yes sir," Douglas complied, gulping his tears into his throat. At Daniel's command, he rose from the bench and walked at a measured pace up the street.

———✦———

"Wow," Midas exclaimed. "That was harsh, even for Daniel."

"He did what he needed to do," Leopold said. He turned to watch Daniel and Raven follow Douglas across the square toward an alley. "The king wants his possessions back and we don't know how close the thieves are to moving them out of the city. Time is of the essence."

"He did what he needed to do?" Midas asked with an incredulous look at his brother. "That sounded an awful lot like Daniel's 'Anything for the money.'"

"You're right, it did," Leopold said in sudden realization. Midas waited for him to say more, but there was nothing.

"I don't get it. You can't stand the way Daniel does things but now you're a lot like him?" Midas asked. "I was hoping for more of a defense from you."

"To what end?" Leopold asked. "You have a good point, and it's something I'm going to have to think about later, but the middle of a job isn't the best time for in-depth analysis of my ideology."

"Fine, but don't expect me to let you off without a discussion at least," Midas said. He got up from the bench, pulled a large bag from underneath, and slung it over his shoulder. "Shall we?"

Leopold led the way across the square and into the alley. Following someone was not always the easiest task in the world, but it became significantly simpler if the person you were following was working with you. The loud sound of Daniel's voice directed Leopold around a corner while a sharp clang of metal told him Douglas had led his friends into the sewer. He waited for a full minute before removing the manhole cover and climbing down the ladder. He stepped out of the niche cut into the wall for the ladder and scanned the pipe in both directions, looking for evidence of Daniel and Raven's passage. A loud splash marked Midas's arrival in the sludge.

"Do you see anything, Leo?" he asked.

"I was looking for ripples in the water, but you just ruined my ability to see anything," Leopold answered.

"Sorry, I wasn't thinking," Midas apologized. "You'll be able to figure something else out, right?"

The question was barely out of his mouth when Daniel's voice echoed back through the pipes.

"I think we'll be able to manage," Leopold said. "Boy, does Daniel have a set of lungs on him!"

The boys took the left branch of the pipe, climbing up onto the raised edges to get out of the sludge running down the center channel. They moved quickly, trying to catch up to the people they were following. The periodic shafts to the surface provided enough light to walk by, though they didn't do much in the way of illuminating the pipe walls which the boys hugged, both to stay out of the sewer sludge as well as to stay hidden in the shadows. In a matter of minutes, they caught sight of the glow of a torch up ahead and slowed their pace to stay far enough behind.

"Say, Leo, I half expected you to refuse to come down here," Midas whispered out of the blue.

"Why?" Leopold whispered back.

"It's a sewer," Midas answered. "You're always whining about how much you dislike sewers. At Rajikline, I thought we were going to have to drag you to the moat and throw you in."

"First of all, I don't *whine*," Leopold said, saying the word with a certain amount of disdain. "My complaints were well founded. I caught illness from the moat and believe me when I say it could have been much worse."

"You say complain, I say whine," Midas said. "It's all fiddle faddle. What I'm saying is, I didn't expect you to agree to this."

"Two things," Leopold said. "First, I may not like getting sick, but I'm committed to the job, and I'll do a lot of things to get it done. Besides, this sewer is very different than the filth I waded through at Rajikline. The water in a moat sits stagnant and festers with bugs and all manner of nastiness. A sewer like this, on the other hand, has storm water wash through it on a regular basis which carries most of the sludge away. It all gets replaced, of course, but at least it's new. To my way of thinking, it's better than what you'd find in a moat. Also, I don't have to swim through this place like I did the moat."

"Oh," Midas said. After a while he added, "You make sewers seem nice by comparison."

"They kind of are," Leopold said. "Now be quiet before somebody hears you."

The going was slow now. Once, on a very long straightaway, they turned a corner just in time to see Daniel, Raven, and Douglas round the next, but otherwise, they had no visual contact with their compatriots. The damp air, slick floors, and awful smell made the trip seem to stretch on, but eventually it was over. Leopold and Midas stuck to the shadows as they spied on the torchlit group staring at the sewer wall.

"So you just pull the catch here and the door pops open?" Daniel said quite loudly. "Clever design. I like it."

"Would you keep your voice down?" Douglas hissed. Ironically, his comment seemed to echo down the pipes more distinctly than Daniel's had.

"Sure," Daniel said, just as loudly as before. "Get me to the man I need to speak to, and we can put all this behind us."

The hidden door popped open and engulfed the three shadows up ahead before snapping shut behind them. Leopold and Midas closed the distance to the door quickly and spent a few anxious moments looking for the catch. Then they were inside, watching the torch light bounce up and down as it disappeared down the tunnel they were now in.

"Let's go over the plan one more time," Midas suggested in a low voice as he followed his brother through the darkness.

"It's simple, really," Leopold said. "You have the bag with the objects we ostensibly need to fence. Stay out of sight until Daniel or Raven gives the signal for you to come out. I'll remain hidden the entire time and keep an eye on the whole situation. Hopefully this won't come to violence, but if it does, I'll be the ace up your sleeve."

"I still don't understand how this is supposed to help us accomplish our mission," Midas said.

"Don't worry about it," Leopold said. "Daniel and Raven have thought this all through, and if we just do what we're supposed to do, everything will work out fine."

"Unless it comes to violence," Midas pointed out. "They must think it is a very real possibility if they told you to stay hidden in the shadows."

"Let's hope it doesn't come to such things," Leopold said. He motioned forward. "I think we're approaching our destination. You go on ahead, and I'll follow you up."

Leopold waited until he was trailing Midas by twenty or so feet before continuing his forward trek. It wasn't long before lanterns, torches, shafts to the surface, and other forms of illumination began to proliferate in the tunnel. The trail expanded into a small room where a barrel of new and partially used torches stood against the wall, indicative that the rest of the way would be lit. This would make things more difficult for Leopold, but it also meant they were getting close to their destination.

The path split, the obvious route running through an archway while there was what appeared to be a secondary way up above. The lack of ladder or stairs might have dissuaded most curious strangers, but for Leopold it was no trouble to scale the wall and take the high ground. Hopefully, it would help keep him hidden as well as offer an advantage if things went bad. It was an elevated track, practically a bridge over the rooms through which Midas was moving. The first few chambers were devoid of guards and appeared to be nothing more than eating, sleeping, and staging areas for whatever men worked for the kingpin to whom Douglas was leading them. They were not in use at the moment. The criminal population of the city was likely lying low after the castle heist.

Leopold was almost through the fourth room when he noticed Midas. He was gesturing frantically to Leopold, trying desperately to get his attention. The older boy pointed to the archway across the room. Leopold noticed it had a door, something not found in the previous chambers, and Midas was making the motion of turning a key. Clearly this was what constituted the real entrance of the hideout and the door was either locked, guarded, or both.

With special attention to the noise he created, Leopold crept forward along his path, entering a short archway. Just ahead, a corner blocked his view of what was to come. Getting down on his hands and knees, he fished a piece of shiny steel from one of his pockets and slowly inched it around the stone wall. He could see a single guard on the catwalk before him, but the reflection didn't give him a view of the situation below. He waited for the guard to turn his back before retracting the mirror and settling on his haunches, leaning against the wall for support.

Leopold played a few scenarios in his head, but there were too many unknowns. In a well-orchestrated situation, any person or people below would regularly check in with the guard on the catwalk. If Leopold took care of the guard, their attention would be on the path above in which case he would have difficulty neutralizing them before they could sound an alarm. Their attention would be diverted from the door, a fact which would be of little use to Midas if it were locked. But what if the plan worked in reverse? It was a gamble since Leopold still didn't know how many people he had to deal with below, but it was the best plan he had.

Moving back out to the fourth chamber, he made a motion of knocking on the door to Midas. The boy made the motion back to which Leopold nodded but held up a hand, indicating Midas should wait before knocking. When he was sure they were on the same page, Leopold crept back to the corner and waited. The seconds dragged on, but eventually he heard the distinct sound of Midas pounding on the door. The ensuing commotion confirmed Leopold's fear: there was a small garrison of guards on the opposite side of the door from Midas.

There was no backing down now, so he dashed around the corner. As expected, the guard on the walkway had been moving to check out the person on the other side of the door and, while he had an arrow nocked on his bow, he wasn't prepared for what confronted him now. Using the moment of surprise, Leopold rushed headlong into his chest, shoving him off the catwalk and riding his body to the floor ten feet below. Everyone's attention was on the door which gave Leopold just enough time to roll to his feet, identify the commander of the guards, and rush forward to put a knife to his throat before he could wrap his head around what was happening.

"There is someone on the other side of the door who wants to come in," Leopold said, maneuvering himself so the commander was between him and the guards who were now advancing threateningly. "If you want to live to see tomorrow, tell your men to back off."

The commander said nothing, and the guards moved closer. Leopold pressed his knife more forcefully against his hostage's neck. Blood beaded along the length of the blade.

"You're running out of time," he said. "Call them off or I slash your throat wide open."

"Stand down," the commander managed to get out. He held up a hand, visually confirming his order.

"Come on, boys, you heard the man," Leopold said, eyeing one of the guards who was still slowly working his way forward. No doubt he thought he was being very sneaky about it. "Back off or I kill him and you'll be next, each the same as the last until you're all lying in pools of your own blood."

"I said stand down!" the commander said in a loud voice. The would-be hero finally stopped his advance.

"And put your weapons on the floor," Leopold commanded. When the guards hesitated to follow the order, he looked to the commander.

"Do as he says," the commander instructed them. Leopold's knife was now pushed so hard against his throat he was practically looking at the ceiling.

The guards weren't happy about the order, but they followed it, placing their swords and shields on the ground. At a word from Leopold, their knives followed in a clanging barrage of metal on stone. One of the guards unlocked and opened the door for Midas while the rest of them made way for him as he entered the room. A moment of sheer panic shot across his face, and he reached for his sword, but his eyes were faster. Realizing nobody was armed, he left his weapon in its sheath and moved to stand beside Leopold.

"What are we going to do with them?" Midas asked his brother. "We can't take them prisoner."

"No, we can't," Leopold agreed. To the guards he said, "It appears our business is almost at an end. If you would be so kind as to place the door keys on the table over there and leave, we can put this all behind us."

"Leo," Midas said and motioned with his head to the inert body of the man Leopold had pushed off the elevated walkway.

"Right," Leopold said. "I don't know if your friend there is alive or dead, but if you could take him out with you, I'd be much obliged."

He shoved the commander forward, knife always at his throat as he corralled the rest of the guards through the door. When they were all out, he pushed the commander toward them while Midas swung the door shut. Leopold stopped it just before it closed and stuck his head out.

"You can, of course, do what you want," he said, "but I have some advice for you. My friends and I will have what we want from your boss long before you can get around to any of the secret entrances and try to stop us, so save yourselves the effort. Also, your boss doesn't seem like the most understanding person. I realize he's done terrible things to people for much less than letting his enemies breach his secret underground hideout, so if I were you, I'd book it out of this place and never look back. As I said, though, the choice is yours."

Midas shut and locked the door behind Leopold who was already looking for an easy way back up to his catwalk. It appeared as though rope ladders were the main method of movement between the upper and lower levels, but they had been retracted to make the walkway more secure.

"So, what now?" Midas asked. "Do we just press forward?"

"Yes, we stick to the plan," Leopold agreed as he searched the wall for an easy path up. "If I had to guess, I'd say the hardest part is behind us."

"Because we're inside?" Midas asked.

"Because the castle heist happened relatively recently," Leopold said. "The criminals in the city are laying low for the time being. If I were whoever is in charge of this place, I'd limit the amount of traffic into and out of my hideout until the vigilance of the royal guard died down. I don't think we'll run into many more people."

The brothers continued their journey through the chambers of the hideout, Leopold once again taking the high road. His prediction proved correct, and they didn't encounter more than half a dozen people. Those they did see were simply patrolling the lower halls, more of a protection against embezzling thieves than outside threats. Their alertness was lacking to say the least, and Midas was able to easily slip past them. It wasn't long before they came to the end of their expedition. It was an ordinary entrance, not the imposing double doors Leopold had envisioned. The only thing giving away its importance were the two guards standing in front of it.

Leopold hurried along the elevated catwalk to the next room, a guard house with a solid set of stairs leading down. It was as abandoned as the rest of the hideout, and he spared little time to examine it closely. He was most interested in people and as there were none, it was time to move on. Midas was in the adjoining room, talking to the guards at the door. The conversation didn't appear to be going well as the voices of the guards continued to get louder. Midas let the bag he was carrying slip from his shoulder and extended his hands as if trying to explain he had come in peace. In a movement so fast Leopold barely saw it coming, he planted a huge, meaty hand over the face of each guard and pressed them up against the wall with his massive body. They struggled for their weapons, but to no avail and in less than a minute, both were stretched out on the floor, unconscious.

"I'll take care of these blokes," Leopold whispered, so close that he startled Midas. "You keep your ear to the door and wait for Daniel's signal."

Midas nodded agreement and moved to the door while Leopold wrestled first one, then the other of the soldiers into the guard house. Actually, referring to them as soldiers was being generous. Their armament showed they were truly nothing more than criminals hired to act as guards. Leopold quickly stripped their weapons and armor and tied them with some rope he found. By the time he had finished and moved back outside the guardhouse, Midas was gone, obviously having entered the room beyond the door on Daniel's signal.

A whisper of a noise, probably nothing more than the scrapping of a scabbard across the stone wall, floated down the hall, and Leopold froze, casting around with his eyes for the source of the sound. No one was in the room with him, so he dashed for the shadows, concealing himself in the darkness cast by the walkway he had been atop only minutes previous. His eyes glued to the doorway, it was only a few moments before another person came into view. He was obviously attempting to stay concealed as he moved, but his actions showed he was quite inept at it.

Leopold waited for the other person to move past him before he detached himself from the wall. Stealthily he crept forward, moving diagonally across the room to fall in behind this new player. As he moved, he happened to notice a ring on the person's finger, not unusual in and of itself, but he'd seen this particular piece of jewelry before. Freeing his knife from its sheath, he grabbed the figure in front of him by the back of his shirt and placed his knife at his throat.

"Captain Payne," Leopold hissed. "What brings you down here?"

The distinctly feminine gasp at his words and the fact his cheek was pressed up against soft skin, combined to form the realization the person before him was definitely not the old, grizzled captain of the royal guard. He pulled the person into the light, revealing the features of a woman Daniel's age or perhaps a bit older. Leopold couldn't tell if the slight reddish tint in her closely cropped, brown hair was just a trick of the light or not.

"Who are you?" Leopold demanded. "I don't like party crashers, so you have about ten seconds to tell me who you are and why I shouldn't slit your throat."

"I'm Evalda Fehn," the woman said, her eyes wide with fear. "I know who you are."

"You're not being very convincing," Leopold said. "Tell me about your ring. I saw Captain Payne with an identical one."

"Yes," Evalda agreed hurriedly. "I work with him. The ring is a symbol of a special group of guards he put together. We investigate strange goings on like the robberies."

"You work for the captain and you're down here," Leopold said. "You know one of the objectives the king gave us was to determine whether or not he was in collaboration with the thieves. This looks pretty incriminating."

"It's not what you think," Evalda said. "I can explain."

A noise came from the room Daniel, Raven, and Midas had disappeared into, and Evalda's speech quickened.

"There isn't much time," she said. "We know what you plan to do, but you can't, not right now at least."

"What do you mean?" Leopold asked.

"The items you stole from the castle," Evalda said. "You have to actually give them to Korbin, the crime kingpin."

"Why should I trust you?" Leopold asked.

"I don't have a reason," Evalda said. "But if you do, Captain Payne will be able to explain everything."

Leopold mulled his options over in his mind. If what Evalda said was correct, she deserved the chance to explain herself. On the other hand, if she was playing him, an army could always be procured from the king later to storm this place. As long as he kept the woman close to make sure she didn't warn anyone, there wasn't really a downside to hearing her out.

"Fine," Leopold said, removing his knife from Evalda's throat. "I'm not saying I believe you, but I'll give you a chance."

The woman gave a sigh of relief.

"Let's get one thing straight, though," Leopold continued. "You don't leave my sight until we've talked to Captain Payne. If you do, I will track you down and take you down. Is that understood?"

She nodded so he led the way back to the door the guards had been standing in front of earlier. Ever so slowly he inched it open and peered through. Daniel, Raven, and Midas were positioned so whoever was in front of them, Korbin presumably, couldn't see the door. Leopold gave a low cough and two clicks with his tongue. Raven turned slightly at the signal, just enough to be able to look at him.

"Give him the stuff," Leopold mouthed to her, motioning with his hands as well. She immediately understood and turned to once again fully face Korbin.

Leopold stood, motioned for Evalda to follow, and back-tracked to the guard house. Taking the upper walkway, they hurried past the remaining guards and into the sewer. When they were finally above ground again, Evalda led the way to the castle.

"I'm Marshall Payne, captain of the royal guard and this is Evalda Fehn, my associate."

"I know who you are, Captain, and frankly, I don't care who she is," Daniel said. "What I want to know is why we just gave some very expensive items to a criminal. Do you realize how angry the king will be when he finds out we didn't find the people who robbed him and that he actually got robbed a second time?"

"He's not going to find out, I'll make sure of it," Captain Payne said.

"Maybe not, but the fact is we have nothing to show for the work we did," Daniel said. "I don't work for free, but he's not going to pay us for what we've done so far. He's also not going to like it when I tell him we let the bad guys get away!"

"I know he's not going to be happy which is why I would suggest figuring out something different to say," Captain Payne said.

"What if I decide to tell him what actually occurred?" Daniel asked. "It wouldn't look very good for you, would it?"

"I'm afraid I can't let you do that," Captain Payne said forcefully.

"Are you threatening me?" Daniel asked, rising from his chair.

"I'm saying we can't afford to let you ruin the work we've put into this investigation," Captain Payne said.

"Tell you what," Daniel said, sitting back down. "I'll allow you to tell your side of the story before I decide what I'm going to do."

"Very gracious of you," Evalda said sarcastically.

"When the robberies started about six months ago," Captain Payne said quickly, "the king assigned me the task of tracking down the people responsible. As my investigation progressed, I came to realize things didn't add up for many of the cases, but you probably already determined as much."

"We did," Midas confirmed. "They were all just practice to see how well using the sewers to break into a building would work. The ultimate goal was always the castle."

"Correct," Captain Payne agreed. "Unfortunately, we were not as quick to figure this out as you were, and by the time we did, the castle had already been struck. We finally put together how the robbery had occurred, but there was still the matter of the king's possessions, one of which is of extreme sentimental value to him.

"We knew the items were too valuable to be easily sold on the street or anywhere in the near vicinity, for that matter. It stood to reason they would be smuggled out of the region. I knew the criminals wouldn't move the stolen goods as long as the heat was on, so I ordered increased security and inspections of all types of transportation. At the same time, I had Evalda infiltrate the criminal society where she easily located the items we were looking for."

"Quick question, if I may," Raven said. "Why have Evalda infiltrate the organization? Why didn't you go yourself?"

"My face is far too well known in the city," Captain Payne explained. "I had considered a few of my most trusted men, but I found there were advantages to sending a woman. First, the vast majority of the guard is composed of men, so a woman immediately dispels suspicion. Secondly, there are some types of robbery which lend themselves to being performed by females. Korbin was in search of people for such activities, so Evalda had an easy time inserting herself into the operation."

"If you found the items, why are we sitting here, having this conversation?" Daniel asked. "Shouldn't you have gotten a hold of them by now? No matter how well fortified Korbin's holding area may be, I'm sure the royal guard could overrun it."

"Yes," Captain Payne agreed. "I have seriously considered that option several times and would have already done so were it not for one problem. When Evalda was undercover, she discovered this thing goes much deeper than we first imagined. We knew there was a smuggling ring but this, well, let's just say we may have bitten off more than we can chew."

"You haven't told the king because you think if he knew the full situation, he would put the stolen possessions ahead of taking down the organization you're going after," Raven said.

"As I said, one of the items is of extreme sentimental value to him," Captain Payne said. "The king is normally a very logical man, but when it comes to his son... I'm not saying I know what he would choose, but I can't afford him blowing the whole operation over a mere bauble."

"This is all fascinating, but you haven't convinced me," Daniel said. "We stand to make a great deal of money by returning the king's possessions, and I'm sure it will be no small feather in my cap when I tell him how you've been going behind his back. It doesn't look good for you, I'm afraid."

"I had hoped we could resolve this without threats, but I'm certainly not beneath making them," Captain Payne said. "If you feel the need to tell the king what I've been up to, I may decide it's necessary to tell him who you really are."

"And who are we?" Daniel asked brazenly. "I'm interested."

"Don't play me for a fool," Captain Payne said. "You may do your best to keep your faces and names a secret, but enough gets around. I think I'm smart enough to tell when The Shadow is standing right in front of me."

A stunned silence fell on the room. Raven and Leopold looked at each other while Midas gaped at the captain, mouth open. Daniel maintained his composure perfectly, glaring at Captain Payne across the room. He crossed and uncrossed his arms several times in the ensuing minutes as silence continued to reign. The captain appeared more than willing to let it last as long as necessary. The message was clear: it was Daniel's move.

"If we were The Shadow, and you had proof, why are we sitting here instead of in the dungeon?" Daniel asked.

"The lady Maria fielded you as her team in the king's tournament," Captain Payne said. "She is a very level-headed person and her faith in you goes a long way. Beyond that, I find myself in need of a group with your particular skill set."

"Does Maria know?" Midas asked.

"That you're The Shadow? No," Captain Payne answered. "And I'm sure everyone here would like to keep it that way."

"You're blackmailing us, Captain, and I can't say I like it very much," Daniel said sullenly.

"It is not nor has it ever been my desire to blackmail you," Captain Payne said. "However, as I said before, I find myself in the unfortunate position of needing your help no matter what it takes."

"Threatening isn't necessary, Captain," Leopold said. "We'll help you out. We'll do it for the king."

"I'll do it for Maria," Midas said.

"And I'll do it so I can finally get my money," Daniel growled.

"I'm glad to hear all you say so," Captain Payne said. He turned to Raven. "What about you? Will you help?"

"Of course I will," Raven answered. She turned to her friends and said, "You all are doing this for your own reasons. Well, I'm doing it for all of you because somebody's got to keep your butts out of trouble!"

"Then it's settled," Captain Payne said. "You do your best to come through for me on this, and your secret is safe with me."

"Great," Leopold said. "When do we start?"

PART 3

◌

Slave Traitor

"We're all here, Evalda," Midas said as Raven walked through the door and settled into a chair on the far wall. The sunlight of high noon streamed through the large bay windows in the common room of one of The Shadow's many bolt holes. Leopold smiled to himself at the term 'bolt hole,' aptly used since this was a hole that they would bolt to and hide in during times of trouble. To be fair, though, it wasn't really a hole in the most derogatory sense. The place was clean and livable, the neighborhood was acceptable, and the décor was palatable. It just didn't have the same hominess to it that their permanent residence did.

"Let's hear it," Raven said. "What's this new information you've got on the smuggling ring? And why are we here in this city?"

"The smuggling ring we've been keeping tabs on finally deemed it safe enough to move the loot from the king's castle," Evalda answered. "We intercepted the caravan less than a day from Kraljevi and managed to extract information on where it was heading."

"Don't tell me, let me guess," Midas said, raising his hand. "Was it heading here?"

"Correct," Evalda said, pointing a finger at him. "Give the boy a pat on the back for his intelligence."

Midas pretended to accept accolades from the others in the room.

"Correct me if I'm wrong, but I thought figuring out where the smuggling ring is located was the whole point of this operation," Raven said. "If you already know they are based out of this city, why do you still need us?"

"A good question," Evalda responded. "We learned from the smugglers we grabbed that their arrival in this city would coincide with a large celebration of the ring. Top operators and bosses of the whole network will be gathered here in just a few days' time."

"Okay, I get it," Daniel said. "This is too good of an opportunity for you to miss. So what do you want us to do? Go mingle with the bad guys and get you names and locations? If you want more information, I'm sure we can get it for you."

"With so many of the smuggling ring's top brass in one place at one time, we can't afford to waste this chance," Evalda agreed. "Of course, my plan is a bit bolder than yours. We'll surround them and take as many prisoners as we can. We'll be rid of them, plus any information we could get might help us root out some more of their kind."

"Surround them and take them prisoner?" Daniel laughed. "I hope you've got a lot more people than us coming in for this party because four assassins and one whatever you are isn't going to cut it."

"Of course we have more people coming, but we can't very well move an army into the city," Evalda said in a tone of condescension. "The smugglers might spook and scatter, and then we'd never find them. The soldiers are coming in a few at a time over the course of several days. They'll be dressed as merchants, peasants, anything which won't draw attention."

"And how many soldiers are we talking about here?" Midas asked, counting on his fingers. Leopold could already see gears turning in his head.

"There will be five hundred all told," Evalda answered smugly. "The first of them will begin arriving three days from now, and the stream will continue for a week. We'll have the whole army in place by the time the party happens."

"Five hundred people entering the city over the course of seven days, and you don't think it'll raise a few eyebrows?" Daniel asked. "I don't care if they're disguised, the bad guys will know something's up."

"You leave it to us," Evalda said. "We've done this sort of thing before, you know."

"Fine, but if the mission is blown because of this, it's on your head," Daniel said. "What I'm really wondering is if this is all going down ten days from now, why are we already here?"

"Reconnaissance," Evalda answered. "I want you to bring me as much information about the location as you can, so we can set up a good strategy for assaulting it. You don't need to have anything to do with the attack if you don't want to."

"Fine by me," Daniel said. "So, where is this thing supposed to be going down?"

"We have substantially more information than just the location, and it's all yours to peruse," Evalda said. "I'll have it brought up as soon as I leave."

"What? Not sticking around for the fun of digging through all the paper?" Daniel asked.

"No," Evalda said. "As much as I would love to, I'll leave it up to you. Now if there aren't any more questions, I have someplace to be."

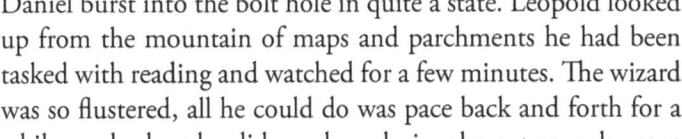

Daniel burst into the bolt hole in quite a state. Leopold looked up from the mountain of maps and parchments he had been tasked with reading and watched for a few minutes. The wizard was so flustered, all he could do was pace back and forth for a while, and when he did speak, only incoherent sounds came out.

"Alright, calm down, Daniel," Midas chuckled, looking up at the wizard. "What's on your mind?"

"Take a deep breath and let it out," Raven suggested, leaving the table behind and going to Daniel. "Calm down and tell us what you found out."

"It's news," Daniel finally managed to get out.

"Good or bad?" Midas asked, suddenly more interested in what was being said.

"Both, I think," Daniel said, then confessed, "Actually, I don't know."

"Well, let's start with what you found out," Raven prodded.

"I know the man who's hosting the party we're supposed to be crashing," Daniel said. "He's a very bad man, and for me to say it, well, even you know it must be true, Leopold."

"What kind of bad are we talking?" Raven asked. "Sadistic, life sucking, or a pain in the butt to infiltrate?"

"All of the above," Daniel answered. "If you don't believe me, let's just say he's bad enough that more than one person wants him taken down. I think I may have found a way to get us back in the game. I never thought this would happen after we broke that contract. It just goes to show that I was right all along about what happens to someone in this business when they grow a conscience. There's no room for nobility in our line of..."

"We've heard it before, Daniel, so you can just stow it," Midas interrupted somewhat rudely. Whether from teenage impudence or some other source, the way in which he treated the older man had changed markedly in the recent past, though he still held a great deal of respect for the wizard.

"Yeah, just tell us what the news is," Leopold spoke up from where he stood in the corner of the room. The others gave a jolt, startled by his voice. Though they knew he was there, his habit of becoming completely silent and nearly motionless was very disarming and had a way of making others forget he was present.

"This is the best news I've had in a while," Daniel said, his anxiety gradually turning into excitement. "I got a second contract on this guy, and it'll put us back in the game!"

"What do you mean 'put us back in the game'?" Raven asked suspiciously. Her eyes narrowed, and she crossed her arms across her chest. "What kind of contract are we talking about, exactly?"

"One that'll put us back doing what we should be doing," Daniel said. "Assassination."

"No," Midas said immediately.

"What do you mean 'no'?" Daniel said. "This is the best opportunity we've had since you three grew consciences! Either we take it, or we'll fade into obscurity. Is that what you want? For the name The Shadow to cease to strike fear into people's hearts?"

"I'm actually not much for people being terrified of me," Midas pointed out, returning to his research. "I'm okay with the jobs we've been doing. They might not be the best in the world, and they don't pay that much sometimes, but at least I can sleep well at night. Besides, now we have an in with the king. I'm sure he can keep us in business if need be."

"Leopold?" Daniel turned to the younger boy.

"Hey, my big brother said it. I kind of like the people we meet when we're not always trying to kill them. I'll help take down this smuggling ring, but count me out of whatever side-job you've dug up."

"Raven, surely you can see what I'm trying to do here," Daniel appealed to the final member of The Shadow. "We were respected and feared before. We were great. Now we're nothing but a bunch of herb gatherers and treasure hunters. We're so much better than that, which is what I want to show the world again."

"We might be great again, but at what cost?" Raven asked sharply. She kept her arms folded across her chest as she stood from her seat. "We leave death and destruction in our wake. We rob children of their parents and parents of their children. We sell our souls for money and fear."

"You like working for the king's men, and it's not like we're turning our backs on them," Daniel said. "We all know there'll be casualties in this raid, and if we just make sure this specific person is one of them, we'll be a heck of a lot richer and back in the game."

"Not interested," Raven reiterated.

"Raven, don't leave," Daniel commanded her back as she strode toward the door. His tone changed to pleading as her movement continued unabated. "I haven't even given you the contract details yet. At least wait until you know the target's name."

"This is based on principle, Daniel," Midas said, standing to block the wizard's movement toward Raven. "Names don't matter."

"Sometimes they do," Daniel countered. "Especially when that name is Dexter Silverstone."

"We just said that names don't matter to us," Leopold said, joining his brother in blocking Daniel's path. Silence briefly fell on the room as the three stared at each other. The sun streaming from behind Daniel made it nearly impossible to look straight at him, but neither of the brothers were about to make their discomfort evident. They would block Daniel for long enough to give Raven time to leave the room. Both were unaware she had frozen on the spot at the target's name.

"How much does the job pay?" her voice finally broke the silence.

"Raven!" Midas exclaimed, looking over his shoulder at the girl. She still hadn't turned to face Daniel.

"Just a little less than the job at Rajikline," Daniel answered, ignoring Midas's interjection. "And that's on top of what Captain Payne is paying us. Pulling this side-job off will be well worth it, both for our reputation and our pocketbooks."

"I'm in," Raven said simply and turned around. "Killing Dexter and taking down his organization will allow me to sleep better at night."

"Hold your horses," Midas interrupted, holding up a hand to both Daniel and Raven. "Raven, what are you talking about?"

"We do things on principle now," Leopold added. "We're not just in it for the money anymore."

"Right, we do things because of the principle of it," Raven agreed. "Believe me when I say we will be killing Dexter on principle. What's wrong with getting paid to do good?"

"We're planning to purposely kill a man we may not have to," Midas argued. "In what universe could we do that based on principle? I don't have a problem with getting paid to do good, but since when is what we're discussing good?"

"If you knew what Dexter is responsible for, what pain and heartache, what atrocities, you wouldn't have any misgivings either," Raven said. "Trust me when I say we would be doing this on principle."

"It's not like you have a choice anyway," Daniel said. "Raven and I choose and plan the jobs. This is going to happen, and we'll make a small fortune by doing it."

"You may be the ones to plan the jobs, but don't forget it's my brother and I who do most of the heavy lifting when it comes to execution," Midas shot back. "We're not going to do it, and without us, nothing's going to come of all your planning!"

"Midas," Leopold said quietly as he reached up to put a hand on his brother's shoulder. The two turned away from Daniel and Raven.

"What's up, little brother?" Midas asked as he bent so that his head was even with Leopold's.

"Raven isn't acting like herself," Leopold said.

"That's true," Midas agreed after a few moments of recollection. "You don't think Daniel has something over on her, do you?"

"No, it's not Daniel," Leopold answered. "It's the target. Dexter Silverstone must be a really bad man for her to agree to this."

Midas looked over his shoulder to where Raven and Daniel stood together, allied against the two brothers in this thing. If only he had the information about Dexter Silverstone they seemed to be privy to, this decision might be easier.

"It's not our place," he argued with Leopold. "He could be the worst man in the realm, but that still wouldn't make this our job. We don't have the authority!"

"Doesn't it?" Leopold asked. "If there is a bad man, one who hurts people, and we can do something to stop him, doesn't that make it our responsibility to do whatever we can?"

"No," Midas said firmly. "The ability to do something does not equate to responsibility."

"Then why'd you rescue me from the bullies who were beating me up when we first met?" Leopold asked. "If you had no responsibility to do something, why did you? What'd you get out of it?"

"You," Midas answered firmly.

"That's not the only reason and you know it," Leopold shot back.

"Okay, fine," Midas conceded. "Let's assume that ability does equate to responsibility. We still have no idea who this Dexter is or what he's done. Responsibility means total responsibility. We can't very well go off blindly after a man whom we know nothing about. Allowing others to make the decisions on how we use our power is certainly not very responsible."

"We can always ask," Leopold said. "Even if they deem it unnecessary to tell us who Dexter is, and we are following blindly, it isn't an irresponsible use of our abilities. Raven believes he's dangerous and needs to be dealt with, and she has certainly earned our trust."

"Fine, we'll go along with it for now," Midas finally agreed. "I'll give the benefit of the doubt, but if our trust has been misplaced…"

"We'll cross that bridge if we come to it," Leopold said.

The two brothers turned around, unconsciously crossing their arms over their chests as they did so.

"We might be in," Midas said after a few moments of silence. "We do want to know who Dexter is, though, before we commit wholeheartedly to this."

"He's a bad man," Daniel answered.

"Very insightful and descriptive of you, Daniel," Midas said sarcastically. "People who cheat at cards can also be considered bad men, but I'd be against killing them for money. What kind of a bad person are we talking about here?"

"He is the worst kind of person you can ever encounter," Raven spoke up.

"You don't have to, Raven," Daniel began, but she held up a hand to silence him.

"Dexter Silverstone is the embodiment of the slimy scum of the earth if there ever was one," Raven explained. "He profits from the misery of others and kills anyone who gets in his way. Most criminals have a code of sorts, maintaining a certain amount of honor. For instance, only the most heartless of thieves would steal what little food a starving family might have, but this is the type of thing Dexter does on a regular basis. He kills, steals, and ruins lives for money."

"So he's kind of like us, then," Leopold spoke up, shocking Raven into temporary silence.

"Well," he continued, "correct me if I'm wrong, but we've done all those things for money. I'm not thrilled with where I've been in my life, but we have killed, stolen, and definitely ruined lives. You said before that we've robbed children of their parents and parents of their children and all for money."

"We've done it all in the past for sure, but we're not like that anymore," Raven argued. Her forceful speech captured Midas and Leopold's attentions so fully that neither noticed the contortions of Daniel's face at these words. The wizard was definitely not thrilled with the new leaf they had turned.

"We aren't just the unprincipled mercenaries we used to be," Raven continued. "We find lost treasure and help people protect their castles from the schemes of evil barons. We aren't the most feared group of assassins in the kingdom anymore."

"I'm not condemning, just trying to get inside the guy's head," Leopold said with a dry laugh. "I need to know the way he thinks if we're going to do this properly."

"If that's your goal, then consider this," Raven said. "He differs from what we were in that he enjoys the pain and misery he causes. When we had to steal something, we only stole what was required. When our job was to kill, we only killed who was necessary. All along the way we've curtailed the wrongs we've committed because to us it was just a job. To Dexter, this is amusement. When someone gets in his way he kills them and their whole family *just for the fun of it*. He's an extreme sadist, causing suffering to others for no other reason than that he enjoys watching them suffer."

"That's quite the profile, Raven," Midas said. "I'm beginning to think you've had first-hand experience with this guy."

"Good guess," Raven said sarcastically. "Now if we're done making stupid comments, let's get down to business. Daniel, I'm assuming Dexter's going to be in town, or we wouldn't be having this conversation."

"That's correct," Daniel confirmed. "His headquarters are here. He's the one hosting the party, actually."

"I know about his headquarters," Raven said quickly.

"Yes, but they don't," Daniel said with a wave toward Leopold and Midas. "As I was saying, he has his headquarters in town and that's where the meeting will take place."

"And when the place gets attacked, we make sure he becomes worm food in all the ruckus," Raven said. "I like it."

"Well, I don't, and I know Midas doesn't either," Leopold said. "I still don't think it's right for us to kill this man."

"I just told you what kind of a man he is," Raven said. "What more would it take to convince you?"

"Nothing will convince us," Midas answered. "Dexter will face justice, but it won't be on the blades of our weapons. We're here to turn him over to the king's judges, not our own devices."

"I can't believe you!" Raven exclaimed, but Daniel held up a hand.

"I think this job would be very good for us and for you personally," he told her. "However, if the whole team isn't on board, we won't do it. No sense in splitting us over something so unimportant."

"What are you…" Raven started, but Daniel cut her off.

"It's decided," he said. "Now, I have some more information on Dexter someplace around here. Come help me find it."

Daniel had to practically pull Raven from the room. She dragged her feet, sputtering over her words as they went. It was clear she was not happy about what had just happened.

"Be quiet and listen to me," the wizard hissed to her when they were in the hallway.

"To you?" Raven asked angrily. "You hung me out to dry! I would have expected you to be on my side if only for the money."

"I am on your side," Daniel said. "Like you say, the money's too good for me to pass up. Besides, I know you want this man dead."

Raven said nothing for several moments after this. When she finally found her voice, it was much quieter and more controlled than before.

"Then why didn't you side with me?"

"The brothers aren't going to see eye to eye with us on this one," Daniel said. "You can beg or plead or argue, but they just won't agree to killing Dexter."

"I don't believe it," Raven said. "I can make them see things my way."

"No, you can't," Daniel said. "I've seen their type before, all high and mighty on their moral code. You won't be able to break them, nor will I. I genuinely believe they've lost the ability to do what is necessary."

"You may be right," Raven said slowly.

"Our work is no place for the squeamish or faint of heart," Daniel said. "Of course, we can still use the brothers' expertise to accomplish our own mission. They would never have to know."

"What's your plan, then?" Raven asked.

"Well, Dexter could die in the fighting no matter what we decide here," the wizard answered. "In fact, he's not the kind of guy to surrender, so it's likely he'll end up going down with the ship, so to speak. All we have to do is give what is likely to happen a push toward becoming reality."

"You're right," Raven agreed. "We could do this and what Leo and Midas don't know won't hurt them."

"You get your dead slaver and we can split the money for the hit between the two of us," Daniel said. "How does that sound?"

"Like a lot better plan than the brothers have," Raven answered coldly.

"We'll do it, then," Daniel said. "Now help me get that information I was talking about before they start to wonder."

———————

"How do you think Raven's attached to this?" Midas asked his brother as they returned to the information on the table. "She's had some sort of run-in with this Dexter character. You could see it in her eyes; this thing may be on principle or it may be business, but it's also personal as well."

"Your guess is as good as mine," Leopold answered. He pulled out a list on parchment and scanned it before returning it to the table. "She's an orphan so I guess it's possible he killed her parents. That'd be a reason to make this personal if there ever was one."

"Or maybe it was her scars," Midas suggested. "She made a point of mentioning how sadistic he is and how he hurts others just to see them in pain."

"And she was particularly vehement about that part," Leopold noted. "Remember how bent out of shape she got when I suggested that he was like us? Honestly, your idea seems to have more credence than mine."

There was a clattering from the hall, and the brothers jumped to their feet in time to see Raven stagger through the doorway and toward the table, her arms heaping with books, posters, rolls of paper, and other assorted odds and ends.

"Daniel dropped his stuff," she grunted as she heaved her burden onto the table. "I'm sure he'd appreciate some help with it."

No sooner had The Shadow gotten all the material onto the table than Daniel began to reorganize it, shoving some of it here and more of it there. Many scrolls, papers, small metal figurines, and other things ended up on the floor by the time he had cleared enough room to spread out the map of the city for which he had been searching.

As Raven and the wizard poured over the parchment, muttering to themselves, Leopold gathered the materials which had been relegated to the floor and moved them to chairs, smaller tables, and any other surface he could find that wasn't the floor. He kept his eyes open as he worked, searching for anything that would be of help to him considering what his role in the job was likely to be. He found several items of use including a smaller map of the city and went to work internalizing the information.

After only a few hours he had memorized the city's layout as well as a floor-plan of Dexter's headquarters. They were housed in a rather unassuming, single story building sprawled across quite a large area in the middle of the city. He realized he had passed the structure many times, often wondering based on the guards at the doors what member of nobility lived inside. Now that he knew, he was less than impressed. The building had but two entrances, the front one on the east side and a smaller one on the south side. There were also two trapdoors in the roof which offered access to a large patio area covering much of the building's footprint. If he could just get to the roof, they would offer him the path of ingress he needed to infiltrate the place. Of course, even getting to the building stealthily would be a test of skill as a wide, open street ringed the entire structure.

"Daniel, I'm going to go scope out the place," Leopold said, standing and stretching. Not only did his muscles need the exercise, but he was about to go stir crazy if he didn't see something besides the inside of the bolt hole.

"That's fine. Take Midas with you," Daniel said, barely looking up from the materials before him on the table.

"See if you can find out how many guards we'll be up against and…" Raven began, but Leopold cut her off.

"I've done this before," he said gently. "I know what I'm looking for."

"I know you do," she said. Silence fell for a moment. "Don't get caught, and be safe."

"I will," Leopold responded.

"I won't get caught either, and I'll be sure to be safe," Midas said, purposefully breaking Raven and Leopold's moment. "You know, if anyone cares about me."

————†————

"This is pretty solid, I'll give it that," Midas said. "It's not going to be easy to get in."

The brothers were walking down the opposite side of the street that ran around the building, stealing occasional glances at the layout, number of guards, and other fortifications. It was a pity they weren't storming the place. The massive numbers of windows combined with the extensive spread of the place would make it easy enough to breach with an army. Too bad they were planning on sneaking in.

"It's solid, but it's no Rajikline," Leopold responded to his brother. "I'd hazard to say even you could sneak into this one if you tried hard enough!"

"Yeah, but why sneak past people when you can just smash them with your sword?" Midas asked. Leopold decided he was only half serious.

"Which is exactly why we're going to split up now," Leopold said. "You'll stay out here. Get up into the buildings around this street and see what kind of view of the target you have from them. Scope it out like you're an archer."

"I'll check 'em out," Midas said, stopping to look up at a four-story turret attached to the corner of the building immediately to his right. It seemed to be the style in this place because at least half the houses had them, though many were not as tall. "Archers would have a good view of the street and building, but why do we care? We don't have any archers."

"Raven's been practicing with her bow," Leopold said. He retrieved a pebble from the ground and tossed it into a sewer grate in the street. "She's no expert, but she's pretty good with it by now."

"Which I'm sure Daniel is thrilled about, but that's not the point," Midas said. "One archer in this situation won't do any good."

"That's certainly true, but imagine twenty of them spread around the turrets," Leopold motioned to the towers around the street. "That'd be pretty effective, don't you think?"

"Yeah, but we don't have twenty archers," Midas said.

"We don't know what we're going to have when it comes down to it," Leopold shot back. "You just scope out the towers and tell me what you find."

"Yes, your lordship," Midas mocked and added an exaggerated bow. "What will you be doing in the meantime?"

"Checking out the inside," Leopold answered. "See, smashing through people may work well in the assault, but it's not so great for reconnoitering."

"How exactly are you going to get inside?" Midas asked. He hopped forward with both feet, landing flat footed in a puddle so as to splash water on Leopold.

"Seriously?" Leopold asked incredulously, swiping the water off his pants. "What are you, five years old?"

"Oh man," Midas stopped suddenly, ignoring Leopold's comment altogether. He looked back at the grate the younger boy had tossed the pebble through then turned wide-eyed to Leopold. "You're going to go through the sewers again like you did at Rajikline, aren't you?"

"Not on your life," Leopold answered. "I got so sick I was vomiting for a week after the last time I did that."

"Then what's the grand plan for getting in?" Midas asked. His eyes widened suddenly, and he pointed excitedly at Leopold. "I bet I know what Raven has against Dexter! She said he wouldn't hesitate to steal from a starving family. I bet she was hungry and he stole her last penny."

Leopold just looked at Midas for several long moments. He shook his head slowly, opened his mouth multiple times as though about to speak but closed it silently each time.

"Really, Midas?" he finally said. "He stole her last penny and that's what she's all fired up about killing him over?"

"Yeah, you're right," Midas agreed. "That would seem to be overkill if it were true. Probably not true."

"Yeah," Leopold agreed. "Now, back to the last thing you said that wasn't ludicrous. I'm going to sneak in right here."

Leopold pointed to the side of the building directly across the street from them. It did not have an entrance but there were plenty of windows scattered along it. A spiky hedge ran down its length, creating a barrier of protection against vandals and thieves. It wouldn't be a problem for Leopold.

"Am I missing something here or are you planning on running across this wide street in broad daylight and climbing in through one of those windows?" Midas said, sounding extremely confused.

"That is indeed the idea, although I plan on entering through one of the access hatches on the roof rather than a window," Leopold said. He tugged on his belt and bent down to test his boots for tightness. "There are four sets of guards who patrol the perimeter of the building. In theory, that should put one group on each of the sides at any given time, but the east and west ends are longer than the north and south. This means that for a period of about fifteen to twenty seconds, there are two groups of guards on the east and west sides and none on the north and south. In that twenty second window, I'll dash across the road, scale the building, and disappear atop it. Once I'm inside they'll never find me."

"Good plan," Midas said with a tinge of sarcasm. "What about bystanders?"

"You're referring to people who see me do this but are not one of the guards?" Leopold asked.

"Or the person who just happens to look out the window while you're scaling it," Midas added.

"Rule number one of stealth: people have a huge capacity to rationalize or forget entirely unusual or unpleasant things," Leopold answered. He slid a piece of leather over the hand guard of his knife to secure it in the sheath. The last thing he wanted was for the weapon to fall out while he was running, jumping, and climbing.

"Do you actually think this is going to work?" Midas asked. "You're going to run across, climb the wall, slip inside, and anyone who sees you do it will just forget about it?"

"Or rationalize it," Leopold added. "Or just not care."

"Leo, I think you might be even braver than I am," Midas told the younger boy. "Or crazy, but I know you're not that."

"Midas, I've found that many times it takes much more courage to sneak than to attack," Leopold said. "In a way, I envy your job. You just put your shield front and center and start your sword swinging. No suspense or uncertainty, just steel on steel."

"Yeah, my job is all vacation and easy sailing!" Midas said with a smile. "You can take it any time you want."

"I never said I wanted to take it, just that I envied you *in a way*," Leopold shot back. "I'll still take this stuff over your work any day."

"That's right," Midas agreed, continuing the friendly argument. "Just as long as we remember whose job is harder, right Leo?"

He turned to rub the comment into his little brother, but Leopold wasn't there anymore. He was dashing across the road at breakneck speed.

Leopold vaulted the hedge, clinging to a window sill instead of landing on the ground. With the agility of a monkey he shot up the side of the building, rolling onto the roof and out of sight of anyone on the ground. He lay there for a moment, catching his breath and wondering whether the patrol had seen him disappear over the edge of the roof. The lack of commotion seemed to indicate they had not, but Leopold was unwilling to visually confirm that assumption. Instead he crawled on all fours to a point about ten feet from the edge where he finally felt comfortable standing up. Based on how far from the wall the patrols walked, his own height, and geometry, he knew they couldn't see him now.

He moved soundlessly across the roof dodging benches, stone statues, and flower beds he hadn't been able to see from below. No doubt they provided a pleasant getaway from the building beneath but would also prove to be a problem for an archer in an adjacent tower trying to take down someone on the roof. No matter. That was a problem for the strategists. He was just here to collect information and evaluate the situation.

A trapdoor finally became visible, hidden inside a small structure of three walls and a roof. The design seemed to have the intention of keeping rain from entering the roof portal, but it would also serve well as a choke point if necessary. Leopold loped toward it, eager to get inside where there was furniture, light, dark, and shadows. This was his preferred habitat, one in which he was almost unbeatable. As he had told Midas, once inside, the enemy would never find him.

The trapdoor lurched upward an inch or so, then slammed back down with a resounding thud. Leopold changed course immediately, dashing around the side of the structure, his feet skidding on the pea-gravel covering the roof as he pressed up against the stone wall. He heard the trapdoor thud open and moved to the rear of the structure before scaling the short wall and lying as flat as possible atop it. One ear was pressed against the stone, not to help him hear but to make his head flatter. He could feel sweat beading on the back of his neck and running down to puddle on the stone. Some of it leaked off the side of his face and into his eyes, but he refused to move a hand to wipe it away. His field of vision was so restricted that he couldn't tell where the person who had come through the trapdoor was, and he refused to give his position away with movement.

There was the sound of the trapdoor thudding shut followed by the laughter of two voices, one male and one female. They were creating quite the ruckus for just the two of them, which was good because it covered the heavy beating of Leopold's heart. It could have been his ears playing tricks on him, but he was convinced their voices were getting farther away which was both good and bad. The good was that eventually they would be far enough away for him to get down while the bad was that the more distance between them made it exceedingly more likely that they would see him if they turned around.

The voices became instantly silent, and Leopold pressed his body even tighter against the stone. This was what he had been referring to when he told his brother it sometimes took more courage to sneak than to attack. He had to trust his skill and his decisions to hide him from the people below. It was imperative that he not move as a single motion could attract attention and highlight his presence. The silence persisted for a long time as he waited anxiously. Against his better judgement, he was just about to make a move for the trapdoor when the couple stepped into his limited field of vision and he froze anew, every muscle in his body tense. The couple walked arm in arm parallel to him so that just one look to the side would reveal his presence. The man wore fine clothes as though he were very rich and was adorned with all manner of rings, necklaces, and other expensive jewelry. The woman, at least ten years the man's junior by Leopold's reckoning, was wearing clothing that seemed to him to be more trashy than fancy. On the other hand, who was he to judge? While he had accumulated a great deal of knowledge across a broad spectrum of subjects over his short life, women's fashion was certainly not an area in which he was well versed.

The couple changed trajectory, moving more fully away from the trapdoor now, and Leopold was finally able to safely crawl forward to the edge of the roof, swing his legs off, and land lightly on the ground. The trapdoor was heavy but not so much so that he couldn't manage it. In less than a minute, he was down the spiral staircase to the roof and hidden among the shadows of the adjacent store room, plotting his next move.

"Just as long as we remember whose job is harder, right Leo?" There was no response, and Midas turned to see his little brother bolt across the street. Leopold jumped the fence like it was nothing and scaled the wall. He'd definitely timed the gap in the patrols correctly and gained the roof with a good two seconds to spare. He was the best at what he did, there was no doubt about that, and as much as Midas might like to rib him about whose job was harder, he wouldn't have traded with him for anything.

Midas watched the guards for a few moments to verify they had not seen Leopold, but they never varied from their predetermined route. A smile crossed his lips as he continued down the far side of the street. There was nothing quite as easy as bypassing guards that never thought for themselves. If the actual job went like this, it would be some of the easiest money they ever earned. On a whim, Midas stopped in front of a particularly tall building, glancing up at it as he moved toward the door. The main structure was three stories tall with a turret extending another floor higher. This would be an ideal spot for an archer to set up if he could convince the owner to allow it.

Two knocks and thirty seconds later, Midas heard footsteps from inside and took two steps back from the door which, moments later, swung inward just enough for a face to show through the crack. It was a middle-aged man, at least six feet tall and not scrawny from what Midas could see. This was the kind of person who should open the door fully, not just half a foot. What was he afraid of?

"My name is Midas," Midas offered after a few long moments. An awkward silence followed the comment which he finally broke with, "Nice building you've got here. It's your residence, right?"

"Yes." The man's monosyllabic answer coupled with a nervous glance at someone or something beyond Midas's range of vision seemed oddly out of place.

"Is this a nice place to live?" Midas asked. The more he talked, the more he thought that small talk wasn't going to get him anywhere. Perhaps money was more this man's speed.

"Nice enough," the man answered shortly. He cast another glance at something behind the door.

"What's going on?" Midas asked.

"Nothing," the man answered quickly, looking back at Midas. "Nothing's going on. I'm not hiding anything."

"Really?" Midas asked as sternly as he could manage. "What's behind the door?"

"Nothing's behind the door," the man answered too quickly.

The answer was clearly nothing even closely resembling the truth, and Midas's mind kicked into over drive. Was this a trap? If so, how? Who would have set it? Instinctively his hand dropped to the hilt of his dagger and his body shifted to a fighting stance.

"Open the door," he commanded in a low voice. When the man hesitated, he added, "Do it. Now!"

Terror and sorrow tore across the man's face as he slowly let the door swing open. Midas's dagger was halfway out of its sheath when he saw them and froze. Pressed up against the wall were two young girls and a woman who was no doubt the man's wife. They cowered there, silent tears running down their faces. Midas was at a loss for words.

"I don't get it," he said, looking back to the man. "What are you hiding from?"

"You mean you're not here to take them?" the man asked suspiciously, motioning to his daughters.

"Of course not," Midas answered. "I just wanted…"

"Get inside, then," the man said, motioning into the house. "Quickly, now."

Midas moved through the doorway and several steps further into the house before turning to look at the family. The father had closed the door and was leaning against it as if to hold it shut against some sort of evil outside. The mother and daughters stared at him, no longer crying but the tears still wet on their cheeks. Midas couldn't think of a single thing to say.

"I'm just here to see what the view from your turret looks like," he finally forced out. "I don't get it? What are you hiding from?"

"You need to use our turret?" the man asked, completely ignoring Midas's question. "For what? To spy on the building across the street?"

"Yeah actually, sort of," Midas answered. "How did you know? Why did you assume that?"

"You don't work for him and yet you look like that," the man said. "Why else would you want to use my turret?"

"I look like what exactly?" Midas shot back.

"You're big and you carry yourself well. You're trying to hide it, but you're obviously a mercenary," the man said. "You said you don't work for Silverstone, so why else would you be here wanting to use my turret unless you're here to…" the man glanced toward his daughters, "…*take care* of him?"

"Is that true?" the woman spoke up. "Did someone finally get enough money together to do something about Mr. Silverstone?"

"Calm yourselves and let's sit down," Midas said. He'd finally regained control of some of his faculties and had an idea of what was going on. "I'm not answering any more questions until we all sit down and take a few moments to process this."

"Of course, sir," the woman directed Midas toward the stairs. "Where are my manners? The sitting room is on the second floor. Garret will show you the way, won't you dear, and I'll be up with tea in a few minutes."

Garret led Midas to the second story sitting room, his two daughters trailing behind, gawking at the young warrior. It was as if they'd never seen anyone before. Or perhaps anyone with quite the same bearing, Midas decided. With as intimidated as their father was, it seemed unlikely that the rest of the town's inhabitants were more courageous. The sitting area was well furnished if a bit small. Midas took a seat in a wing-backed chair leaving its twin and a couch for the others. Garret sat on the couch while his two daughters stole peeks at Midas through the doorway. Silence reigned in the area, heavy as a blanket draped over everything. It was so complete that Midas felt uncomfortable breaking it. Instead he busied himself with taking in the arrangement of the chamber. It was small, miniscule for a sitting room, and contained only the two wingback chairs, the couch, two end tables, and some wall hangings. After observing all there was to see, Midas began rearranging his legs and twiddling his thumbs.

All this activity, though it seemed to take forever, actually passed less a minute and with Garret still unwilling to start the conversation, Midas found it necessary to turn to other avenues of amusing himself. The next time the girls poked their heads around the doorframe to get a look at him, he stuck his tongue out at them. Startled by the unexpected action, they failed to retreat back into hiding as soon as he spotted them but stood, staring at him for several long seconds. He held their gaze, wondering all the while what his next move would be.

"You'll have to excuse my girls' gawking," Garret finally spoke up. "They've never really seen anyone outside the family much less someone like you."

"Oh, that's quite alright," Midas said generously. "I like kids. Was one once, believe it or not!"

Garret smiled at the joke.

"Where are you from originally?" he asked. "I mean, where did you grow up?"

"Here and there," Midas answered. "I don't rightly know most of the places I've lived in my life. Moved around a lot as a kid and now, well, you can imagine that my job doesn't lend itself to settling down in one place too long."

"Then you are a mercenary!" Garret exclaimed.

"I never said that," Midas answered with a shake of his head. "Tell me, Garret, why so many floors in this house?"

"What do you mean?" Garret asked, thrown by the sudden change in topic.

"Usually multiple floors are associated with wealthy people," Midas said. "No offense, but it doesn't really seem like you're wildly wealthy."

"Oh, we're not," Garret assured him. "When this town was founded, the land inside the walls was prime real estate, so it was very expensive. People who wanted to set up shop in town could only afford a very small plot of land like the one my house is built on. They were forced to build up instead of out which is why you see so many tall houses around here."

"And the land was too precious to waste any of it, which is why the buildings are built wall-to-wall, butted right up against each other?" Midas asked. "That's what makes them look larger than they actually are."

"Yes," Garret agreed. "That's not to say the houses are small. My family is very blessed. On a footprint the size of a kitchen we've managed to fit a kitchen, sitting room, bedroom, and workshop."

"The fourth floor is the workshop?" Midas asked.

"Yes. How did you know?" Garret asked in surprise.

"The fourth floor of a turret doesn't go unnoticed, and you don't want anyone to know they exist," Midas said, smiling and waving at the girls. They giggled in response and disappeared out of sight again. "The kitchen is on the first floor, sitting room on the second which means the bedroom must be on the third."

"That's very astute of you, sir," Garret conceded. "That is indeed the layout."

"The one thing I don't get is why you don't want anyone to see your daughters," Midas commented. "If I had children as pretty as them…"

"Daddy says we have to stay inside or they'll come and take us away."

The younger girl stood only a few feet from Midas, hands clasped behind her back and eyes elevated toward him. She couldn't have been more than five or six years old, Midas decided just before the realization of what she'd said crashed down on him.

"Gabriella, what have I told you about talking to strangers?" Garret asked his daughter.

"But this one is good, Daddy," Gabriella said, never taking her eyes off Midas. "He's going to help make our problems go away."

"Sarah, take your sister and go to your room," Garret told his older daughter. With a nod she grabbed Gabriella's hand and tugged her toward the stairs.

"You're gonna help us, right mister?" Gabriella asked even as she was pulled out of sight.

"Yes," Midas answered under his breath, his eyes still glued to the stairs where the small girl had disappeared. He stayed that way until Garret's wife entered the room with a tea kettle and some cups, though he couldn't say how much time had passed. As the tea was poured, he spoke again, this time in a quiet voice.

"It makes sense now. I get why you're so scared and why you hide your daughters." Garret and his wife exchanged glances. "Dexter Silverstone buys and sells flesh. Doesn't he?"

———┤————

Leopold strode brazenly into the room, the only room he had yet to visit if he didn't miss his mark. It was spacious and mostly empty, containing little more than a large, round table with impressive oak chairs spaced evenly around it. A few book shelves and small tables positioned against the walls completed the décor without making it feel crowded. There were no papers, scrolls, or other things that appeared to contain interesting information, so Leopold skirted the furniture and headed for the doorway on the far side of the room. The connected study was more to his liking. One portion of it had been converted into a sitting area with several chairs and couches positioned around some low tables. Leopold looked for doors, windows, and any other avenues of exit but found none. The lack of windows made sense since this room, by his best estimation, was directly in the center of the building, but the lack of doors surprised him somewhat. Out of the entire building, he had yet to find a single dead-end, but here was one in what appeared to be the office of whoever ran the place. Maybe they thought it afforded some sort of privacy. This was the type of information which could be invaluable later on when they needed to trap Dexter.

Leopold rounded a partition at the back of the room and was unable to stop before thumping headlong into a surprisingly conservative wooden desk. He planted his hands on the paper-strewn surface to stop himself, staring at the treasure trove of information for a few seconds before sliding around to the chair. There was no telling what he would find in here. People left the most interesting things out on their desks when they thought the room was secure. In minutes he had uncovered dozens of nuggets, most of which would appear to be useless to the casual observer, but Leopold knew better. A financial statement could tell a much larger story than where someone was earning and spending his money. Well-kept books, as Dexter had, could provide information such as the approximate number of guards he hired, when supplies were usually delivered to the compound, and, with a bit of deciphering, what his favorite foods were. On the other hand, a guest list for the upcoming event was much easier to interpret.

With his ears alert for sounds from the next room, he poured over the documents, ledgers, scribblings, and other papers for a long time. This was one of the rare occasions that he had plenty of time to search and read as much as he wanted, gleaning whatever information was available. Apparently this room was off-limits to the guards and common servants which made sense the more he discovered. Mr. Silverstone was certainly no upstanding citizen but was involved in a number of shady business dealings. With as many people as no doubt would like to bring a case against him, the fewer that had access to this information the better. But then why did he leave all this out on his desk? Leopold rocked the simple wooden chair onto its back legs as he pondered the question. Perhaps pride had led him to believe that he was impervious to the law. Or maybe the tedium of keeping everything hidden had become too much. It didn't matter though. Silverstone's slip-up was The Shadow's blessing.

The chair slipped suddenly, and Leopold found himself plunging backwards. His head collided heavily with the wood paneled wall behind him, splashing sparks across his vision. He shook his head several times and waited for his vision to return before he realized the hard surface pressing against his back was not the wall but the floor. He sat up, groaning as his skull protested the movement. Once he was able he righted the chair and returned the contents of the desk to the way he had found them but as he turned to leave the study, something held him in place. There was something odd about what had just happened, something that seemed out of place. Even with the blunt force trauma to his head, he had picked up on it, though he wouldn't know for sure until he tested it.

Leopold's fist thudded against the wall panels with a dull, hollow thud. A smile broke out on his face as he scanned the wooden slats. So this was why there was no way out! It was a hidden exit no one seemed to know about except for Dexter

Silverstone. He found the anomaly in the wood and placed his hands in position. The latch wasn't very well hidden, and as he tugged at it, he had the sudden feeling that he was opening…

"A closet," he said aloud, disgust heavy in his voice. Here he thought he'd found something of great importance when all he'd discovered was Dexter's personal stash of extravagant fur coats. With an annoyed tug, he jerked the closet closed and headed around the partition to the sitting area. As he headed for the door, a large mural he hadn't noticed before caught his eye. On closer examination, he saw that it wasn't a mural at all but a very thin tapestry hung against the wall near the door. It depicted a scene Leopold wasn't familiar with. A large god-like figure with a twisted face was set at the top of the scene. Under him were what appeared to be giants, all decked out in battle gear. In their hands they held whips with which they drove the masses of small, bound and chained humans beneath them.

"Giants enslaving humans?" Leopold asked no one. "And what god is that supposed to be? I've never heard of him in any mythology."

He stepped forward to examine the hanging more closely but snapped his head upright at the sound of voices in the next room. Dodging chairs, couches, and low tables, he shot back through the room, hiding himself behind the lattice by the desk. He forced his breathing to steady and willed his heart to cease its incessant pounding all while keeping one ear pressed against the lattice. Time seemed to slow down and stand still. For one surreal moment, he realized that he was trapped in a room with no second avenue of escape. Not that he was worried for himself. He'd gotten out of worse spots than this before, but it had always involved fighting. If he was so much as spotted, this job could be over before it ever began. Was that a problem? He and Midas had been against it from the beginning. Killing was a business they'd wanted to get out of and getting spotted would be the perfect excuse to not do it. No one would blame him.

A vision of Raven flashed before him, begging him with her eyes to do this thing for her. He didn't know what her connection to Dexter was, but he trusted her. Beyond that, he'd seen the ledgers and knew where the man got his money from. If there was ever a person in the world who deserved, no *needed* to be killed, it was Dexter Silverstone.

"Is Silverstone insane?!" a voice said. "I know he's built his business on taking risks, but this one is stupid with nothing to gain from it."

"That's not for us to decide," the other voice, a woman, said in a more reasonable tone. "This is his place, and he called this meeting, so we play by his rules."

"I still think he's crazy," the first voice said. There was a huff of air as the man flopped onto a sofa. "If he keeps toeing this line, eventually someone is going to decide that enough is enough. Then we're all going to be in trouble."

"Who's going to do it?" the woman. "The town guard?"

"The people of the city," the man shot back. "We may outnumber the guard two to one, but if the whole city rose up against us, we wouldn't stand a chance."

"He's been dealing with these people for a long time," the woman said. "I'm sure he knows how to handle them."

"People can do some unexpected things with the right stimuli," the man said. "The Smiths, the Millers, and the Schaffers. Silverstone has brought the daughters of all three back into town."

"Have some faith," the woman said. "He knows what he's doing."

"I know what I'm doing? Well that's good to hear!" a third voice broke in with a note of mirth.

"Mr. Silverstone!"

There was some scraping and thudding and Leopold guessed that the two original occupants had jumped to their feet.

"Oh, take a seat and don't mind me," Dexter Silverstone said jovially. "I'm just here to grab something from my desk."

Leopold scrambled backwards, looking every which way for someplace to hide. There was nothing except for the wall behind him so he slid the closet open, blessing its silent latch, and climbed inside. The doors closed as silently as they had opened, and the last he saw as they slid shut was Dexter Silverstone rounding the corner and looking right at him. But that wasn't possible, was it? He pressed to the back of the closet and moved as far as he could to the right, holding his breath and waiting. His heart was pounding so loudly he was sure Silverstone would hear it if he just opened the door. For an eternity he waited and nothing happened. It was all in his head. He hadn't been spotted after all. All he needed to do now was wait for the other two to leave and...

The closet doors slammed open causing Leopold to jerk backwards.

"Come out you little rat." The voice was still that of Dexter Silverstone but all the humor and joviality was gone from it. "I know you're in here. If you don't come out now, I'm just going to have to find you the hard way. And it won't go well for you if that's the case."

"Hey boss, what's up?" the man from before asked.

"There wasn't anyone in here," the woman put in. "We would have seen them if there had been."

"You looked in my closet?" Dexter asked, sarcasm in his voice.

"Fair point, Mr. Silverstone," the woman said.

"Come out," Dexter said again. This time there was open hostility in his voice, and Leopold didn't doubt that he would be killed if he were found. Any normal person would have shrunk back further into the corner trying to make the impenetrable walls of the closet give way. Leopold was not any normal person. Wedging his fingers into a chink between the back wall and the top of the closet and grabbing the bar the clothes were hanging on with the other hand, he lifted himself silently into the air and among the shadows near the roof.

"Check the floor," Dexter said before Leopold could situate himself comfortably. "His feet should show beneath the coats."

There was some rustling followed by silence.

"There's no one here, boss," the man said.

"They've gone through the secret passage," Dexter said coldly. "Get after them and bring them back alive. I'd like to have a word with whoever it is that's been in among my clothes."

"Down the secret passage, Mr. Silverstone?" the woman asked incredulously.

"Yes. The catch is in the back left corner of the closet," Dexter said, his voice rising with each word. "You know the one I'm talking about. Heck, I only have one secret passage in this whole blasted place!"

"Boss, slow down and think about this a second," the man said. "Who do you think it was? The help? One of the girls? No one knows that passage is there."

"Look, Mr. Silverstone," the woman added reasonably. "I didn't hear anything from here. Let's check the door to the passage and see if it looks like it has been opened recently."

"Why are you fighting so hard against this?" Dexter asked suddenly. "It almost makes me think that you're trying to hide something."

"In all honesty, sir, I just don't want to spend a few hours on a wild goose chase that I'm pretty sure I'll come back empty-handed from," the woman answered.

"Fair enough," Dexter said after a pause. "I guess you're right. I'll check the door."

From his high perch, Leopold saw Dexter Silverstone for the first time as he forced the coats apart and ran his eyes down the seams of the secret door. *Don't look up*, was the only thing running through Leopold's mind.

"You're right. No signs of anyone coming through here," Dexter said as he straightened the coats back out. "I guess I'm just a little jumpy these days."

155

"Don't worry, boss," the man said as the closet doors slid shut. "We've got your back."

Leopold's muscles were burning by now, but he knew better than to give them a rest and let himself down now. That would be to fall for the oldest trick in the book: close the doors like you're done looking, give the prey long enough to come out of hiding, and then throw the doors wide just in time to catch them. Well, he was the best sneaker in the whole realm, and he wasn't about to fall for something so juvenile. Sure enough, a minute after the closet closed, Dexter threw the doors open and checked everywhere again. When he left this time, it was for good.

Leopold lowered himself quietly to the ground and felt around the back corner of the closet for the catch to the secret passage door. It was skill that had got him this particular nugget, but skill couldn't account for all of it. He smiled to himself, thanking heaven for human nature that would assume someone had found a secret passage before it would simply look up and see the real cause of their problems. He found the latch, depressed it, and the door hissed open. Now it was time to find where this thing led to and take the information back to Daniel and Raven.

———————————

"He doesn't sell flesh," Garret told Midas. "He rents it out."

"And only the youngest and prettiest, I'm guessing," Midas added. "He pulls straight from the city he works out of? Is the guy insane?"

"Why?" Garret's wife asked. "Who's going to stop him? The guard is too small to do anything and the people…well, we're so frightened he could enslave us instead of our daughters and we probably wouldn't resist."

"This is not going to continue," Midas said slowly, almost painfully. There was a knot the size of his fist in his stomach and his facial muscles refused to obey him anymore. He couldn't see his expression, but he didn't doubt it was frightening to behold.

"What are you going to do about it?" Garret challenged. "Are you the mercenary I think you are or not?"

"I am," Midas said darkly. "I kill for money, and he's the one with the price on his head. I was brought here by the money, and I will collect the bounty afterwards but even were that not so…"

Midas looked from Garret to his wife and back again.

"Your daughters deserve better than this," Midas said. "They deserve to grow up in a city where they can go outside without fear that they will be abducted. And you deserve to not have to live under the thumb of this monster. I'm going to take care of this, but you're going to have to help me."

"Help you how?" Garret asked. "I'll do what I can, but I'm no warrior."

"In many cases it isn't the warriors who are the tipping force in a battle," Midas said. "Soldiers, equipment, and strength of arms can be assessed and measured and accounted for if you have the right information."

"And what information would that be?" Garret asked.

"This city guard," Midas said. "Where might I find them?"

"I told you already, the guard is outnumbered," Garret's wife said. "They can't stand against the sell-swords Mr. Silverstone has."

"You leave that to me," Midas said. "Just tell me where I can find the guard."

"Their headquarters is two blocks west in the precise center of the city," Garret said. "If there's anything else I can do, just tell me. As I said before, I'm no warrior, but I'd do anything for my daughters."

Strong words for someone who showed them to me when he thought I worked for Dexter, Midas thought to himself. He decided to let the fact slide. People were much more apt to acts of heroism when in groups.

"I don't expect you to fight," he said. "That's what I'm paid to do, and I intend to earn my keep. Stay ready, though. We'll be back to use your turret when the time comes."

"'We,' sir?" Garret asked. "How many of you are there? Who are you?"

"Who are we?" Midas asked. He let the silence grow for a few moments before answering his own question. "We are The Shadow."

―――――――――

"Do you want the bad news or the worse news first?" Leopold asked. The Shadow was congregated in the bolt hole again, gathered in the same room as before. Most of the clutter had been cleared off the table near the window and moved to the floor under and around it. Now all that remained atop were large maps of the city and Dexter's headquarters.

"Bad news, I guess," Raven answered, looking up from the maps and twirling a small figurine between her fingers. This was one of the many tools she used to plan the jobs, small figures that represented different people and different times. Leopold was never sure how, but they seemed to give her super planning powers. Not that she was bad at her job without them, but with them she could plan anything, even an excursion into Castle Rajikline. The fact they were out again meant she knew something the brothers didn't.

"The bad news is we'll be up against a lot more people than I originally thought," Leopold said. "Dexter alone has a hundred and twenty guards on the payroll."

"Right, but that's just the base figure for how many we'll be up against," Daniel interrupted, looking up from the paper Leopold had transcribed from what he remembered of Dexter's guest list. "From the names you wrote down, it seems like this meeting is of all the top players in this particular business."

"That's good," Raven said simply. "The more birds we can get with one stone, the better."

"It's good but hard," Daniel said. "Each of these people is big enough that they'll all likely bring a bodyguard or two. That could put the total number of enemies as high as two hundred. Maybe a few more."

"We can take two hundred easily when we're joined by the five hundred soldiers Evalda promised us," Midas dismissed the concern. The others had to turn to look at him as he was the only member of The Shadow who had elected to lounge elsewhere in the room besides near the strategy table. His sword lay across his knees, and he occasionally ran a whetstone down the blade, producing quite an unpleasant noise.

"Which brings me to the worse news," Leopold said. "Her sources were wrong because this party is happening within the next couple days."

"That's a lot sooner than Evalda had anticipated," Raven said, her brow creasing in worry and concentration. "Her army won't have even started to arrive yet. Daniel, any chance we can get a message to Evalda and tell her to hurry the men up?"

"No," Daniel said. "She skipped town on some other assignment and was supposed to be back with the first of her army. We wouldn't be able to get a message to her quickly enough even if I did know where she was."

"So it's four against two hundred?" Midas spoke up, once again rubbing stone against metal. "That's only fifty apiece, right?"

"Midas, do you have to do that right now?" Raven asked.

"Hear me out," Leopold interrupted. "The situation isn't the best, but it's not all bad news. At least get all the information before you start picking everything apart."

"Right," Raven conceded. "What else do you have for me?"

"A few things that'll be really nice to know," Leopold answered. "First, since the building is only a single story tall, that makes it pretty easy to infiltrate. I was able to do it today just by scaling the wall between these guard patrols." He pointed to the path indicated by a few figurines.

"What's the feasibility for the rest of us getting in that way?" Raven asked.

"Not good, but there're other ways inside you could utilize," Leopold answered. "Windows can be broken if necessary and there's also sewer access if anyone besides me wants to try that for once."

"What do you mean?" Raven asked. "We all took a trip through the sewers back in Kraljevi."

"Yes, but those sewers were different than the ones you're always so gung-ho for me to use when I'm sneaking into castles and the like," Leopold explained. "They had a lot more open space and less fecal matter. The ones here would be different. A lot tighter and lined with filth you wouldn't even want to imagine."

"You make it sound so appealing, but I'll pass," Raven said. "Anything else?"

"Are you sure?" Leopold persisted. "I thought it might give you some perspective on the whole thing."

"There's a reason we make you do stuff like that," Midas said as he ran the whet stone down his blade again. "*I* don't want to be the one walking knee deep in someone else's feces just to get inside a building."

"I can respect that," Leopold told his brother. "Just so long as we remember whose job is harder."

"I didn't say it was hard, just unpleasant," Midas retorted. No one was listening but were back to discussing the matter at hand.

"We have sewer access. Anything else I should know?" Raven asked.

"Either way, I don't think we'll need to use the sewer," Daniel said. "I've managed to lay my hands on an invitation to the meeting. If we disguise ourselves to play the part, we might be able to get in the front door."

"What kind of disguises are we talking about?" Midas asked.

"The invitation is to a Lord Sauvage whom I can play the part of," Daniel answered. "As I said before, everyone attending will likely bring some bodyguards and servants, so we should all be able to get in that way."

"We'll be the hired help, and no one cares what we look like, but what about you?" Midas asked belligerently. "How are you supposed to disguise yourself as someone you've never met before?"

"He's nobility," Daniel shot back over the rasping of Midas's whetstone. "It's my job to know this stuff. Do you have to keep doing that?"

"Only if you want my sword to be sharp when it matters," Midas answered easily. "You said you acquired this lord's invitation. Won't he be missing it?"

"No, and don't ask how because I don't feel like explaining it," Daniel said. "Suffice it to say, this is my job, and I'm really good at it."

"Boys, let's stop fighting," Raven cut in. "So what's Sauvage look like?"

"Fortunately, it turns out he looks a lot like me," Daniel answered. "It shouldn't be a problem for me to portray him, and as I said before, the rest of you will play my bodyguards and servants."

"Fine with me," Midas said. He dropped the whetstone into his lap and used his finger to test the edge of his sword's blade. "I'm better at playing the muscly guard than the stuck up noble any day of the week."

"Really, Midas?" Raven asked. "I have no words for you. Leo, do you have anything else?"

"Yeah, one really big thing," Leopold answered. "Dexter has an office located in the center of the building right here." He tapped the map. "In a closet in the back of the room is a panel that opens to a secret passage which comes out almost a quarter of a mile east of the building. I know where the exit of the tunnel is and how to open it from the inside."

"That *is* useful," Raven said evenly, though the sparkle in her eyes betrayed her true emotions.

"It's all useful," Daniel said. "Good job on the recon, guys. The problem, though, is that while this is valuable, it doesn't really help us. Remember, we don't want to just get Dexter, we want to capture all of them. Even with all this information, we can't do that with just four people."

"And that's where I finally have something worthwhile to say," Midas commented, standing up and sliding his sword into its scabbard. "We may only have an army of four, but there're sixty warriors in the city just waiting to be called upon."

"Sixty warriors in this city?" Daniel asked incredulously. "Where?"

"Right here," Midas answered, crossing the room to the table and stabbing a finger at the center of the city map. "The city guard."

"We're not here officially, Midas," Daniel pointed out. "For all the guard knows, we're acting on our own. They won't believe any story we spin about working covertly for the king, so why would the guard help us?"

"Because Dexter Silverstone has skirted the law and been a pain in their side for far too long," Midas answered. "The only reason they haven't dealt with him before this is because he has more men than they do. If we can convince them that together we'll win, they'll help us."

"Set up the meeting," Daniel told Midas after some thought. "My word, I never thought I'd see the day we linked up with a city guard!"

"Or the day we'd be working for the king," Raven agreed. "Anything for the money, right Daniel?"

"Right you are. Anything for the money."

"I can appreciate where you're coming from, I really can," Captain Miller, leader of the city guard, said. He stood across the table from Daniel, hands planted firmly on the north wall of the city map. "I've wanted to take out this joker for a long time, but it's just not possible."

"Of course it is," Daniel contradicted. "Anything's possible if you know what you're doing."

"Really?" Captain Miller asked. "You're telling me that flying is possible?"

"Okay, some things are beyond the grasp of humans, but this isn't one of them," Daniel said. "We can take Dexter Silverstone down if we work together."

"You don't understand me," Captain Miller said. "Even if we had the manpower to deal with him, we don't have the authority. Technically we don't have any proof that he's done anything against the law."

"Kidnapping isn't against the law?" Raven asked rhetorically.

"Of course it is," Captain Miller said in an irritated voice.

"There are dozens of families in this city that will verify he took their children," Daniel said. "What more proof do you need?"

"None of those families have proof he was the one that did the taking," Captain Miller explained. "You don't know how much it kills me to watch him continue day after day, doing what we all know he's doing but unable to prove it. The safety of this city is my responsibility and it pains me more than you can know to let this continue."

"Actually, I know exactly what you're going through, Captain," Leopold spoke up for the first time since the meeting had convened. "Your daughter was one of the many girls taken by him, wasn't she?"

"Everyone knows that," Captain Miller said morosely. "That should tell you the extent to which I've tried to bring him down. There just isn't a way to do it."

"You know he took your daughter, but what you don't know is that she's going to be back in the city during the meeting Dexter called," Leopold said matter-of-factly.

"What?!" Captain Miller exclaimed, standing up straight and gripping the hilt of his sword tightly in his left fist. "How do you know this?"

"Including her, there will be at least three girls from this city at the meeting," Leopold said. "The proof in his headquarters will make this mission completely legal. All we have to do is actually pull it off."

"If that's the case, I'm in," Captain Miller said, "but I refuse to send my men on a suicide mission. We need a way to get in, get Dexter, and get out with minimal danger."

"If you cut the head off a snake, the body still twitches for a long time afterwards," Leopold said.

"And that's assuming the head doesn't grow back, in which case all you have is a really ticked off snake," Raven added. "For this to work, we need to tear this organization up by the roots or someone else will just take Dexter's place."

"We don't have the facilities to keep all of them while they await their trials," Captain Miller pointed out.

"We don't have the manpower to take them all into custody either," Daniel said.

"Then we request reinforcements," Captain Miller said. "I can have five hundred soldiers here within two weeks."

"Captain, let me make myself very clear," Daniel said, ignoring the irony of what the captain was saying. If they had *one* week of time, there would be as many soldiers in the city. "The window of opportunity we have is incredibly small. If you want to see your daughter again, we need to plan and mobilize *now*, not two weeks from now."

"I told you, we don't have the facilities to hold them all," Captain Miller said. "What would you have me do?"

"Not hold them," Daniel said simply.

"I won't be party to killing them," Captain Miller said. "That's not the way the law works. Every man, no matter how vile, should have his day before the judge."

"We'll take into custody whoever surrenders, but there are always casualties in an assault like this," Raven said. "By the time we're done, there may be enough room for everyone still left alive; otherwise, send the call for reinforcements now. You'll only have to hold them for two weeks."

"I hope as many of them survive as possible so they can be tried for their crimes," Midas said, "but some people always die in war. It can't be helped."

"This isn't war," Captain Miller said forcefully.

"Of course it is," Midas contradicted. "Think about it. The people of this city are afraid for their lives and the lives of their children. The guard isn't strong enough to protect them and the council isn't in control any more. Dexter Silverstone is in charge whether you want to admit it or not. This isn't typical crime to be dealt with in the courts. This is a city under an occupation which can only be defeated by fighting in the streets, metaphorically speaking of course. Have you walked around the city recently and seen the people? This isn't life wrapped up in a nice little bow any more. This is war."

There was a drawn-out silence as The Shadow stared down Captain Miller. The guardsman held their gazes for a long time, but eventually his eyes faltered and dropped. He pulled his sword an inch out of its sheath then let it slide back with a loud clack that broke the heavy silence.

"In war, collateral damage is unavoidable, and innocents are killed," Captain Miller said. "I will not allow war to come to my city."

"Innocents have been killed and collateral damage has occurred already," Raven said vehemently. "Captain, war is in the city whether you want to face the fact or not. The only question now is what you're going to do about it. Are you going to let the city wallow in this undeclared war, or will you do what needs to be done to protect the people?"

"Let's say I agree with you," Captain Miller said. "We don't have the troops to take Mr. Silverstone head on, and we don't have the time to wait for reinforcements. What are we supposed to do?"

"You supply the men, and Raven will supply the strategy," Daniel answered. "We've never worked with so many people before, but with your people and mine together, we'll be unstoppable."

"Beyond that, you have a whole city of people waiting to be freed from this curse," Midas said. "Sure, most of them might not be warriors or soldiers, but if you put pitchforks or even hammers in their hands, you'll have a formidable army."

"Okay," Captain Miller finally conceded. "When do we do it and how?"

"Tomorrow night is when the festivities really kick off, so we'll make our move then," Daniel said, leaning over the table. "We only have your sixty trained soldiers plus the four of us, so we'll have to be careful about how we position each person. Raven, can you start us off telling Captain Miller what we have so far?"

"Sure thing, boss," Raven said. "Okay, Captain. The building only has two doors. There're a lot of windows which could theoretically be broken, but we'll deal with that later. For right now, let's assume the doors are the only way in and out of the structure."

"There's a third way as well, though it'll be handled a bit differently," Leopold seamlessly transitioned from Raven. "A secret passage runs from this room in the center of the building to what looks like a warehouse about a quarter mile east. This will be our main source of entry into Dexter's headquarters."

"Back to the two main doors," Midas took over. "Since most of the people attending this get-together are unaware of the secret passage, when we attack, they'll try to get out either the west or the south entrance. Twelve of your men will be assigned to hold either entrance. The doors are small enough that they should be able to establish a good choke point and prevent anyone from escaping. Even assuming a few casualties, they'll still be able to do their job."

"As I said before, the secret passage will be our main mode of entry into the building," Leopold said. "To begin our plan, fifteen of your men will take and hold the warehouse. This shouldn't be a very hard task since it's largely abandoned. The key here will be making sure no one escapes to tell Dexter. Once this is accomplished, Raven and I will infiltrate the building by way of the passage."

"At the same time, Midas and I will be entering the building through the south entrance," Daniel said. "We have in our possession a stolen invitation to the event as well as costumes to pass ourselves off as the invited guests. Once inside, we'll link up with Raven and Leopold. Midas will move to the roof and be the main source of information as to what's going on inside. We don't want the soldiers to block up the south and west entrances until the people inside are already alerted to our presence. Midas will communicate this and other important things through use of colored sparks on the roof."

"While Midas is getting into position, Leo and I will start to pick people off one by one," Raven said. "While we're whittling down the numbers, Daniel will be collecting as much information as possible and passing it on to Midas."

"Obviously we'll only be able to deal with so many people before someone notices," Leopold said. "When that happens, Midas will signal the attack, and your men will move up to block the building's entrances."

"What about the fifteen who will be guarding the secret passage?" Captain Miller asked.

"Good question," Raven said. "They'll follow Leo and myself by thirty minutes so ideally they should be in Dexter's closet when the attack commences."

"And what about the windows?" Captain Miller asked. "How are we preventing people from escaping through them?"

"The plan is to rally the city's people," Midas answered. "We haven't started this yet since we don't know if Dexter has spies in the city. I have some contacts who will gather an army before the attack begins and use it to create a perimeter surrounding the building. If anyone gets past your men, the villagers will take care of them."

"If the citizen army doesn't materialize, we'll go to plan B," Raven added. "The remaining twenty of your men we haven't assigned yet, the best archers you have, will be positioned in the tallest buildings surrounding Dexter's headquarters. If anyone makes it out alive and runs for it, the wide-open area surrounding the building should provide your marksmen with plenty of time to take them down. The added bonus, of course, is that they'll have good angles on anyone who manages to make it to the roof of the building."

"Wow," Captain Miller said after the rapid-fire barrage of information. "This is a surprisingly thorough plan."

"What did you expect?" Raven asked. "This is what we do, and we're the best at it."

"I'll take your word for it next time," Captain Miller said.

"And I'll pray to God there isn't a next time," Raven responded.

"It looks like this place is secure," Raven said to Leopold. They stood in the center of the empty warehouse while Captain Miller's fifteen guardsmen searched all the cracks and crevices for enemy survivors. The two guards posted there had been ill-equipped but had attacked them nonetheless. Now they lay dead in pools of their own blood where they had been unceremoniously killed.

"Alright, time for part two," Leopold said. "Are you ready to go?"

"Ready as I'll ever be," Raven answered. "So, where's this door to the secret passage?"

"Over there," Leopold answered, pointing and walking toward a plain looking door set into one of the warehouse's many walls.

"It's just a door?" Raven asked incredulously. "It's not hidden or anything."

"It is hidden," Leopold disagreed. "It just happens to be hidden in a warehouse instead of a closet."

"That's a fair point," Raven said.

"Do you have the lantern?" Leopold asked when they reached the door.

"Right here," Raven answered and pulled a small lamp from where it hung on her belt. It was designed with a shutter that could be dropped to prevent any light from escaping. This was ideal for sneaking in pitch black situations when light was necessary but could give you away in a second. Raven lit the lantern and followed Leopold into the pitch-black hole of the secret tunnel. The door thudded shut behind them with a sense of finality. One way or the other, nothing would be the same for this city after what transpired tonight.

"I wanted to talk to you before we started this, and I figured this was as good a place as any," Leopold said after a minute.

"What is it, Leo?" Raven asked. "Don't tell me you've got nerves."

"Of course not," Leopold responded. "It's about this job and all the killing it's turning out to be."

"Come on, Leo," Raven said, exasperation in her voice. "You know we don't have a choice. We're outnumbered with no hope of reinforcements. If we don't move now, we lose the opportunity."

"I know," Leopold agreed. "I knew there would be casualties, and with the changing situation, there will be even more now. I just want to make sure we're doing this the right way for the right reason. I want Dexter to stand trial for what he's done."

Raven sighed inwardly at the statement. Even after everything he knew and everything that had changed, Leopold was still in favor of keeping the scum of the earth alive. Daniel had been right when he said Leopold lacked the ability to do what was necessary. She didn't really hold it against him, but she also didn't understand why he was so insistent.

"There will be casualties as you mentioned, and it's possible Dexter will be one of them," Raven said. "He's stubborn that way."

"I just want to make sure we're not going in to assassinate him," Leopold said.

"I won't kill him if I don't have to," Raven lied. Dexter was the worst of the worst, and she would do whatever was necessary to make sure his journey to hell started here. "Are you happy?"

"I am," Leopold said. "Just wanted to make sure we're on the same page. Now, let's go get some bad guys."

The quarter mile to Dexter's headquarters went by much faster than when Leopold had traversed it the first time in utter darkness. In less than ten minutes they were at the stairs which led to the panel in the closet. Raven extinguished the lantern and stashed it under the first step. She took a position behind Leopold who was listening intently at the wall. A tug on the lever mounted in the stair banister caused the panel to slide open, revealing Mr. Silverstone's private fur coat collection. Leopold stepped through these and silently eased the closet doors open a fraction of an inch. The coast was clear, so he stepped into the room, perking his ears up for sounds of people. A peek through the lattice by the desk confirmed what his ears had determined: the study and sitting area were devoid of life.

Upon closing the secret panel and closet, Leopold and Raven hurried through the sitting area, the adjoining room with the large table, and into the rest of the building. Keeping bowed heads and cowed demeanors, they moved quickly through halls much more crowded and boisterous than the last time Leopold had been here. Blending in was child's play with all the servants, guests, and body guards running every which way. Moving about was easy but picking people off would be difficult. It wasn't anything The Shadow couldn't manage, but it would at least be a challenge.

"Glad to see you two made it," Raven told Midas and Daniel at the predetermined meeting place. "How'd the disguises work?"

"Like a charm," Midas answered. "The guards took one look at the invitation and let us in. They didn't even do a double take of Daniel."

"I have a question, Midas," Leopold said. "I understand why Daniel had to be in disguise, but you were just playing his bodyguard. Why do you have a fake mustache on?"

"Because mustaches are cool, and I can't grow good facial hair," Midas answered immediately.

"Enough of the chit chat, you two," Daniel cut in. "Raven and Leo, you know what your job is. Do what you do. Midas, you're going to move back and forth between inside and the roof. Transfer any information you need to by way of the colored sparks I gave you. I'll meet you here once every half hour to keep you updated on what I've discovered."

"Those sparks are really cool, Daniel," Raven said. "You'll have to show me how they work someday."

"It's magic," Daniel responded with a smile and mystical wave of his hand. "A wizard never reveals his secrets. Alright, let's get this done and don't screw up." He left the gathering.

"You two, stay safe," Midas said. "Like Daniel said, do what you do but remember that no servants or slaves are to be harmed unless they draw weapons on you." After silent acknowledgement from his friends, he moved off in the direction of the roof stairs.

"And then there were two," Raven said, looking at Leopold. "So what's the best way to do this?"

"Kill the bad guys and collect the payment?" Leopold offered.

"Jerk," Raven muttered.

"There's a storeroom near the east wall of the structure," Leopold explained. "Last time I was here, it was full, but I think most of it was supplies for this get-together. It might have some empty space where we could hide bodies."

"Let's go check it out," Raven said.

The next forty-five minutes were as tedious as they were stressful. Raven and Leopold worked their way back and forth across the length and breadth of the building, dispatching Dexter's guards and associates as often as possible and hiding the bodies as best they could. The party which had been boisterous upon their arrival had only increased in debauchery since. The number of intoxicated people continued to rise, though the guards abstained from the drink entirely. Even with alcohol in full effect, the people were still so numerous that chances were few and far between to pick them off, and Leopold and Raven only succeeded in collecting nineteen kills before the alarm was raised.

"Back to the study," Raven said as the sounds of battle ensued.

Leopold nodded, drawing his dagger and short sword. He led the way back toward Dexter's office, unimpeded for the most part. This far into the building, the people were still unsure of what was going on, and the bulk of the guards had already been deployed to the entrances of the building. Suddenly, out of nowhere, five armed men blocked their path. Two of them wore the garb of guards, though who the others were, Leopold had no idea. He lengthened his stride until he was running down the hall at them, both blades tucked to his sides, ready for use but currently out of the way. The attack from the first man was sloppy, and Leopold sidestepped it, sliding his dagger easily across the poor fool's throat as he passed. The next sword he met with crossed blades. Ducking and moving inside the enemy's defenses, he rammed his dagger to the hilt in the man's throat.

The next man was a guard as seen by the armor he wore. Leopold exchanged two sets of blows with him before rolling past and slashing his calf. The man went to his knees with a cry of pain and Leopold finished him with a jab to the neck. Raven was currently locked in combat with the only remaining enemy, the other guard. Leopold stepped in, blocking a swipe with his blade and forcing it up in a wide arc away from the man's body. Raven easily dispatched the man through the gaping hole left in his defenses.

"Raven, Leopold, over here!"

Daniel was back the way they had come, and they hurried to his side. His sword was out and stained with blood, and he bent over, catching his breath.

"Dexter and at least forty of his men are making for the study," Daniel panted.

"Our fifteen will never hold it," Raven said in alarm. "If we hit them from behind, we might be able to sow enough confusion that our people will have a chance."

"Right," Daniel confirmed. "But we need to hurry if we're going to get there in time."

The three took off down the hall, Leopold leading the way. Already the sounds of fighting were audible up ahead, the clash of steel on steel, and the angry and pain-filled shouts of men. He could feel the residual heat lingering in the air of forty sweating men passing through such a confined area. He saw them ahead, forming a wall, all with their backs to him, trying to forge ahead through the city's guardsmen who were resolutely holding their ground. Something small and dark flew past him and skidded down the hall among the feet of Dexter's men. It was one of Daniel's contraptions, a new one from the look of it. It began to spew smoke in all directions throwing Dexter's guards into confusion. Leopold hit their backs with a roar, laying into any exposed flesh he could see, dodging blades, and dancing over the bodies of the fallen.

The smoke quickly filled the hall, obscuring the view of everything which was happening. Leopold adopted a crouched stance to stay below the haze, stabbing at legs and stomachs when they were exposed and simply upending the guards when they were not. With his back pressed to the wall, he found himself tied up in a frantic struggle with a guard. Moments later, Raven put down the enemy from the rear. As the fighting subsided a bit, the members of The Shadow formed a triangle with their backs to the center, taking on whatever shapes accosted them from the rapidly diminishing smoke. Leopold dispatched three more before the fog had cleared enough for them to be able to see. They were in the room just outside the study now, the carnage of the recent skirmish all about them. The shapes of the city guard could just be made out at the edge of the smoke cloud. They had made their stand behind an overturned sofa and, though several of their number had fallen, had managed to quell the tide of enemies. The blood painting their weapons and armor served to make them look like creatures from a nightmare.

"On me!" Daniel called, waving his sword in the air. Hopped up on adrenaline from the battle, the city guards swarmed him, shouting and banging their swords against their shields.

"You, stay here and guard the tunnel," Daniel ordered three of their number. "The rest of you will sweep this entire building. Don't leave a single one of Dexter's men alive!"

With a battle cry, the guards rushed out of the room and down the halls of the building.

"Where to now, Daniel?" Leopold asked. He was somewhat out of breath from the fight but still in condition to continue.

"By now the soldiers at the doors of the house will have breached and will be sweeping the halls," Daniel answered. "The bulk of this job is done. Let's head to the roof to meet up with Midas and get a bird's eye view of the situation."

The halls to the roof stairs looked quite different now than just fifteen minutes previous. Signs of battle, dead and broken bodies, and streaks of blood were everywhere. Groups of the dead indicated where the enemy had attempted to make their stands and trails of them showed where they had been cut down as they retreated. After all Leopold had seen in his life, this didn't even phase him and somewhere deep in his soul, that worried him. The stairs to the roof were no less stained, containing the blood and bodies of dozens who had tried to escape upward only to meet the formidable sword of Leopold's brother.

"Midas, how's the battle going?" Daniel called across the roof to the silhouette standing at the edge of the building.

"There should be a man with a crossbow near the stairs," Midas called back, ignoring the question. "Bring it here quickly."

Leopold snatched the weapon from where it was wedged under the body of its late owner and sprinted with it to his brother. Midas took the weapon and sighted down its length at something on the road. A man on a horse had forced his way through the army of city folk and was making a break for it down the avenue.

Midas exhaled half a breath and held what remained in his lungs for just a moment before pulling the crossbow trigger. The bolt arced through the air, dropping just in time to connect solidly with the rider's back. The man stayed astride the horse for a short distance before slumping sideways and off of it. The horse cantered to a halt shortly after, realizing that it didn't have a rider anymore. Midas hung the crossbow limply at his side, a smile gracing his features.

"Tell me, Leo, could you have made that shot?" he asked smugly. "Remind me again whose job is harder."

Raven stomped through the bodies in Dexter's office, looking at the face of each in turn. The exertion of the recent battle had gotten her blood flowing which made her scar stand out in stark whiteness against her flushed face. She finally stopped by a man and stared at him for a long time. Then, without looking up, she spoke.

"Are you ready to hear the rest of my story, Leo?"

"I'm not sure this is the best time for that," Leopold answered.

"This is the perfect time," Raven told the dead man before her. "This is where it started and ended. This is the perfect setting and I'm ready to talk."

"Alright, then let's hear it," Midas spoke for his brother.

"The last I told Leo, I was an orphan at an orphanage, playing politician at a really young age," she said, quickly catching Midas up. "Thing was, I was about to learn that charisma and intelligence won't get you out of some predicaments. The man who ran the orphanage was an unpleasant individual and one who had, let's just say 'unwholesome' addictions that were expensive to sustain. Luckily for him, he had the perfect source of money."

Raven paused meaningfully.

"One of his friends was a buyer and seller of human livestock," she continued. "Many of the orphans went to be sold off one by one as the trader traveled the realm. I saw some children go to easier jobs, squires or house servants. I also saw others go to much worse. I have no doubt that some of my friends died in the mines they were bought to work. I, myself, didn't sell quickly, which was somewhat of a surprise since I was pretty back then. I didn't have these scars yet."

Raven paused here and self-consciously touched the scars on her face. This was the first time since Leopold had known her that she seemed to care about them.

"You're still beautiful even with the scars," he interjected. "Maybe even because of them."

"Smooth," Midas approved in a low voice.

"Thanks, Leo," Raven acknowledged the compliment. "Anyway, I was one of the last children sold, and I went to an awful lot. They made me take a profession that, well, let's just say parents wouldn't be proud to hear that their daughter was doing. Things continued like that for a while, and I lost track of time. It was all routine for me: do my job, eat, sleep, go to work again. For those of us who were a bit too high spirited, they had a solution. Nightshade can kill a person, but in small enough doses, it just causes paralysis, perfect for slavers trying to control their livestock. With as much trouble as I caused, I was practically on a diet of the stuff.

"Daniel changed it all one day. I was in a room with the head honcho, Dexter as you may have guessed, and some other top people in his business network when a commotion broke out in the corridor outside. It started with a sound like a steel-clad giant's fist knocking on the door followed by the splintering of wood, the clash of steel, and shrieks of men.

"The men in the room with me had thoughts only for themselves and began to leave through the room's windows. Since we were on the second story, some of them injured themselves in the fall, but many got away. Dexter was one of the last to go, but before he could escape, the door caved in and a flood of armed men poured in with Daniel leading the charge. Dexter grabbed me by the throat and held a knife to my eye, threatening to kill me if anyone came closer. The soldiers backed off, but Dexter, spiteful man that he was, slashed me three times across the face before throwing himself out the window. I guess he figured that if he couldn't have me, I wasn't going to keep my looks."

"He was trying to kill you and almost succeeded," Daniel cut in. "You were laid up in bed for almost a week before we were sure you wouldn't die from the wounds he gave you."

"Whatever the case," Raven said, "he survived the jump through the window and escaped to continue his infernal business. Daniel and I have been looking for him ever since."

"For revenge," Leopold stated.

"No, for the sake of the girls he still had and the people whose lives he continued to ruin," Raven corrected. "I hated him for what he did to me, but more than that, I hated that he was allowed to continue to destroy people's lives. Not that it matters now, but I didn't want to take him down for myself but for everyone else."

"You're a better person that I am, Raven," said Leopold, crossing the room to put a hand on her shoulder. "I think I'd want revenge after all you went through, but you didn't. You even agreed to not kill him if you didn't have to. Of course, he ended up dead anyway, but that's not the point."

"Well, what do you think now?" Raven asked, turning to face Leopold finally. "Now that you know about my past, what do you think of me?"

There was a quavering note in her voice as if she might cry at any second. He looked into her eyes and saw something he had never expected from her. Behind her strategies and schemes and beyond her rough and tumble attitude was a girl who was lost and didn't know what to do. She liked Leopold a lot, loved him even, and she didn't think he'd be able to look at her the same way now that this was all out in the open.

"I think I love you even more now than I did before," Leopold said, pulling her into a hug. She lost it then, crying profusely into his shoulder. Midas encircled both of them in his massive arms, holding them tightly. They stood like this for several moments.

"We've got you, Raven," Midas said gently. "You're one of us and we'll always have your back. We'll always love you no matter what. I mean, I don't love you the same way Leopold does or anything and I'm sure Daniel's a little more reserved about the whole thing. I mean, he isn't even over here giving you a hug…"

"Midas, shut up," Leopold said. "You're ruining the moment."

"Am I interrupting something?" Captain Miller's voice came from the doorway. A smile was on his face and he stood straight and tall, his left arm wrapped around a teenage girl.

"The moment's gone," Raven announced. "You two can let me go now."

"I *am* interrupting something, aren't I?" the captain said. "I can come back later if that would be better."

"Not anymore, sir," Raven said as she wiped a stray tear from her face. "What've you got for us?"

"First of all, I'd like to introduce all of you to my daughter, Faith," Captain Miller said. Faith waved shyly. "Darling, this is Leopold, Midas, Raven, and Daniel. They're largely responsible for your rescue. Which reminds me, Midas, the horse of the rider you took down with that crossbow – nice shot, by the way – is yours as far as I'm concerned. I had it taken to the guard stables, so you can pick it up from there whenever you want. Now, as to all of you, I couldn't help but notice how well you handled yourselves in this situation."

"Oh, come on," Midas said with a wave of his hand. "That's just because we're amazing."

"I concur," Captain Miller said. "Which is why I'd like to offer you a job in the guard, if you want it."

"No," Daniel said immediately.

"If guard life isn't your idea of a good time, I'm sure I could also hook you up with something a little more exciting. A job in the army, perhaps?"

"You misunderstand me, sir," Daniel said. "I appreciate your offer of a job very much, but military life isn't for us. I prefer to not be told what to do by someone else."

"That's understandable, sir," Captain Miller said. He turned to the young people. "What about you three? What do you say? Can I interest you in a job?"

There was silence in the room as the three considered what had just been asked of them. Without realizing it, Captain Miller had changed the whole dynamic of the situation. Daniel had always been the uncontested leader of The Shadow, but by failing to acknowledge this, the guardsman had shifted things about. For the first time in his life, Leopold realized that his future was in his own hands. Just like Daniel, he didn't want to let someone else tell him what to do and when to do it. He looked at Midas, practically able to read his brother's mind.

"It would be nice to have a steady paycheck," Leopold said seriously.

"And to always be working for the good guys instead of freelancing," Midas added.

"Plus, I think I've had my fair share of adventure and excitement already," Leopold said. "I could get used to a nice, boring city guard job."

"We'd get to put on uniforms every day and know we're making a difference," Midas agreed. "Now that'd be the life!"

"What my knuckle-headed associates are trying to enunciate," Raven said with a roll of her eyes, "is that while we appreciate the offer, we can't accept."

"I've got no desire to break up the group, so I'll have to decline as well," Leopold said, surprised to find it was the truth. Despite his disagreements with Daniel, he didn't want to leave his friends.

"Then it's got to be a no from me as well," Midas added. "Without me, who would keep them out of trouble?"

"Very well," Captain Miller said amiably. "Keep me in mind, though, if you ever want to settle down. Oh, and go see the citizens before you leave. There's a lot of them who want to thank you, many of them in a substantial fashion."

"Meaning?" Daniel asked.

"Meaning you'll easily be able to resupply for free before you leave this place," Captain Miller answered.

The next day, Evalda arrived with the first of her army and took over what remained of the operation. Those criminals who had survived the attack were cataloged and scheduled to be transported back to Kraljevi for their trials while the others were thrown into a mass grave outside the city walls. Evalda didn't even seem too upset that many of the top-ranking villains, including Dexter, had died in the attack. She simply told The Shadow they had done a good job and gave them their payment, so after a good night's sleep, they left the city.

Leopold reined his horse to a halt and looked behind him at the city receding into the distance. Now that he knew the story, had lived it and helped write it, he understood what the walls around it stood for. They represented the strength of the city, and now that Dexter was gone, they were not a lie anymore. The city was strong once again and was another footnote in the legacy The Shadow was leaving behind, some of it good, some of it bad, but all of it important. One more city free and a lot more gold in their pockets. Could life get any better than this?

Leopold urged his horse forward, following the path Midas and his new horse, Arrow, were blazing across the countryside.

The road would have been easier, of course, but where was the fun in that? Besides, Daniel had decided they would go cross-country so cross-country they would go, because what Leopold had told Captain Miller had been the truth. He had no desire to leave his friends, so as long as they followed Daniel, he would too, for better or for worse.

PART 4

Fire and Stone

No one said anything as The Shadow trudged down the deserted caravan route. The sun beat down on them from overhead, and with no vegetation over two feet tall for miles around, there was no reprieve from the sweltering heat. It was nearing the hottest time of the year, and many of the streams on Daniel's map didn't exist. Even the water had retreated into the earth to escape the sun.

The Shadow had drunk the last of their water hours ago, and they were anxious to find more. At first they had been hopeful, continuing cheerfully and expectantly on their way, but after four dead streams, worry set in accompanied by their thirst. Panic followed soon after, but it gave way to pure exhaustion. Still they trudged on, hoping to God they would find a flowing stream soon.

There was no hiding from the heat, and it did not abate quickly. The sun sailed across the sky as leisurely today as any other day, calloused against the suffering the four individuals beneath it were enduring. They pressed forward across the sand under their feet, silently cursing the day they had set eyes on this desert and praying desperately for water.

The day seemed almost unending, but the sun eventually set, hiding beneath the horizon to the west. As it disappeared, Leopold expected darkness to settle across the whole area, but the darkness didn't come. The stars, simply waiting for the sun to hide its face, shone out in all their glory, and the moon was soon to follow. There were no clouds in the sky to hide even an iota of the heavenly light. The night was almost as bright as the day.

Though the light did not fade with the setting of the sun, the heat certainly did. Almost immediately, as if snuffing a flame, the warmth disappeared from the air, and the cold which took its place was nearly as brutal as the heat had been. Now The Shadow was caught between the cold of the night and the heat still radiating from the sand beneath their feet. It was strange, this sensation Leopold had never before experienced. It confused his body greatly as to whether it should be sweating or shivering, so it did both.

As he staggered along under the weight of his pack, Leopold thought back to the reason they were in this situation. It wasn't his place to blame any member of The Shadow for failure since they succeeded or failed together, but if he were forced to pass judgement, he knew this was Midas's fault. He was the only one who hadn't done his job, and now the horses were gone. With nothing to ride, what should have been a two-day journey had dragged on for four already with no end in sight. On the other hand, the end was already upon them if they didn't find water soon.

The moon was high in the sky when Daniel stopped and motioned for the others to gather around him. No words were uttered, there was no saliva to form the sounds, but with gestures he told Leopold and Midas to dig up a short, barrel-like plant from the ground. The task should have been simple for the brothers but was complicated by the presence of long, sharp spines which covered the entire plant. Nevertheless, they succeeded in freeing it from the dirt and laid it on its side in front of Daniel.

The wizard cut the plant in half with a long knife, revealing the surprisingly moist and pulpy interior flesh which he proceeded to scoop out into a bowl from Raven's pack. He used the blade of the knife to mash the contents of the bowl until it was a thin, soupy mess. He took a swig of the liquid and passed it to Raven. Midas was next, and when the bowl reached Leopold, he didn't even hesitate to suck down some of what remained. It carried an unfamiliar flavor so strong it probably would have caused him to gag and retch if he hadn't been so thirsty. It took several passes around the circle, but eventually their thirst was slaked, at least for the moment, and Daniel motioned them onward.

As the night passed, the sand cooled until, just before dawn, it practically reflected the cold up into their faces. Then, as if stepping from a cold, winter night into a fire warmed house, the sun peeked above the horizon and the heat was back. They continued walking for a few more hours before stopping to sleep. Under the suggestion of Raven, they carved shallow ditches in the sand, crawled into them, and covered themselves with their bedrolls. Though Leopold was skeptical at first, the sand beneath the surface was considerably cooler than that on which they had been walking. His blankets served the dual role of blocking the sun and retaining the cool air, and though the situation was somewhat less than comfortable, it was much better than yesterday's march through the midday sun. He was so exhausted, he fell asleep straightaway.

As he slept, the memory of their last contract played before his mind's eye. The job was simple as was the plan. Daniel was in charge of the distraction, Raven provided over-watch with her bow, Leopold was tasked with doing the job, and Midas was in charge of the horses. Everything had gone off without a hitch. Daniel's diversion, involving fires, colored sparks, and loud noises, was effective if not a bit showy and drew the attention of every guard in the place. It was ridiculously easy for Leopold to get past the simple, wooden pickets, finish the job, and retreat to the rendezvous point where the others had already gathered.

The first thing he noticed as he approached was how strangely quiet it was. When they brought horses, they always had to keep them some distance from their target because of the ruckus they made, but now there was no sound except the occasional crunch of Leopold's boot. Something was wrong. He gave a long, low whistle followed by three short ones and another long one. The response was delivered, and three figures melted out of the shadows.

"There you are," Leopold said in relief. "For a moment there, I thought you had left without me!"

"No, we're still here," Raven said. "The only problem is, the horses aren't."

"What do you mean?" Leopold asked, not comprehending what was going on.

"She means I've managed to let the horses give me the slip," Midas said morosely.

"Then we wait for them to come back and if they don't, find them in the morning," Leopold said, still not seeing what all the fuss was about. "We've had to track down horses before. It's not the end of the world."

"We can't stay here," Daniel said. "Apparently the commotion I caused warranted an investigation. Raven spotted what amounts to a small army leaving the gates just before you got away. If we stay here, they'll find us for sure."

Leopold was about to suggest hiding, but as he looked at his barren surroundings, the ludicrousness of the idea was apparent. Inwardly he cursed himself for not being faster, Midas for losing the horses, and Daniel for insisting on a distraction which was in no way vital to the mission's success. Leopold had told him as much, but the wizard wouldn't listen. It seemed the only person he didn't have reason to be angry with was Raven; in fact, she was the one who had warned them of the search party.

"So what do we do?" Leopold asked.

"We head out," Daniel said simply. "On foot."

"It took us two days to ride across the desert, and now you want us to walk it?" Leopold asked. "We don't have any water skins, food, blankets. How do you expect us to make it alive?"

"Luckily we're not as bad off as you would think," Raven interjected. "Right after you left, Daniel had Midas unload the horses to allow them to roam a little more comfortably. We still have all the supplies, but they're in horse packs."

"Great," Leopold grumbled. "Because horse packs are definitely designed for humans to carry!"

"Later, you can gripe about it until you're blue in the face, but not right now," Daniel said. "The search party is out looking for us as we speak, and we need to put as much distance between us and them as we can. When dawn breaks, they'll be able to spot us from a mile away."

Seeing the logic of Daniel's statement, The Shadow took what they could carry and headed out into the desert.

Leopold awoke with a start, realizing a moment later the bedroll, which had covered him when he went to sleep, had been removed. Midas's face loomed above him as the older boy continued to shake him awake. Leopold batted his brother's hands away and pushed himself to a seated position. He tried to rub the sleep from his eyes, but they were so dry and gritty he only succeeded in irritating them.

The others were packing their gear, so Leopold followed suit. The sun had already set, but the sand was still hot from it and kneeling to roll blankets was uncomfortable. It was only a matter of minutes before The Shadow was packed and ready to move out. Before they began the next leg of their journey, Raven distributed food, of which they had plenty, and the much more precious mashed pulp of another barrel cactus.

They left their make-shift campsite, moving in single file across the seemingly endless desert. Daniel took the lead, his map in one hand and star charts in the other. It was an unusual method of travel on solid ground, a fact which the wizard did not deny. Though star charts were largely used for traversing the sea, he insisted on bringing them into the desert because, as he put it, "The desert is nothing more than a sea of sand and just as difficult to navigate as one of water. Star charts are the easiest way to do it."

This wasn't the first of his idiosyncrasies with which The Shadow had learned to put up. Anyway, at the moment it appeared to be paying dividends. Daniel plunged ahead at an unchecked pace, carving a path across the desert in a confident manner. Of course, any good leader acted with confidence even when they weren't, so as to keep the spirits of their troops high, but Leopold had known the wizard long enough to distinguish between his confidence and bravado. Right now, he was displaying the first.

The Shadow stopped to rest when the moon was high in the sky, and Daniel motioned for them to gather around him as they tried to gum their way through dried meat and tough bread. He laid his map out on the sand, orienting it in accordance with the star chart. When this was accomplished, he had the others get closer so they could hear his rough, raspy voice. Lack of water had not been kind to his vocal cords, and Leopold wondered what would come out of his own mouth if he attempted to speak.

"We are approximately here," Daniel said, tearing off a piece of his bread and dropping it on the map. "As you can see, there isn't much around except this city right here."

The marking indicating a city was located near the edge of the desert, a few miles away from the sloping base of a mountain range. Depending on how accurate the map was, it appeared to be situated on an oasis fed by naturally occurring springs. It also sat in the flow path of a river running off from the mountains.

"I've never been here before," Daniel admitted. "I don't know who rules this place, nor do I have any contacts in the criminal underground, but it's still our best bet. You can see they have dependable water supplies, plus we should be able to trade for or buy more horses. If you don't have any problems with this plan, simply give me a thumbs up. Otherwise, you'll have to speak to let me know what your reservations are."

There were thumbs up all around, so Daniel continued.

"If we keep up the pace we've been moving at, it shouldn't take but another day's worth of walking. That means if we walk straight through the night and into the morning, we should be there before midday. Otherwise, we'll have to set up camp again and make the rest of the trek tomorrow night. I'm personally in favor of continuing into the morning, but this choice affects all of us. Is anyone in favor of stopping before daybreak? If so, raise your hand now."

No one did.

"It's settled then," Daniel said, dusting off his charts and map and rolling them up. "We should see the city by the time the sun rises, so it'll give us some encouragement. For now, we'll just keep plugging along as we have been. I promise, this journey is almost over."

The Shadow rested for another ten minutes before shouldering their packs again and following Daniel across the trackless sand. The mere mention of an end to this miserable experience was a veritable transfusion of energy into their bodies, and their pace moving forward was faster than it had been before. The miles practically flew beneath their boots as all four people continually scanned the horizon for a glimpse of the city. The night dragged on, and as signs of the city continued to evade them, their pace fell with their hopes.

But the desert can play tricks on the vision, especially at night, and it wasn't until the sunrise that the city became visible, much closer than they had expected. It was still several hours away, and they stopped once more to pillage water from a cactus. Nevertheless, their hearts were encouraged, and the pace increased once again. Long before the sun had reached its zenith, they were walking through fields of wheat which gradually turned into vineyards, orchards, and many other types of farms outside the city walls. The shade from the trees was enough to revitalize them. They also saw hundreds of irrigation streams, branching off from the river flowing from the mountains. At the first of these they met, they exchanged what remained of the disgusting, pulpy cactus mush in their bottles and skins for real water.

Filling their bellies with the cool liquid invigorated them, and they pressed on as quickly as ever toward the city gates which were thrown wide. A single contingent of soldiers guarded them, but they were quite lax in their duties. This wasn't unexpected since the only people around were those who worked the fields outside the walls. Any would-be invading armies could be seen coming for miles and in the light of day, there would be plenty of warning against them. Though The Shadow received wary looks from some of the soldiers, the prevailing wisdom seemed to be that four strangers couldn't do much harm to the city, and they were not impeded.

The interior of the city was much different than the ones Leopold had seen in the past. In the desert and with the nearest stone quarry a considerable distance off, most of the buildings were constructed not of stone or even wood. The most common material was animal skins which had been stitched together and propped up with poles of various substances to make shelters. These tents seemed to serve as everything from houses to blacksmith shops and even market stalls. Were it not for the city walls, these people might well have been taken for a tribe of nomads.

The walls were of an unusual design, one Leopold had never encountered before but which made sense given the situation. Stone made up the lowest section of the fortification from the ground to a height of about eight feet. Some sections were built higher, evidence of the ongoing nature of the project. Stone might be hard to come by out here, but it was still ideal for defending a city, and little by little, it was being imported and used. Everywhere the wall was not being assembled, the short stone base was topped with pickets and barricades of wood, bone, animal skin, and whatever other substances made themselves available to these desert dwellers.

"We may have a slight problem," Daniel said. He had moved off to the side of the beaten track and was going through the saddle bags he carried.

"I don't like the sounds of that," Midas said, moving over to the wizard and dumping his bags on the ground. "What's wrong?"

"I can't find any of the money we brought," Daniel answered, his search through the bags becoming more frantic.

"What do you mean you can't find the money?" Raven asked.

"I mean it's not here," Daniel repeated. "Everyone, look through your bags and see if you can find it."

Leopold, Midas, and Raven rummaged through their bags for signs of any coins. Raven realized the futility of the search early on and gave up long before the brothers did.

"It's not going to help to keep looking through the same stuff you've gone through a hundred times already," she finally said.

"I don't understand how you can give up so easily," Leopold shot back. "Don't you realize that without money, we're barely better off here than out in the desert?"

"Probably because we're *still* out in the desert," Midas said. "We've got quite a way to go before we reach the mountains, and then it's still a journey to the next civilized town. We need horses which isn't going to happen without money."

"We can trade for them," Raven suggested.

"Come on, Raven," Leopold said, looking up at her in disbelief at her ludicrous statement. "Taking the sum total of everything we have between the four of us, it probably isn't even enough for a single horse, much less four."

"Hold onto that thought," Daniel said. Something across the street had caught his attention, and he made a beeline for it, so focused on where he was going that he walked directly into the path of an oncoming wagon.

"Watch where you're going, idiot!" the wagon driver yelled as he tried to calm his flustered oxen.

"Where's he going?" Midas asked, watching the wizard stop in front of a large wooden board covered in pieces of parchment.

"It's a signboard," Raven explained. "People who need to hire someone for a given task will often post the jobs there. Checking it out may be our best bet at finding work here."

"I've never heard you mention a signboard before," Leopold said.

"We've never used them in the past since anyone who wanted our services came to us," Raven said. "Of course, desperate times call for desperate measures. It may help us earn enough money to get out of this place and back home."

"I think I found something," Daniel called from the other side of the road, waving a sheet of parchment in the air. This time, he watched for traffic as he dodged his way back to his compatriots.

"Did you find a job?" Raven asked when he was reunited with them.

"Yes," Daniel answered. "It's not exactly the type of work we normally do, but it's at least somewhat up our alley. It pays well, too."

"Enough to buy four horses?" Leopold asked.

"And then some," Daniel said.

"Alright, I'll bite," Midas said. "What's this job? Given that it was posted on a signboard, I can't imagine it caters to our skillset."

"No, but we should still be able to do it easily," Daniel said, turning the handbill so the others could see the writing scrawled across it. "It appears a large beast of some sort has been plaguing the city. They refer to it here as a demon dog, but I imagine it's nothing more than a large wolf. Probably leads a pack which makes it seem more imposing."

"We're going to be simple pest exterminators," Midas said.

"Hey, anything for the money, right?" Daniel said. "I'm sure we can all agree this is the time to live by that motto if there ever was one."

"For once I agree with you on that point," Leopold conceded. "So, who do we go talk to about this?"

"It looks like this problem has gotten a bit out of hand," Daniel answered after scanning the parchment in his hand. "It's the baron himself who's going to pay the reward."

"The baron? Great," Leopold said sarcastically. "I just love castles. Can't wait to be in another one."

The stone castle was certainly an aberration in a city mostly comprised of animal hide tents. It rose five stories above the ground with turrets on each corner continuing to climb for another two. The structure was of an older design than the city wall currently under construction. Though impressive in its own right, it was not of remarkable size when compared to other castles The Shadow had seen. Most likely, it had been intended as a simple outpost for an advance-warning garrison of one of the bordering lands. Now, however, it had been converted to be the seat of power for the surrounding area.

A moat encircled the building, fed by an underwater spring which surfaced inside the courtyard. The constant flow of liquid filled the moat and spilled out of it through half a dozen streams which fed more irrigation ditches of the farms round about. Leopold noted that the flowing nature of the watery defense eliminated the possibility of stagnant algae and festering disease. But in the absence of this deterrent, another had taken its place. The fast pace at which the water moved would make it very difficult to use floating platforms to reach the castle walls.

Unlike the city gates, those of the castle were shut tight, a fact Leopold found interesting. Perhaps the baron feared something he deemed not important enough from which to protect his citizens. Or maybe it was the residents themselves whom he feared. He filed the observation away for later, knowing it could make the difference between helpful or belligerent citizens.

"Halt! Who goes there?"

The question came from the top of the wall, so Daniel inclined his head upward.

"We are travelers," he answered. "On our way through town we noticed this handbill put out by the baron and thought we might be of assistance."

The wizard stood with his head inclined for several moments of silence before a rasping of metal brought his attention back to the gate before him. A small, sliding window had opened, and a pair of suspicious eyes stared through it.

"Step forward and hold up the handbill."

Daniel obeyed the command and moved up to the gate, passing the parchment through the sliding window. It slammed shut, and Daniel stepped back to fall in with the young people again. They stood there, staring at the closed gates for several, long minutes.

"I think we're wasting our time here," Midas finally spoke up. "We could have walked back home in the time it's taking them to do whatever it is they're doing."

Daniel held up his hand for silence.

"They're checking us out over the wall and through peepholes they probably have throughout the gate," he said in a low voice. "Give it a little while longer. They'll admit us eventually."

As if in response to this claim, a small door set into the middle of the right gate swung open and a single, unarmed man stepped through it. By his apparel, he was probably the steward of the castle, appointed by the baron to deal with all matters of this type.

"I understand you are here about the contract out on the demon dog," the steward said in a condescending tone. Though just an employee of the baron, he apparently saw himself as being above the common folk.

"That's correct," Daniel answered shortly. He was unaccustomed to being talked down to, especially by those he saw as his inferiors.

"Then I fail to understand why you are here," the steward said. "Was the posting not clear enough? Come back when you have killed the dog and you'll be paid. It's as simple as that."

"Not so fast, steward," Daniel called after the man who had already turned to reenter the castle. "It's not my habit to do business for a man I have never met. This is a principle which holds for any employer whether of the nobility or not."

The steward turned slowly to face The Shadow. The look on his face said he was both astonished and disgusted by the impertinence of the man standing before him.

"Then I guess you'll just have to find another job," he said haughtily. "Baron Bendel does not wish to be bothered with such menial matters as a contract of this nature. Either complete the task and get paid or don't. Your decision is of little consequence to me."

"The fact that the baron himself has set a reward on this beast tells me something," Daniel said. "If the problem has gotten bad enough to warrant his attention, it must be a serious plague on the city. How do you think he'll take it when he finds out you turned away people who were willing to rid him of the problem?"

"He will never hear about it," the steward answered as he turned to leave a second time. "Your part in this matter ends here."

"I wouldn't be so sure," Daniel said, freezing the steward in his tracks. "I've done work for many very influential people, all of whom are extremely indebted to me. I guarantee you at least one of them has the ear of your master."

"Why are you so intent on this job?" the steward asked. "If you're as connected as you claim, the amount this contract pays would be beneath your notice."

"Suffice it to say the amount is very important to us," Daniel said. "Now get us an audience with your master, or I swear I will not stop until I've ruined your life."

"I'd listen to him," Leopold said. "As much as you may doubt it by looking at him, he's actually quite vindictive."

The steward said nothing for a moment as he considered his options. Finally, he gestured for The Shadow to follow him into the castle courtyard. Upon stepping through the gate door, they were immediately flanked on either side by an entire detachment of guards. Whatever else there was to Baron Bendel, he certainly didn't appear to be a very trusting person. The steward's next words drove this point home.

"You will leave your weapons with the guards here at the gate," he said. "Then you will follow me."

"Very well," Daniel said. He unstrapped his sword and handed it to one of the soldiers. Leopold and Raven followed suit, handing their weapons over without complaint. Midas removed his large, two handed claymore from his back, but didn't let go of it when a soldier moved to take it.

"You take good care of this weapon," he growled, pulling the soldier forward for emphasis. "If I come back and find it has a single scratch on it that I didn't put there…"

"It'll be alright, Midas," Daniel said. "I'm sure they'll take care of our weapons while we're gone."

Midas let go of his sword and gave one last glare at the soldier who held it before turning to follow his friends and the steward further into the castle. A contingent of guards accompanied them inside the central keep and along the few short halls. They stopped in front of large, double doors which, though closed to block the view of what lay inside, obviously led to a room of great importance. Leopold guessed it was the throne room.

"Wait here while I go speak to Baron Bendel," the steward said. "Don't hold your breath. I think he'll have you thrown out like the vermin you are."

The steward disappeared through the large doors, and they boomed shut behind him with an odd finality.

"Nice guy, isn't he?" Midas commented to the guard immediately beside him. The man simply glowered back, so Midas turned to his brother. "What would you say, Leo? On a scale of one to ten."

"I'd say a four," Leopold answered immediately.

"A four?" Midas asked in surprise. "Please, explain."

"To be sure he is an egotistical blowhard who affords only a snobbish demeanor to those whom he deems to be beneath him," Leopold said. "On the other hand, his manners meet the letter of the etiquette law even if they completely miss the intent."

"His manners?" Midas asked. "He's been nothing but rude to us since we arrived."

"Agreed, but he sees us as inferiors," Leopold explained. "Obviously he would treat us poorly. On the other hand, I have no doubt he treats those above him with the utmost respect. This, in my opinion, ranks him at least a two."

"I don't really agree with your assessment of him as a blowhard," Raven said. It was unusual for her to engage in one of these exchanges which essentially amounted to being multi-person rants. "A blowhard is someone who is excessively talkative and boastful. While the steward no doubt meets the second criteria in his actions, he doesn't seem to talk a lot."

"Ah, but wait until you see him around the baron," Leopold said, lifting a finger to underscore his point. "That's when you'll see the talking and groveling begin."

"Okay, so his manners earn him a two, so why did you rank him a four?" Midas asked. "Where did the other two points come from?"

"I don't know," Leopold said with a shrug. "I guess I like his haircut."

"His haircut?" Midas asked in consternation. "How does hair factor into niceness?"

"I don't know," Leopold answered. "Would you be happy if I cut him down to a three instead?"

"Make it a two and a half and we'll call it even," Midas said, extending his hand to shake.

"You do realize he doesn't care what we rank him on the niceness scale, right?" Leopold asked.

"Two and a half," Midas reiterated, his hand still extended.

"Fine, two and a half it is," Leopold said, shaking his brother's hand as if to seal the deal. After this, the brothers turned to face the throne room doors in a silence which reigned for several minutes until it was unexpectedly broken by one of the guards.

"You gave him a two and a half?" he asked in a low voice. "I think I'd give him a one."

"How about a zero?" a guard from the other side of the group said. "Is it possible to give him a zero?"

This question elicited snickers from many of the soldiers.

"That depends," Leopold answered. Apparently the steward wasn't the most popular person in the castle. "If you can provide enough evidence to make me lower my rating, I'll consider it."

"He smells bad most of the time," someone said.

"No good," Leopold responded. "I've known plenty of nobility who have the same condition. Even the king does from time to time."

"Hold on a second there, brother," Midas said. "We're ranking him on a scale of niceness, not one having to do with nobility."

"True," Leopold agreed. "Very well, the point stands. Would anyone else like to make a case?"

"He turns beggars away from the castle gates and throws them in the dungeons sometimes," another of the guards said.

"Wow, that would be cold hearted even for someone as evil as an assassin," Leopold said. "It's pretty damning for a steward. Okay, I'll decrease my rating by a point. Does anyone object to one and a half?"

There was no response for at this exact moment, the doors in front of the group swung open, and the steward stepped through them. The guards pretended to be incredibly alert as they watched The Shadow.

"The baron will see you," the steward said. Though his face remained neutral, his tone indicated he was not happy about the message he had been forced to deliver.

The guards remained outside, and the steward escorted The Shadow through the double doors which shut behind them with a loud bang. A new breed of guard, probably the baron's personal contingent, secured this room at the doors and at stations along the walls. They even guarded the foot of the throne on which Baron Bendel sat. It was a very ornate and comfortable looking throne, a fixture which stood at odds with the room's design. By the look of it, this chamber was probably originally used as a barracks of some sort and had later been converted into the seat of power of this baron's land. Though much time and money had been spent adorning the walls in elaborate tapestries and furnishing the place with expensive pieces, they could not hide the essentially Spartan nature of the room.

"I understand you have come to take care of my problem," Baron Bendel boomed as The Shadow reached the foot of the steps to his throne. They bowed out of respect before Daniel spoke.

"Yes sir, we have," the wizard said. "We were just passing through and noticed you have a varmint problem. Something about a demon dog I understand."

"Indeed," the baron agreed. "The beast has been plaguing my lands for several months now. Chickens, livestock, and pets are all at risk. He's even been known to prey on humans caught outside the city walls after dark.

"Does he strike only at night or during the day as well?" Daniel asked thoughtfully.

"Only at night," the baron answered. "If he comes around during daylight hours, I've never heard of it."

"And does he work alone or with a pack?" Daniel asked.

"I don't know for certain," the baron answered. "I've never personally seen the beast, but some people report seeing him with other dogs while others report he wreaks his carnage alone. I don't know who to believe. If you need more information on him, I would recommend questioning the people of the city. Many of them have firsthand experience."

"Thank you, sir," Daniel said.

"What, no more questions?" the baron asked. "This is usually the part where people like yourselves begin to haggle about the reward amount."

"No, sir, the reward is quite up to our expectations," Daniel said. "I do, however, have one request."

"Of course you do," the baron said. "Well, out with it."

"My associates and I have fallen on a spot of bad luck," Daniel explained. "We have no place to stay and no money to rent a room at the inn."

"And you want me to put you up, is that it?" the baron asked.

"Yes, sir," Daniel answered. For the first time he could remember, Leopold saw Daniel's eyes lower as though intimidated by the man before him.

"I'll do it," the baron said, "but only because of the reputation you have. Many of my allies speak highly of your work. I will warn you, however, that if I am to put you up, I expect results."

"Oh, you needn't worry about that, sir," Daniel answered quickly, lifting his eyes to look up at the baron. "We will rid you of your pest problem or die trying."

"I sincerely hope it's the former," the baron said. "I have no use for dead bodies in my city. Steward, show them to their rooms."

"Right away, your highness," the steward said with a low bow. He gestured for The Shadow to follow him and led them from the room so quickly, the guards barely had time to open the doors for him. As much of a show as this man put on for others, it was evident he was terrified of Baron Bendel.

"Explain to me again how we got stuck doing the legwork while Daniel sits back at the castle and does nothing," Midas said. He, Raven, and Leopold were making the short trip from the castle to the town square, a place where several taverns were located. If there was any place to gather information in a city, it was the tavern.

"He's not doing nothing," Raven argued. "He's questioning the castle staff while we work the populace."

"I still don't understand why he always gets the easier jobs while we're stuck with the harder ones," Midas complained. He touched the handle of his claymore, once again protruding from over his shoulder, glad they had at least been allowed to reclaim their weapons while they were outside the castle.

"Forget your gripes and focus on the job at hand," Leopold said, snapping his fingers in front of his brother's face. "We need information on the demon dog if we're going to take it down. What's our strategy for asking questions?"

"A lot more straightforward than many of our jobs," Raven answered. "The people here need this thing gone more than the baron does. We should each take a different tavern and just start asking people about it. If they think we can help, they'll tell us everything they know."

"I guess you're right," Leopold agreed. "It's not like we're trying to kill their beloved baron or anything. People tend to be a lot more helpful when you're helping them."

"So we divide and conquer. I like it," Midas said. He pointed to the nearest tavern and said, "I claim that one."

"Whatever," Leopold said. "I'll take the far one."

"Meet back at the fountain in the middle of the square," Raven called after the departing boys. "If you take too long, I'm coming in after you."

Leopold waved his acknowledgment as he hurried across the open, cobblestone covered area and opened the door to the tavern. He hadn't realized how dark it had become until the light spilled out across the threshold accompanied by a wave of noise and the somewhat unpleasant smell of bodies. With a grimace at the latter two, he wrinkled his nose slightly and headed inside.

There were a lot of people crowded into the small building, everyone shouting, smiling, and above all, drinking. At least a few tables accommodated various gambling games, some involving cards and others dice. A dart board on one wall provided distraction for some of the patrons who by and large seemed better at drinking than throwing the projectiles. Scanning the room, Leopold decided the barman would be a good place to start and began to force his way through the crowd. Upon reaching the bar, he motioned for the bartender who, after taking care of a few other patrons, came over to see what the boy wanted. Leopold ordered a drink.

"I was actually looking for some information as well," Leopold said as the bartender pulled a stein from under the counter and poured liquid into it from a pitcher.

"Information about what?" the man shouted over the clamber of the tavern.

"About this demon dog which is supposedly terrorizing the city," Leopold answered as the barman turned to stash his pitcher.

"Say again," the bartender said, turning back to face him.

"What can you tell me about the demon dog?!" Leopold yelled.

Apparently everyone inside decided to stop talking simultaneously because Leopold's query blasted across the room, freezing everyone in their tracks. Everyone except the bartender who took a rag from his belt and began to wipe down the counter. Even so, he was suspiciously silent as he avoided eye contact with Leopold.

"Well, let's not have everyone speak at once," Leopold said sarcastically. "I can't understand a word you're saying!"

"The beast is a giant dog of some sort," the bartender said as he continued to wipe down the counter. "Attacks and kills livestock, people, even a traveling soldier from time to time. It's certainly nothing to be trifled with."

"Have you come to rid us of it, then?" one of the tavern patrons asked. "It's been a blight on this land for far too long."

"Yeah, I'm here to help," Leopold answered.

"I'd take care if I were you," someone called. "The beast is likely to think you're just a snack given how big you are! He might not take you as seriously as you might like."

The laughter over the comment quickly turned into regular, loud mouthed conversation, and in no time, the tavern was as loud as ever. Leopold turned back to the bartender who was still wiping down the counter. No matter where he moved, he studiously avoided looking at the boy.

"Do you want to tell me about the dog?" Leopold asked. "I'm afraid what little you've said so far won't be of much help when I try to track it down."

"What do you want to know?" the man asked, finally looking at Leopold.

"Well, several things," Leopold said. "Let's start with where the thing can usually be found. Where have the sightings been, in general?"

"It strikes all over, but it seems to like the farms and fields on the southwest side of the city," the barkeep said, tucking his rag into his belt. "Tends to avoid the city gates, probably because of all the soldiers, light, and torches."

"Torches?" Leopold said. "Do you think it doesn't like fire?"

"It definitely doesn't," the barman answered. "I've heard plenty of stories about people keeping it away from their farms using torches and other sources of fire."

"It doesn't care a lick about fire," the large, slightly tipsy man in front of Midas said. "One poor sap built a ring of fires around his house to keep the thing at bay, but the flames only served to trap the family. I saw the demon dog stomp right through the fire and tear apart everyone in the house."

"So no to the fire," Midas said. "How about common weapons? Pitchforks, swords, spears?"

"They don't do a blasted thing to this monster," the man said. "I think it's ethe…I mean etheri…it's a bloody ghost!"

"If it's a ghost, how did it tear apart a whole family?" Midas asked curiously.

"I don't know," the man answered. "Next time I see it, I'll be sure to ask for you!"

"And approximately how large of a beast is this?" Midas asked.

"Huge," the man answered, blasting Midas with beer-ridden breath. He stood and stretched his arms to indicate the size of the beast. Evidently it was too large for his gestures to capture because he toppled over backwards.

"Don't let my brother tell you tall tales," another man butted into the conversation, helping the fallen fellow back to his seat. "I'm Ian."

"Midas," Midas said and shook the proffered hand. "If he's been embellishing, what's the real story about this creature? Is it actually impervious to fire and conventional weapons?"

"Not at all," Ian answered. "Pitchforks will certainly pierce his hide if you can get close enough. He's just a regular, flesh-and-blood wolf."

"Then what makes him special enough to have a bounty on his head?" Midas asked.

"It's big for a wolf and the leader of a particularly vicious pack," Ian answered. "He's brazen enough to scoff at fire, and the others follow him, sometimes to the death. Several of his followers have been killed, but he seems to find more as quickly as they can be dealt with. It's given rise to the idea that they're invincible."

"I see," Midas said, nodding in understanding.

———†———

"It's a single beast, I swear," the woman before Raven affirmed. She downed a shot glass of something clear in one gulp and slapped it on the bar, indicating to the bartender to refill it.

"Then you've seen it before," Raven concluded.

"To be sure," the woman agreed. She picked up her freshly charged glass and gulped down its contents again.

"When, if you don't mind my asking?" Raven said.

"A little over a week ago," the woman answered, turning to face Raven for the first time since the conversation began. She propped her arm on the bar, inadvertently flexing the substantial muscles in her forearm and shoulder. "I work as a blacksmith which, in this area, means I make a lot of house calls to farmers whose horses have thrown shoes or whatnot.

"Anyway, about a week ago, I took a call late in the day, so it was dark by the time I headed back to the city. Everything was quiet until just before I reached the gates when suddenly, all hell seemed to break loose. A sound so terrible it practically made my ears bleed tore through the night. I hurried around a farmhouse which blocked my view of the gate and laid eyes on a sight I'll never forget. The largest beast I've ever seen was at the city gate, trying to tear through them with its claws. The whole area was illuminated by the guards' campfires and torches, giving me a perfect view of what was happening.

"The gates were closed, but as I watched, the demon managed to wedge his claws into the seams and began to wrestle them back open. Its hide was already peppered with arrows from the gate guards who continued to rain the projectiles down on the thing. They were throwing everything they had against it, but it just kept coming.

"I was scared, but there was only one thing to do. Taking two of my heaviest hammers in my hands, I rushed at the beast, giving as loud of a battle cry as I could. It was so intent on getting into the city it ignored me until I reached it and started bashing away at it. Suddenly, it turned on me and let out the loudest, most terrifying sound I have ever heard. It swatted me away with a paw giving me a scar for my trouble."

At this point, the blacksmith pulled the neck of her shirt down low enough to reveal a nasty looking cut. It was puffy

and had an angry red look about it. Raven noted the semi-cir-
cular shape of the wound and surmised it was actually from a
horseshoe, not this demon dog. She wasn't about to point it
out, though. If this large blacksmith wanted to pretend she had
gone up against the beast rather than hiding from it in terror,
Raven wasn't going to contradict her.

"I must have hit something hard because I blacked out,"
the woman said, straightening her shirt. "When I came to, it
was raining, and the beast was gone."

"Well, I don't see how we're going to track this thing if it's as
elusive as everyone claims," Leopold commented after he had
reunited with his friends at the fountain. "Apparently it doesn't
even make a sound when it hunts."

"I'm going to have to call malarkey on that one," Raven
said. "One woman told me a very convincing story about it
attacking the city gate. Said it made, and I'm quoting here, 'the
loudest, most terrifying sound' she'd ever heard."

"The city gate?" Leopold said. "I was told it favored the
southwest side of the city and avoided the gate like the plague.
Something about it not liking the guards' torches."

"Why are we talking about 'it'?" Midas asked. "I was told
the thing was no more than an overlarge wolf which led a particularly vicious pack."

"Definitely just one creature and apparently indifferent to
fire according to the blacksmith I interviewed," Raven argued.

"I had one person claim it ignored fire and was ethereal
in nature," Midas said. "I mean, he was so tipsy at the time he
couldn't quite get the word out and settled on ghostly instead."

"Why all the contradictions?" Raven wondered aloud. "I
would expect a few of the details to be in dispute, but this is
ridiculous. One person says it avoids fire while another claims
it ignores it. Some people claim it's one wolf while others have
seen a whole pack. We even have some people claiming it attacks the city gates while others say it avoids them like the

plague. Every story is so different, we can't rectify them all. Which one are we to believe?"

"None of them," a voice spoke from the darkness.

Leopold, Raven, and Midas looked around for the source of the statement, but there was no one to be seen. Midas stood from his seat, swung his claymore from his back, and started toward the shadows from which the voice had come. He kept the sword in its sheath but ready to draw at a moment's notice.

"Who said that?" he asked in as imposing a voice as he could muster. "Show yourself or I'm coming after you."

"I'm right here."

This time the voice sounded frightened and urgent. Midas turned towards it to see a pair of empty hands extending from a group of particularly deep shadows.

"Show yourself," Raven demanded, hopping down from the fountain and moving toward the shadows.

"I can't," the voice said. The speaker was male, though from the pitch of his voice either young or very frightened. Perhaps both. "I've taken a huge risk just to tell you what I have so far, and I can't afford for anyone to see my face. If you want me to tell you more, you'll have to come into the shadows with me."

"Who's going to see your face out here?" Raven asked, looking around. "There's no one outdoors at this time of night."

"You can never be too careful," the voice said. "Someone always seems to be watching in this city."

"Fine, we'll humor you," Raven said. "But be warned: if you try to jump us, we have weapons and will strike back."

"I mean you no harm," the voice said. "I just want to talk."

"Very well," Raven called. "We're coming in."

Midas led the way, keeping his weapon in its sheath but always at the ready while Leopold brought up the rear. His hands rested on the hilts of his knife and short sword, almost an act of neutrality to anyone who didn't know how fast he was. Raven strode forward into the shadows, hands not on her weapons, but ready to move quickly if the need arose.

They stepped into the darkness one at a time, taking a moment for their eyes to adjust before continuing. They could now see the person who had spoken to them, a protrusion barely discernable from the shadows of the tent wall behind. The mysterious stranger wore a cloak to mask his features, and Leopold could make out very little at first. After the members of The Shadow were in the alley, the figure looked all around, even moving to the edge of the building to peer out into the square.

"I have information for you," the gravelly voice of an older woman startled Midas, Leopold, and Raven. They whirled about and were just able to make out the shape of a frizzy haired lady making her way toward them with the aid of a walking stick.

"I have information," she repeated. "I do not understand what it means, but I think it may bear ill tidings for you."

"I assume it has to do with the demon dog we've been asking around about," Raven said.

"It does," the woman affirmed. "As my grandson said, you should trust none of the accounts you heard today."

"If we believe none of them, then what are we to do about finding the beast which has plagued this city?" Raven asked.

"The demon dog which you have been contracted to kill is not real," the woman said. "It is a story, though for what purpose it was invented I can only guess."

"Not real," Raven said. "How do you know?"

"The handbill you picked up today and followed to the castle was placed there no more than three days ago by the baron's guards," the woman explained. "At the same time, they went through the city, knocking on every door and telling the folk here about the ruse which was about to happen. People would come through shortly, they said, asking about a beast which was terrorizing the city. Under the penalty of imprisonment or some other punishment, we were instructed to play along when you came through asking. What you heard today was the inventions of a lot of scared citizens."

"If the dog is just a ploy, and we're here under a false pretense, what should we do?" Leopold asked his friends.

"Run," the old lady answered. "I don't know why the baron should wish to lure you into this city, but no good can come of it for you. Get as far from here as possible before the sun rises, and you may have a chance."

"We can't do that," Raven said. "All our supplies are at the castle."

"They aren't worth risking your life for, are they?" the woman asked. "You can follow the river all the way to the mountains from here, so water shouldn't be a problem."

"One of our number is back at the castle," Raven said. "If what you say is true, we would be condemning him to a fate probably worse than death."

"Do what you must," the woman said with a shrug. "I have warned you. Now it is time for you to make your own decision."

"Yes," Midas agreed. "Thank you for your help, ma'am."

"I just wish I could have been of more assistance," the woman said apologetically. "Jason, it's time to go."

The cloaked figure detached itself from the shadows of the wall and hurried to his grandmother's side. She took his arm and allowed him to help her down the alley, turn a corner, and disappear into the night.

"What are we going to do?" Leopold asked when they were alone once more. "If Daniel was here, I'd vote to run like the lady suggested, but I can't see leaving him to the baron."

"What do you think we're going to do, Leo?" Midas asked. "I'm good, but not even I can take on the whole castle guard."

"We may not have to storm the castle," Raven pointed out. "The baron hasn't made a move for us yet. That may hold true until we can get to Daniel and get out together."

"Or it may not," Leopold interjected. "We have to plan for the worst case scenario."

"We can't take weapons in with us," Midas said. "If we go through the front gate, we'll be entering unarmed."

"Do you think you could sneak in, Leo?" Raven asked.

"Of course I can," Leopold answered. "What exactly do you have in mind?"

"Midas and I could give you our weapons and go through the front gate," Raven said. "You can sneak in with the swords and we'll re-arm ourselves once we're inside."

"What will the guards at the gate think when we come back without weapons?" Midas asked. "They know we checked them out when we left."

"The guard shift has changed since we left," Leopold said. "If you tell them you never got the weapons on the way out, they probably won't check. It's quite a production for them to get in and out of the cabinets they stored our stuff in."

"How good do you think our chances are of that succeeding?" Raven asked.

"Pretty good," Leopold replied. "I wouldn't mind doing it if one of you could sneak in with the weapons."

"Good enough for me," Raven said. She unbelted her sword and handed it to Leopold. "I guess I'll have to say goodbye to my bow. The gate guards still have it."

"No use crying over spilt milk," Midas said. He handed his weapon to Leopold and moved out toward the square. "Come on, Raven, let's get this show on the road. The sooner we get in, the sooner we can get away from this place."

"Be there in a second," Raven called after him. She turned back to Leopold, opening her mouth to say something, closing it before any words came out. Finally, she said, "Be careful, Leo."

She leaned in to kiss him on the cheek before heading after Midas.

———————

"You were right about the guards," Midas said when he and Raven met up with Leopold inside the castle walls. "They were more concerned with not having to open the weapons cabinet than anything else."

"And human laziness wins again," Leopold said dryly. He handed Midas and Raven their swords, now wrapped in some sheets of cloth he had lifted from the drying lines of an establishment in the city. "Keep your weapons wrapped and hidden but somewhat easy to get to. You never know when we may have to use them."

"Right-o, brother," Midas agreed, tucking the bundle his claymore made under his arm. "So what's the plan from here?"

"Obviously we have to go into the castle and locate Daniel," Raven said. "Should we use the front door, or is there a less obtrusive way for us to get inside?"

"The front door is our best option," Leopold answered. "I don't know what plans the baron has for this trap of his, but we have no reason to believe he wants to spring it yet. It's better for us to continue as if nothing has changed. With luck, we may be able to hide the fact we know anything until we're already gone."

"Okay, front door it is," Midas said. "Who's going to take the lead?"

"You are," Leopold answered. "You look the most imposing out of all of us, so people are less likely to question you."

"Sounds good," Midas said. His body assumed a slightly stooped posture as though he were getting ready to sneak someplace. "You ready to move out?"

"Only if you can manage to look a little less guilty," Raven answered. "Straighten up and act normal. You're supposed to look big and mean, not like you're trying to sneak into a castle."

Midas corrected his posture and took a few deep breaths.

"Here goes nothing," he muttered under his breath as he stepped out of the shadows into the main thoroughfare and headed straight for the castle gates. It was interesting, Leopold noted, how much his brother was sweating. It wasn't like this was the first time he had infiltrated a castle, but it was the first time he had knowingly walked into a trap.

"High chin and mean face," Leopold whispered to his brother as they approached the doors to the keep.

In the event someone's emotions were impossible to mask, it was better to cover them with a different emotion. Anger would work well in this case. Midas must have done a good job of it because neither of the guards said a thing as he passed. It looked as if they would make a clean entrance when disaster struck.

"I'm going to need to see what you've got there, sweetheart," one of the guards told Raven, moving toward her.

"You'll do nothing of the sort," Midas roared, turning to intercept the guard who was unable to check his progress in time. He bumped face-first into the boy's chest. It was kind of scary to see how Midas measured up to the fully-grown man.

"Actually, I will be seeing what's in it," the guard blustered. He had to tilt his head back to look up at Midas. "It's our job to keep this place safe, and I think her package looks suspicious. In fact, all your packages look suspicious. Why don't you open them all up for me?"

"Not going to happen," Midas said again.

"Don't make me hurt you," the guard said, though now he looked a little worried.

"I would *love* to show you what's inside our bundles," Midas said, obvious sarcasm hanging on every word. "The only problem is, they're for the baron himself, and we have instructions not to let anyone see except for him."

"I wasn't informed of such a delivery," the guard said.

"Probably because you're one of about a hundred other peons guarding this place," Midas retorted. "I can't help it if someone decided you didn't need to know about it, but I'm under strict orders not to show these to anyone but the baron."

"That's a nice story, but it won't fly with me," the guard snapped.

"I don't care," Midas shot back. "I need to get these to him as soon as possible. If you try to stop me, you'll just be a stupid casualty along the way."

"You are not going any further until you show me what's in the packages," the guard said resolutely.

"I'll be glad to wait for your friend there to go get the baron and have him verify my story," Midas said with a grim smile. "On the other hand, I don't think he'll be too pleased about being disturbed. Otherwise, let me pass, but I am not letting you peek inside our delivery."

"We'll do it," the guard threatened. "We'll get the baron."

"Fine," Midas said with a shrug of his shoulders. "It's up to you, it being your funeral and all."

The guard stared at Midas for a few moments, sizing up the situation at hand.

"Time's a-wasting," Midas said, thumping the guard on the head to simulate the passing of the seconds. "The baron wants these soon, and if we're late, I'm going to blame you."

"You're going straight to the baron?" the guard asked. "You won't stop anywhere else along the way?"

"Of course," Midas said. He gave an exaggeratedly low bow. "Whatever you say."

"Get out of here," the guard said, jerking a thumb down the hall.

"Your wish is my command," Midas said in a mocking tone.

Leopold followed Midas down the hall, not letting out the breath he was holding until they had turned a corner and were out of sight. Midas promptly let his shoulders sag a little as though carrying a heavy weight on them. He turned to Leopold who beamed up at him.

"That was awesome!" he congratulated his older brother in a low voice.

"Yeah, Midas, I never knew you had it in you," Raven said. "You can officially bluff with the best of us."

"Good," Midas said. "I was hoping I did alright."

"You did better than alright," Leopold said, clapping him on the shoulder. "Now get us up to Daniel's room."

The trip to the various sleeping chambers on the third floor of the castle was short and uninterrupted. A spiral staircase took them up, and a few turns of the hall later, they stood in front of the doors to their quarters. The baron had assigned the four of them two separate rooms, and Daniel had insisted on having one to himself. It didn't really make sense, but they had long since learned not to question such idiosyncrasies and lack of consideration from the wizard.

"The door is open," Leopold said as he turned the latch and pushed the door in.

"Daniel, are you in here?" Raven called as they stepped across the threshold. "We have new information. It's urgent."

"I don't think he's here," Midas said. "But what's that chest on the table over there?"

Leopold crossed the room to the table and examined the ordinary box. He tried to lift the lid, but it wouldn't raise, no doubt secured by virtue of the large keyhole on the front of the chest. Retrieving two long, slender pieces of metal from one of his pockets, he stuck them into the lock and began to wiggle them about.

"Locked, huh?" Midas asked.

Leopold grunted in response as he continued to work at the lock.

"Where's the box from?" Raven asked the obvious question. "It can't be Daniel's. We didn't bring anything like it in from the desert."

"But if it's not Daniel's then whose?" Midas asked.

"I don't know," Raven said, bowing her head as she paced back and forth. "Let me think."

Midas looked between her and Leopold, one pacing the room while the other continued to scratch away at the lock of the chest. The silence made Midas feel uncomfortable and useless. He was trained to fight enemies he could meet head on and bash with his sword. Not understanding what was going on was not his natural habitat.

"Guys," Raven said, halting dead in her tracks and looking at the brothers. "We need to get out of here *now*!"

"What about Daniel?" Midas asked. "He's in this trap as much as we are, and we need to get him out."

"He's not in the trap, he *set* it!" Raven said.

"I got it!" Leopold called simultaneously.

"Wait, what?!" Midas asked, looking back and forth between his friends.

"I got the lock, but the only thing in the box is black sand," Leopold said. He dipped his hand into the chest and extracted a handful of the stuff, letting it drain from his fist like grains through an hourglass.

"I said we need to get out of here without Daniel," Raven reiterated. "He's the one who led us into this trap."

"What are you saying, Raven?" Leopold asked, looking up for the first time from the black grains in his hand. "How could you know?"

"Because I helped him," Raven answered emphatically. "I didn't know what I was doing, but I'm the one who put us in this city at this time. And that black sand in your hands, Leo. It seems I heard stories about it recently."

"The rumors about the spell book! The one we fought evil men and bug monsters to get!" Midas exclaimed. "Supposedly the witches developed a black sand which could rip apart mountains and destroy castle walls! Do you really think this is it?"

"If it is," Leopold began, "that means..."

"The book isn't actually gone," Raven finished.

"And the last one to have possession of it was Daniel," Leopold said.

"That doesn't make sense," Midas interjected. "Even if he was the last one to have it, we destroyed the book. We all saw it burn, so how could he have the spells from it? Did he copy them down?"

"No," Leopold answered. "A reproduction of the book, not the book itself, was destroyed. I can see it in my mind, the covers of the two. What we destroyed was a passable reproduction but not perfect."

"How can you be sure?" Raven asked. "It was so long ago."

"Do you remember when I told you how I remembered things so well?" Leopold asked. "My memory is like a bunch of pictures dancing through my mind. I see a picture of both books side-by-side in my head, and they are not the same."

"That's bad, very bad," Midas said. "If Daniel took the book, he must have an agenda we don't know about. We've been tricked all along."

"Let's not jump to conclusions," Raven said. "It's possible he simply sold the book to the highest bidder. You know what a miser he is."

"We can't assume that," Midas interjected vehemently. "There's the matter of, as Baron Bendel would put it, our reputation proceeding us. He said his allies spoke highly of us, but how would he know? Clearly he was referring to us being The Shadow, but we were never introduced to him as such."

"And what about the other jobs we've done but were never actually completed?" Leopold continued hastily.

"Such as?" Raven said.

"You know the kid we rescued from castle Rajikline?" Leopold asked.

"Yeah, Benny," Midas answered. "He was the same kid who you were prisoners with a long time ago."

"Do you know who he really is?" Leopold asked. There was silence in response, so he answered his own question. "He's the King's son! And if you'll recall from when we were in Kraljevi, there was an astounding lack of Benny in the castle. He never made it home."

"I don't buy it," Raven said. "What do Benny and the book have in common? Isn't it more likely Benny was an unfortunate casualty somewhere along the way and that Daniel sold the spell book? He spoke of selling it before. Why wouldn't he if he actually switched it out for a fake?"

"Or perhaps 'selling' things was only a way I kept you doing my bidding without letting on what was actually happening."

The three young people spun around to see Daniel standing in the open door to the room. He was smiling though it was an insincere look which graced his face.

"I don't understand," Leopold said slowly. "You mean Benny, the book..."

"Everything," Daniel interrupted. "Everything you did, the contracts you fulfilled were all for me. Granted there were a few which were exactly as they seemed, but that was just to keep you from guessing what was really going on."

"I don't get it," Midas said. "What was really happening? Weren't we making enough money to satisfy your infernal thirst for riches?"

"You really don't know anything, do you?" Daniel laughed. "Money isn't an end, not really. Human nature dictates it is power which motivates people, so money is only as good as the power it can buy."

"And you want the throne," Raven said in sudden revelation. "You've been relegated to nothing more than a fake your entire life and now when you have the means to make a name for yourself, you intend to make use of them."

"I wouldn't put it quite that way, but you've got the right idea," Daniel said with a laugh.

"Then you're going after the king!" Leopold exclaimed.

"No, not right away," Daniel admitted. "He's too strong at the moment with all the support he currently has from his barons. I'll have to do something about it before I go after his head."

"The barons will never side with you," Midas growled. "They aren't traitors."

"You'd be surprised what the promise of riches and power will do to most people," Daniel answered smugly. "Of course, there are those who won't turn on him no matter what, and they'll have to be dealt with more forcefully." He looked at Midas and gave an evil smile. "I think I might start with his niece, Maria, and you know what? There's nothing you can do to stop me."

"Are you sure about that?" Midas asked. "We have you outnumbered three to one. Besides which, I could easily take you out myself." He lumbered across the room toward the wizard who just smiled lazily at him.

"Midas, no!" Leopold shouted, but it was too late. A knife flashed in Daniel's fist, stabbing deep into Midas's stomach. The boy staggered backwards, clutching at the wound as Daniel fled the room and locked the door behind him. He leaned back against the wall, smiling. Extracting some flint and steel from his pocket, he bent down to find the fuse.

If the three young people in the room had been more observant, they would have seen the black cord stretching across the floor to disappear under the door. Then again, this was Daniel's room, so why would they have noticed? It was of no consequence. Once the fuse was lit, it would burn quickly across the room, splitting several times until it reached the bombs of black sand scattered throughout the room. Then those three, troublesome friends would be gone forever.

Daniel lit the black string and watched as it quickly burned under the door. He took several steps down the hall and plugged his ears. He had been careful when he measured the amount of explosive into the boxes, but it was a volatile, ill-known material. In large enough quantities it could take down castles, and the last thing he wanted was to be too close when it went off. A massive shock ran through the stone of the castle followed moments later by smoke boiling out from beneath the door. The wizard smiled to himself. Those irritating children he had worked with for so long were finally gone.

"The sneaky dog!" Midas gasped as he looked in shock at the red spot growing on his shirt.

"It's locked," Raven called as she tried the door knob. "Do you think we can break it down?" She was so distracted that she didn't even notice the cord on the floor burn past her.

Leopold saw it and instantly followed it to the box. If the black sand was actually the explosive which could take down castles, the fire was clearly intended to set it off. If he could cut the cord, he could prevent the fire from reaching the box.

"Raven, open the window!" Leopold yelled even as he drew his knife from the bundle in his hands and slashed the cord well ahead of the sparks. Nothing happened. He tried again with the same result but this time as he brought the knife down he spied some sparkles from the rope. There was metal woven into it, making it impossible to sever. The window was their only hope.

Sheathing the knife, Leopold grabbed his brother and helped him quickly toward the window, ignoring the obvious pain of the larger boy. Raven had the shutters open and was looking back to Leopold for some indication as to what to do next.

"Out!" Leopold said and sent his brother lurching toward the girl. Midas toppled into her, sending them both tumbling out of the window. Leopold was moments behind. The sound of three forms splashing into the moat below was masked by that of the explosion above them, and as they surfaced, they could feel and see bits of stone and wood raining down around them. Truly, the explosive concoction was every bit as volatile as Baron Dietrich had indicated. The current in the moat pulled the three figures downstream as they fought to stay afloat against the weight of their clothes and weapons. Eventually they thrashed their way to the bank and pulled themselves out on it, gasping from the exertion. Luckily, the explosion had blinded the sentries on the wall, temporarily removing their night vision. Even if every one of them were not employed in looking at the flaming remains of the room, they would still not have been able to see the young people scurrying to get as far away from the place as they could.

PART 5

Out of the Shadows

In the bright starlight of the desert, three shadows could be seen blazing a trail as fast as they could go away from Baron Bendel's castle. The smooth, sparkling surface of the river to their left guided them unerringly toward the mountains which bordered the large expanse of sand. Adrenaline fueled their flight, and they made good time as they fled in relative silence.

"We need to stop and take a break," Leopold finally said.

"No time," Midas gasped. The effort of marching was clearly taking its toll on him. "Daniel's going after Maria, and she still thinks he's a friend. We need to get there first and warn her."

"You're not going to do the baroness any good if you never reach her at all," Leopold countered. "You've just been stabbed. We need to take care of it, or you'll die before we get much past the mountains."

"Don't worry about me," Midas waved his brother away. "It's just a scratch. I'll be fine."

"No, you won't," Leopold disagreed. "You've already lost a lot of blood, and not dealing with it now is going to kill you. Raven, back me up on this."

"He's right, Midas," Raven said. "We need to take care of it now, while we still can."

"I'll be fine," Midas began, but Raven silenced him with a raised finger and a stern look.

"Sit down and stop whining like a baby," she said. "The sooner you cooperate, the sooner we can keep moving forward, and the sooner we'll eventually reach Maria's lands."

"Fine," Midas said. His tone might have been sullen if he hadn't sounded so exhausted. "I just don't see why we're wasting time on this when someone is in danger."

"Relax, Midas," Raven said as she rolled up his shirt high enough to expose the wound. "Daniel thinks we're dead and isn't likely to put his plans into action at least until tomorrow. He might have even been talking about the distant future when he said what he did about Maria."

The knife had driven some of the cloth into the hole in Midas's stomach, and though Raven was gentle as she tugged it out, he still inhaled sharply in pain.

"It didn't sound like the distant future when he mentioned it," Midas said. "I got the impression he was close to moving on the crown. That's why he could afford to dust us. We've already done all the heavy lifting for him."

"Will this work for bandages?" Leopold asked, holding forth his undershirt which he had extracted from beneath his outer garments.

"It'll have to do," she answered. "Cut it into strips, take one of them, and go wet it in the river."

Leopold hurried to do as he was told. As he bent over the water, soaking the rag, he caught sight of his face and froze at what he saw. Rarely did he see his own reflection, but this was much different than what he had seen last time. He looked older than before, considerably so with the stubble covering his face, something he had never had to deal with in the past. Soot and small cuts masked his features, giving them the appearance of someone much more intimidating than a sixteen-year-old boy.

For goodness sake! He was barely a young man. How had he managed to see and do everything he had in the past sixteen years? There were old men who had endured less in sixty. It wasn't fair what life had given him. Trouble had been his lot from the day he was born, or at least from the first day he could remember. And now the fate of the kingdom rested on his shoulders and those of his friends. They were just kids for heaven's sake! How were they supposed to stand up under all this?

Leopold slapped the water angrily, and his reflection disappeared from the surface, now turbid with the agitation. He glanced up at the stars above him and suddenly felt very small. With as large as the world was, the multitudes of people who walked the surface, and the number of stars in the sky, how could he, one person, make a difference?

And what about the God Raven had spoken of? Jesus was his name, wasn't it? It was because of him The Shadow had turned to doing good things, so didn't he owe them help in their endeavors? On the other hand, with so many people in the world to oversee, how could he possibly have time to look out for three young adults, practically still children? Leopold wanted to justify the idea of God owing them something, but deep down inside, he couldn't. It was their own sinful ways which had landed them in this line of work and their current predicament, so how could he expect a divine being to care about what happened to them?

In the end, it wasn't from a place of self-proclaimed righteousness but one of complete helplessness which he sent up an appeal to Jesus. It wasn't for himself but for his brother and Maria he was asking this favor, so perhaps God would answer it if only for its unselfish nature. Leopold looked back down into the water and though his reflection hadn't changed, the feeling of hopelessness was gone. This burden wasn't on his shoulders alone nor on those of his friends. Alone, they couldn't accomplish the task set before them, but God could help them succeed.

And if he didn't, they would do their best, no matter the result. After all, what more could a mortal do?

Leopold carried the wet rag to Raven who had finally succeeded in digging a few fragments of cloth from Midas's wound. She cleaned the skin of blood and pressed a wad of cloth to it. Blood soaked the material quickly, but she continued to add more until the bleeding subsided. Taking what remained of the cloth, she bound the wound tightly, rocking back on her heels to examine the final product.

"See, what did I tell you?" Midas asked. "Nothing to worry about, is there? I feel fine. Could walk another hundred miles today if I had to."

He tried to rise to his feet, but his pain flared, forcing him to sink back down onto the ground.

"You're tough, Midas, I'll give you that," Raven observed. "But not even you can walk away from a stabbing unimpeded. You need to rest for a while and recover your strength."

"Fine, but if you want to rest, you're going to do some explaining," Midas said. "Back at the castle you said you knew Daniel had double crossed us because you helped him do it? What did you mean?"

Leopold didn't say anything but perked up his ears at the question. Though earlier he had ignored her statement in favor of the more pressing issue of getting out of the castle alive, the importance of it was not lost on him.

"I didn't know what I was doing," Raven said evasively. "I was a pawn in this as much as you were."

"What exactly did you do?" Midas persisted. "It must have been something pretty significant for you to jump to the conclusion that Daniel was trying to kill us!"

"I'm with Midas on this," Leopold said. "I understand being used as a pawn, I think now we all do, but whatever it is you did, you kept secret from us. Why?"

"Please, don't make me tell you," Raven pleaded. "I thought it was for your own good. I didn't know what he had planned."

"Apparently, because he tried to kill you, too," Midas said. "But I'm not interested in what you thought, I want to know what you did. I need to know if I can still trust you!"

"I made a mistake," Raven said in a cracking voice. She looked imploringly to the younger brother. "Leo, please…"

"I know we've had differences of opinions in the past as to what jobs we were willing to take, but I never figured you to betray your own team," Leopold said stiffly. "I still don't think you would, but you're not making me confident in my trust in you. Just tell us what you did."

"It could mean the end for us," Raven said. Tears were in her eyes, but she kept her voice in check.

"If we can't trust you, it'll mean the end for us anyway," Leopold said. "No relationship can withstand secrets. Just tell us what you did. Get it out in the open."

"I was the one who let the horses go on our last mission," Raven blurted.

"What?!" Leopold exclaimed. "I thought Midas was in charge of them."

"He was, and he did exactly what he should have," Raven said. He put hobbles on them so they couldn't wander off and turned them loose. I cut their restraints and spooked them so they would run away."

"Why?" Midas asked.

"Daniel was always planning on stopping at Baron Bendel's city," Raven answered. "It was a bit out of our way, but by releasing the horses, I gave him a reason to lead us there."

"Why not just tell us?" Leopold demanded. Though he was trying his best to keep his anger in check, it was beginning to flare. Betrayal hurt, especially when it came at the hands of one of his closest friends.

"You and I haven't exactly seen eye to eye for some time when it comes to our work," Raven said defensively. "Daniel said it was for a job, one which you might not agree with one hundred percent."

"And you went along with it?" Leopold asked angrily. "When did you stop caring what Midas and I thought?"

"Since you've lost your ability to do whatever is necessary," Raven shot back.

"You think I can't still do whatever is necessary?" Leopold asked. He was going to add a statement about what made something necessary, but Raven cut him off.

"Yes, I think you lack the ability," she answered. "You proved as much when you refused to let me kill Dexter Silverstone!"

"He's dead," Midas said. "You got what you wanted anyway."

"Yes, he's dead, but *in spite* of you, not with your help!" Raven shouted. "I like you guys, but I can't always be tripping over your idea of what's right and what's wrong!"

"It's because of our ideas of right and wrong that we're on our way to help Maria," Midas said. "Do you not want to do that? Just leave if you want to go!"

"I'm helping Maria because that's what friends do for each other," Raven snarled. "Speaking of which, she needs our help. We should get going."

She jumped to her feet and hurried off into the night, following the river toward the mountains. Leopold helped his brother to his feet, and together they hobbled along after her. Leopold knew Midas didn't need all the help he was giving, but at the moment, with everything falling apart around them, he wanted to feel close to his brother. As they traveled, Midas continued to grumble about Raven until Leopold couldn't take it anymore.

"Please don't be too hard on her," he said. It hadn't taken long for his anger with Raven to evaporate as he began to see things from her perspective. "She's had the hardest time out of all of us."

"Yeah, betraying your friends is quite the ordeal," Midas grumbled. "I'd be exhausted and confused too if I were leading her double life."

"That's not what I mean," Leopold said. "You and I never owed Daniel as much as she did. He saved her life and she's been indebted to him ever since. He's always been there telling her what to do, and she's been doing it. She recognizes right and wrong as well as we do, but she's conflicted because of her duty to Daniel."

"Her duty to him is just an excuse," Midas said.

"You wouldn't understand," Leopold said. "You saved my life once, so I get what she feels. I owe you my life, just like she owes hers to Daniel."

"A fat lot of good it did her in the long run," Midas said. "The mongrel turned on her just as he did on us."

"Which is another reason to go easy on her," Leopold said. "Her world is falling down around her ears right now, and what she thinks is being violently rewritten. She's understandably shaken up and is bound to say things she'll regret later."

"No matter what you say, Leo, the fact remains you're putting a gold coating on a pile of horse manure," Midas said. "It doesn't matter why she did what she did, the real question is: Do you trust her?"

Leopold's silence was more than enough of an answer for Midas.

"That's my point," the older brother said. He shook off Leopold's helping arm and strode ahead.

"You're right," Leopold whispered to no one but the night. "I don't trust her."

As he followed his brother's massive outline, he realized the words he had spoken were true. It didn't matter how much he liked Raven, the fact was, he didn't trust her anymore.

The Shadow arrived in a small, mountain town as the sun was just poking above the horizon. Midas was understandably fatigued by the trip, though not nearly as much as Leopold would have expected. Clearly his brother was made of much hardier stock than even he imagined. A stab wound of any sort was nothing to be taken lightly, and one to the stomach was very painful and often fatal. In contradiction to all these facts, Midas had stood up impressively under the injury and the strenuous exertion immediately following it.

"I'll go see if I can find out anything," he said a bit deliriously as they entered the town limits. "Just point me to the tavern. You know that's where we'll find people willing to talk."

"Really? The tavern this early in the morning?" Raven asked. She reached a hand up toward his forehead. "Are you sure you don't have a fever?"

"I'm fine," Midas growled, swatting her hand away. "The tavern's my best bet. What's yours?"

"Midas, sit down right here," Leopold indicated a survey stone, no doubt marking something of significance. It was nowhere near the center of town, so what it was, Leopold hadn't the slightest idea.

"We need to figure out where we are," the larger boy argued, trying to push past his brother.

"I know we do," Leopold agreed, holding his brother back. Though Midas put on a good show, the ease with which Leopold restrained him showed how much of his strength was gone.

"What you need to do right now is rest," Raven said.

"I do not," Midas retorted. "I'm as strong as ever. Good to go when you are."

"She's right," Leopold interjected. "We'll need you as well rested as possible when we reach our destination. Sit down and take a load off."

"Fine," Midas grumbled when he realized his claims of being well were falling on deaf ears. He sat down, leaned back against the survey marker, and crossed his arms.

"Excellent," Leopold said. "Now Raven, I'll go see about finding out where we are, and you see if you can rustle up some new horses."

"We don't have any money, if you hadn't noticed," Raven said, chasing down Leopold as he walked toward the tavern.

"And are you seriously going to try the tavern for information? No one is going to be there."

"I understand your opinion on the matter," Leopold said. "If you have a better idea, let me hear it." Raven was silent so he continued. "As for horses, see if you can barter for delayed payment. I'm sure Maria will be more than happy to reimburse whoever we get them from."

"And if no one wants to give up their horse for promise of coin?" Raven asked.

"Then we do what we have to do," Leopold said with a sigh. He turned to face Raven. "I don't like the idea of stealing from these people, it looks like they have enough problems already, but this is a matter of life and death."

"Understood," Raven said. "I just wanted to make sure we were on the same page."

Leopold walked the rest of the way to the tavern and threw open the doors. The inn keeper was behind the counter cleaning dishes in a pot of steaming water and looked up to see who was gracing his establishment with their presence.

"Good morning to you," he said. "What can I do for you, young sir?"

"I need to know where I am," Leopold answered, making a beeline for the man. "And no, as much as it may sound like I have, I have not been drinking. Just got lost and need to get my bearings."

"Town's name is Treble Gap," the man said. He spit on the plate in his hands and polished it with a rag.

"Doesn't ring any bells," Leopold said. He leaned on the bar and looked the barkeep right in the eyes. "I need to know how to get to the Mountain Manor. It's Lady Maria's seat of power."

"A lady in a seat of power?" the man behind the counter laughed. "Ruling land is a man's job. Everyone knows the ladies sit beside them only to make them look better!"

"Sir, I don't know how long you've been cooped up in this little town of yours, but clearly things have changed since you last checked," Leopold said. "Do you know any of the barons of the surrounding lands? Who's your ruler?"

"Who can tell?" the bartender asked. "This close to the border of the land of two barons, we keep changing hands back and forth. I could never keep up with who was in charge, so one day I decided to stop wasting my time. My life's been a lot better since I decided I don't care. I just pay taxes to whichever group of soldiers rolls through town."

"Our host there hasn't gotten out much in the last few decades," a patron at one of the many tables scattered about the place said. "I travel a significant amount, though, and may be able to help you out. Where was it you were looking for again?"

"Mountain Manor," Leopold answered, crossing the room to the patron's table. "I'm looking to reach Lady Maria's land."

"I'm actually headed that way myself," the man said. He brushed the greying hair out of his eyes, revealing weathered features. "You're welcome to come along if you'd like."

"Walking?" Leopold asked.

"Heavens no!" the man exclaimed, looking up in surprise. "How would I carry all my wares if I walked? I've got a wagon in the stables around back."

"You're a peddler, then," Leopold said. "I have two friends with me. Would you be able to take us all?"

"I don't see why not," the man answered. "The more the merrier is what I always say."

"And how quickly could you take us there?" Leopold asked. "We're in quite a hurry as it is."

"It's two weeks' journey by cart," the man answered.

"It'll have to do," Leopold muttered to himself. Out loud he said, "Thank you for your offer. Where should my friends and I meet you?"

"After I finish my meal, I'll be heading around back to hook up the old horse and wagon," the man said. "You can meet me out there if you'd like."

"We'll do that, sir," Leopold said, bowing slightly. "Thank you again for your help."

"Think nothing of it," the man said with a wave of his hand. Leopold nodded and hurried outside to where Midas was still sitting against the survey stone. "Come on, big guy. I got us a ride to Maria's castle. All we have to do is get you around the back of the tavern."

"That's good," Midas said. "Suddenly, I don't feel so good. I may need to sleep for a while."

"I should say so," Leopold said with a smile. "You were stabbed just a few hours ago. That puts most people out a lot sooner than the next morning!"

"Yeah, well I ain't most people," Midas said, his words slurring slightly.

"I noticed as much," Leopold managed to get out as he struggled under the ponderous weight of his brother. He staggered forward a few more steps when the weight suddenly lessened, and he looked over to see Raven with Midas's other arm thrown over her shoulders.

"No, I don't need your help," Midas said groggily and tried to push her away.

"Shut up, idiot," Leopold retorted. "You're not getting to the wagon under your own strength, and you're a bit too heavy for just me."

By the time Raven and Leopold got Midas around behind the tavern, the peddler had already hooked his horses up to the wagon and was climbing onto it.

"There you are," he said cheerfully as they came around the corner. "I was beginning to wonder if you were actually going to take me up on my offer."

"Of course," Leopold groaned under Midas's weight. "My brother just happens to be the world's heaviest person, apparently. We had a bit of trouble getting him back here."

"I see," the peddler said. "Well, get him on the back of the cart and we'll be off. One of you can sit up here with me if you like."

Getting Midas onto the cart was easier said than done, and his efforts to speed the process along didn't help. Every time Raven and Leopold almost got him onto the wagon, he would try to pull himself up, end up pushing against something, and sending all three toppling into the dirt. The peddler sat atop his cart, not offering his assistance but waiting patiently until Midas was finally securely situated in the wagon. Raven crawled up to sit in the front with him, and they were off.

The wagon was certainly not the most comfortable Leopold had ever ridden on, or perhaps it was the poor state of the road. The periodic jolts were sometimes bad enough to make the now only semi-conscious Midas cry out in pain. By now sweat was standing out on his forehead, indicating the ill effects of his wound had finally caught up to him. Leopold did his best to ease his brother's discomfort, but in the end there simply wasn't a lot he could do. To block out the groans of pain, he curled up on some of the peddler's softer wares and drifted off into some much needed sleep.

In all, the journey was simultaneously boring and nerve racking. At first there was Midas's condition to worry about. He sweated, groaned, and tossed restlessly in his sleep, but by noon of the second day his fever broke. He was out of the woods in that he was certainly not going to die from his wound, but there was still a long road to recovery. It would be quite a while before he was back to full strength.

After Leopold's concern for his brother had subsided, his thoughts turned to Maria. Though there was a chance Daniel wasn't planning to move against her for some time, it was also possible they had misjudged him. He could be moving against his enemies even now, and they would never know it until they reached Maria's castle. In every town they stopped, Leopold asked for news of unrest in the realm, but many of these places were just as secluded and cut off from current events as the one in which they had met the peddler. They were left with no choice but to wait patiently, trying to mentally prepare for every possible situation they might encounter when they arrived.

Raven and Leopold took turns riding in the front of the wagon with the peddler while the other stayed in the rear with Midas. Though the wounded boy was certainly not much for company, he was still better than the peddler who clearly didn't often have companions on his trips. It seemed he could talk non-stop, spinning yarns and recounting tales too tall to be true. Nevertheless, the stories made the time pass more quickly, so there was always much contention about whose turn it was to sit up front. On other occasions, Leopold and Raven would both sit in the back with Midas, leaving the peddler up front by himself.

"What do you think is going to be waiting for us when we arrive?" Raven asked on one of these occasions. She had just scrambled back over the mound of wares in the cart and took a seat on the back lip of the wagon, allowing the soles of her boots to just scrape the ground as it passed beneath her.

"I don't know," Leopold answered. "Part of me wants to believe Daniel wasn't talking about the near future when he said what he did about Maria, but I can't shake the feeling we're on the brink of war. I just hope we aren't too late to warn her."

"We owe her that at least," Raven agreed. "But what if we get there, warn her, and Daniel still decides to attack? She'd need all the help she could get, but a siege isn't really our natural habitat if you know what I mean."

"I do," Leopold agreed. "We've never been tied to one place for very long, and this probably isn't the time to make huge life changes. On the other hand, if Maria needs help, I have a feeling I know what Midas is going to do."

"I understand how hard of a decision it'll be for you," Raven said.

"Choosing between a person to whom you owe your life and what you think is the best thing to do?" Leopold said, looking at Raven. For the first time since the desert, he noticed how haggard and worn her features had become. "Yeah, I have a feeling you know exactly what it's like."

"Of course, the big difference is the person you look up to isn't hatching a plot to blow you into a hundred tiny pieces," Raven pointed out with a humorless laugh.

"Well, as far as I know," Leopold agreed. He looked back at the sleeping form of Midas. "To be fair, you thought the same thing until just a couple of days ago."

"Fair, or do you mean forgiving?" Raven asked. "Because the fact is, I had a conscience, two of them actually, trying to tell me what I needed to do, and I just wouldn't listen. What happened was my fault. I messed up and we're all paying for it."

"Don't beat yourself up," Leopold said magnanimously. "What's past is past. You can't change it, but you are in control of what happens from here on out."

"What if I can't change the results of the decisions I've already made?" Raven asked.

"I don't believe in a point of no return," Leopold answered after several moments of thought. "Someway, somehow, we can change what's going to happen. The future isn't written in stone."

"But can you and I change it?" Raven asked. "I used to think we were important people who controlled our own destinies, but now I'm beginning to realize we're just cogs in a machine much larger than I ever imagined."

"Mere pawns may be unable to change anything, but I know someone who might be able to," Leopold said, pointing toward the sky. "If Maria's God can't change what's about to happen, He's not worth following, and my faith in everything will be gone. But I think He can do it, and I intend to do whatever I can to help Him."

"He doesn't need our help," Raven said. "Supposedly he's powerful enough to do whatever he wants without our intervention."

"You may be right," Leopold said, nodding. "He may not need my help, but he's going to get it anyway. My hope for the future depends on him, and I intend to give whatever pathetic assistance I can."

"Are you saying you've become religious, Leo?" Raven asked in mock surprise.

"I wouldn't say I have yet, but I want an excuse to," Leopold said.

"That's a big change," Raven said.

"I've followed Daniel, scratch that, I've followed *money* all my life and look what it's done for me," Leopold said, stretching his hands out to indicate their current predicament. "When life chews you up and spits you out, maybe it's time for a change."

"You're right," Raven agreed.

For a while they watched the scenery slowly pass, letting the silence between them grow.

"What about us?" Raven finally asked.

"I don't know," Leopold admitted. He thought carefully before pressing on. "I understand what you did, Raven, I really do, but that doesn't change the facts."

He waited for Raven to ask him what he meant. He half expected her to get defensive, or angry, or sad, but she didn't. She didn't say anything at all, so he continued.

"The fact of the matter is, you betrayed me and Midas. I know Daniel was manipulating you, but you went behind our backs. You thought we somehow weren't worthy of the same information you had. You didn't trust us, and that's what hurts me the most."

"Leo…" Raven stammered at the accusation, but he held up a hand.

"Let me finish. I know you didn't mean for all of this to happen, and I know you're sorry. I forgive you for what happened, but I just don't, I *can't* trust you anymore."

"I don't know what to say," Raven murmured.

"There's nothing you can say," Leopold responded. "I still love you, but my trust in you is gone, and there's nothing you or I can do about it."

"Leo, I promise I would never intentionally hurt you," Raven whispered so her voice wouldn't betray her emotion.

"Trust isn't begged for, nor is it given," Leopold said. "You have to earn someone's trust. Over time, you may earn it back, and I'm willing to give you that chance, but right now, I've lost faith in you."

"I get it, Leo," Raven said. "Thank you for at least giving me the chance to prove myself again."

"Hey, little missy, did you get lost crawling over all my stuff?" the peddler called from the front seat of the wagon, interrupting whatever it was Leopold was about to say.

"I guess that's my cue," he said instead. "Have a good time back here in the peace and quiet."

Raven nodded to him as he crawled back to the front of the wagon. She sat watching the road go by for a long time until a particularly forceful jolt pitched her forward onto the dirt road. She scrambled to her feet and easily chased down the wagon, but as she resumed her seat, this time a bit further from the edge, her mind began to work in a different direction. As thankful as she was to the peddler for letting them hitch a ride, they needed a faster and quieter mode of transport. She got her wish in the town they stopped at when night fell.

"Hey Leo, come over here!"

Leopold looked up from the mug of cider he was nursing, courtesy of the peddler with whom they were traveling. Midas, recently conscious again after his long bout of fever, was as active as ever if not a bit weaker from his wound. He sat amongst a group of farmers who could have undoubtedly been his family. Every single one of them was just as large as he and uglier to boot.

Leopold picked up his mug and headed toward his brother. He didn't know where this was going or what he might be walking into, so his attitude was wary. He scanned the group, picking out the strongest as well as the one who was most likely in charge. They parted to make way for him as he approached, though he did not get the feeling it was out of respect.

"What's going on, Midas?" Leopold asked. "You'd better have a good reason for making me walk all the way from the bar."

"Guys," Midas said, throwing his arm around Leopold's shoulders. "Meet my little brother, Leo. He's the one I was telling you about. What do you think?"

"I think he looks like someone forgot to add the main ingredient when they were making him," the man in charge quipped. "Not much to look at, is there?"

"You just might be underestimating him if you judge simply based on his size," Midas said. "I think he could lay your butt out on the ground. Leo, how long do think it would take to do that?"

Leopold took a swig of his mug as he pretended to size up the man in front of him. He didn't know what was going on or what his brother had in mind; however, it was his experience in these situations that it was best to just play along.

"The count of one hundred and thirty," he finally said, giving the man one last, dismissive look. "I could do it even faster if I were feeling particularly inspired."

"You, take me down?!" the man demanded with a laugh. "In your dreams, little man!"

"The dreams will be yours," Leopold said. When only puzzled looks accosted him, he explained. "They'll be your dreams because you'll be unconscious when I knock you out. Oh, never mind. Wit is lost on the wrong crowd."

"I think he's insulting you, boss," one of the crowd said. "You want us to show him who's the real boss around here?"

"Hold on there, big shot. This is no way for civilized people to behave!" Midas said, rising to his feet and holding out his hands. "Let's place some money on it. I bet my brother here can lay you out by the count of one hundred and thirty."

The man in charge named an amount.

"Deal," Midas said shaking his hand.

"Easy money," Leopold muttered loud enough for every-one to hear.

"Well, how about this?" the man in charge said. "If fighting me is such easy money, how about you take on Joel over there." He pointed to the largest person in the group. "I'll even give you as much time as you need to whoop him!"

There were laughs from around the surrounding crowd which had grown substantially through the course of the con-versation. Clearly Joel was a town champion of sorts.

"I'll lay out your boy for you," Leopold agreed. "I'm raising my price, though. I don't like changes."

The man in charge looked at the people behind him as if to confirm what he had just heard. He turned back to Leopold with a look of condescension.

"You realize by increasing the bet, you'll have to pay more when you lose, right?"

"Double it and you've got yourself a deal," Leopold said.

"Doubled it is," the man said with a shrug. "You ready to kick this upstart's tiny little butt, Joel?"

"You have an interesting way of making money," Leopold said, turning to Midas.

"Oh, come on," his brother said. "You know we need it, and this was the fastest way to get it. They wouldn't have bet if it was me in the fight. Besides, in my condition, I don't know if I could win or not."

"Well, thanks so much for throwing my name in the ring," Leopold said sarcastically. "I enjoy a good fight where the odds are stacked against me."

"Come on, Leo, I saw you in the sword fighting competi-tion," Midas responded. "After what I've seen of you, if you can't put down this country bumpkin, I'll be severely disappointed."

"That'll be the least of your worries," Leopold said. He ro-tated his neck to stretch it, then did the same with his shoul-ders. "If I lose, slab-o-meat over there isn't going to be too hap-py to find out we don't have the coin to pay him."

"I guess you'd better not lose," Midas said.

"And I hope you've got some horses lined up for us to purchase," Leopold said. "We need to get to Maria's as fast as possible. Besides, I don't really want to stick around to see if these people are sore losers or not."

"I've got it sorted out," Midas answered. "You win this fight and we'll be riding out of town an hour from now." He pointed behind Leopold. "Looks like Joel is ready to go. Good luck, brother."

Leopold drew the short sword and knife from the scabbards on his legs and dropped them on Midas's table. He stepped into the ring which the tavern patrons had moved tables to create and walked to the center. Joel was over near the edge, stretching his arms, back, and legs to an extent which Leopold found excessive. By this point, either they were stretched or they weren't.

"Are we going to get on with this, or are you going to stand there all night doing nothing?" Leopold called.

Joel didn't say anything as he continued to stretch, looking meaningfully at Leopold as he took much longer than necessary.

"Boy, if I had known this was going to be a stretching competition, I wouldn't have agreed to it," Leopold taunted. "I was under the impression we were going to fight like men not stretch like…"

The first blow came so quickly, Leopold never saw it. Joel's foot snapped out in a kick, catching Leopold in the chin and sending him spinning into the tables behind him.

"Pretty good kick for a child," Leopold said, rubbing his jaws and trying desperately not to wobble too much on his feet. This guy was a lot faster than he looked, a fact on which Leopold had underestimated him. It wouldn't happen again.

"Pretty good tumble for a little girl," Joel retorted.

"Thanks, I've been practicing," Leopold shot back. The next two blows were slower and more predictable. The combination punch, first left then right, would have been devastating had Joel managed to land either of them. Leopold didn't find the opening he was looking for and simply danced away and backwards, avoiding the fists altogether.

"Leo, we're running on borrowed time as it is," Midas called. "Finish this quickly."

It sounded like Midas was showing a lack of faith in his brother as if Leopold didn't finish this quickly, Joel would certainly defeat him. But Leopold caught the real message. Lady Maria might well already be under fire from Daniel and his allies in which case she would need all the help she could get. The Shadow needed to get horses and get moving to offer her their help as quickly as possible.

Leopold gave a thumbs up to his brother and watched for the next opening. He dodged a few more blows, always sliding backwards and sideways, drawing the fight to the edge of the circle. Joel's blows managed to catch him a few times, and with each successful strike, he became cockier. There was no way the kid in front of him could take him down! Even if he managed to land a blow with his short arms, it was sure to be little more than a tap compared to what Joel was dealing out.

The opening came suddenly as Leopold knew it would, and he was ready for it. Ducking under one of Joel's punches, he shot past him, jabbing him in the ribs for good measure. Stepping off one of the tables at the edge of the ring for height, he jumped onto Joel's back, wrapping one arm around the large man's neck. It took only a split second to position his other arm so he had his opponent in the rear naked choke. His feet dangled above the floor, but he tightened his grip, squeezing as hard as he could with his arms. This was a finishing move, one which could end the fight in a few seconds. All he had to do was hold on.

Joel felt the buzzing in his head as the flow of blood to his brain was cut off. He clawed ineffectually at Leopold's arms for a few seconds before resorting to one last ditch effort. Jumping up and backwards, he directed all his weight down as hard as possible on Leopold. The two bodies hit the floor and for a moment, the breath was driven out of Leopold's lungs. Even as he gasped for air, he squeezed tighter with his arms, knowing he was done for if Joel got loose. The big man flopped about like a dying fish for a few seconds before his body went entirely limp.

Leopold finally allowed himself to relax and take a few, deep breaths. He rolled Joel's unconscious form off of him and stood up, dusting himself off as though the whole thing had been a walk in the park for him.

"Collect your money and let's get out of here," he told Midas as he passed him. I'll be outside with Raven, trying to recover."

True to Midas's word, it was less than an hour before they were on the road, astride new steeds and making good time. Raven, the lead horseman, carried a lantern to illuminate the road while the other two followed closely behind.

"So, how do you feel?" Midas asked Leopold. "Some of those hits you took looked pretty bad."

"Let's just say next time you need money, get it yourself," Leopold responded. "I think I must feel as bad as you, and I didn't get stabbed in the stomach."

"Look at the bright side," Midas said. "We're going to reach Maria a lot faster this way."

"Yeah," Leopold agreed. "The peddler seemed sad to see us go, but there wasn't anything to be done about it. I wish he had taken payment for the assistance he gave us."

"He's old fashioned," Midas said. "I could tell by one look at him. He believes helping people is its own reward."

"My heart wants to agree with him," Leopold said. "Unfortunately, my brain keeps pointing out it seems to just be a thorn in our side which grows with every good deed we do."

The remainder of the trip to Maria's castle was shorter than expected, and on the third day The Shadow rode through the gates of Mountain Manor less than an hour after sunset. Upon recognizing the familiar faces, the gate guards let them pass without a word, and stable boys met them, taking the reins of their horses. They slid off their mounts, looking around at the flurry of activity which was evident throughout the courtyard.

"Captain, what's going on?" Midas called, striding toward the gate guards.

"I thought you of all people would know," the captain answered. "Your colleague arrived not a quarter hour in front of you with some other people in tow. Unsavory characters, if you ask me, but nobody did."

"Daniel's here already?" Raven said. "Where is he?"

"Lady Maria was going to meet them in the throne room," the captain answered. "I would imagine their meeting has already begun."

"I don't know what he's got planned, but you need to shut the gates right now!" Midas said.

"I'm not shutting the gates," the captain said. "There's no reason to do so, and I'll have to answer for why I did."

"If you have any loyalty to Lady Maria, you will shut the gates right away and stay on the lookout," Midas said emphatically. "I'll take full responsibility if she asks what happened."

The urgency in Midas's voice must have convinced the captain because he motioned to his soldiers and the gates began to close.

"What exactly are we preparing for?" he asked Midas.

"I don't know," Midas answered over his shoulder. He was already heading for the keep. "It could be an attack from outside or one from within, so stay vigilant!"

"What of your companions?" Maria asked Daniel.

"I regret to inform you, they are no longer with us," Daniel answered.

"What?!" Maria exclaimed, rising suddenly to her feet. "What are you saying?"

"They met their demise at the hands of a devilishly clever man," Daniel said with false sadness. "It was a weapon we've never seen before, and they stumbled right on top of it. I barely made it out alive myself."

Maria sank back into her chair, the burst of energy now gone.

"I must urge you, your ladyship," Daniel said, putting one foot on the steps to Maria's throne and leaning forward. "I have a hunch whoever did this to my friends is coming for you next. We must move quickly."

The doors at the entrance of the room suddenly slammed open, drawing the attention of every person in the place. Three figures burst into the hall, making for Maria at top speed.

"Don't believe a word he's telling you, Maria!" Midas called. "He can't be trusted."

"I don't believe it," Daniel shouted. "What do I have to do to be rid of you?"

"You," Maria said, glaring at him. "You're the devilishly clever man, aren't you?"

"Yes, but it's not what you think," Daniel said. "What I did, I did for your own protection."

"Whatever he says, it's a lie!" Midas shouted. "He may sound convincing, but if you just give me a chance to explain..."

"They are the notorious criminal group known as The Shadow," Daniel said. Midas, Leopold, and Raven were so surprised, they stopped dead in their tracks.

"Well?" Maria said, looking at Midas. "Tell me it's not true."

"Okay, that part is actually true," Midas said. "But he was the ring leader. You can't trust him!"

"You just admitted to me that you are criminals, so how can I trust you?" Maria asked.

"He tried to kill us because he knew we wouldn't go along with his worst plan," Raven said. "He intends to take control of the throne from the king, and anyone in his way, yourself included, must go to pave the way for the new king."

"That's a lie, your ladyship," Daniel said. "I don't know where they got this idea, perhaps they themselves were going to do as much, but I can assure you, I am not who they say I am."

"The creator and mastermind of The Shadow?" Raven asked. "All three of us will swear to the fact."

"You've already admitted to being criminals, and now you're just trying to take me down with you," Daniel said. "I don't know what plan you've cooked up inside your heads, but it's over. You can't win."

"Our only plan is to save this kingdom and Lady Maria," Midas retorted. "We're willing to do whatever is necessary to make it happen. Get out of our way, or I'll tear your head off with my bare hands!"

"I don't believe you've got the strength left in you after I stabbed you!" Daniel taunted. "Frankly, I'm surprised you're even standing."

"Enough!" Maria bellowed, silencing everyone in the hall. "Guards, take them all into custody. Lock them in the jail so I can question them later. And for God's sake, see to Midas's wound." To Daniel and The Shadow she said, "I can assure you I will get the truth, but it will be on my terms, not yours."

"I don't have time for this," Daniel snarled, hurtling up the stairs to Maria's throne, grabbing the baroness, and putting a knife to her throat. "Take them, and then go open the gates."

For the first time, The Shadow noticed the substantial number of soldiers Daniel had brought with him. Their overlooking of this fact was understandable given these peoples' armor was similar in make and color to Maria's guards. The only real difference was the seals which the breastplates bore. Midas felt something push into his back and, in a move faster than the eye could follow, flipped the man over his knee, took his crossbow, and pointed it at Daniel.

"Let her go or I swear I'll plant this right in your heart," he told the wizard.

"Oh, come on!" Daniel exclaimed, shaking his head in frustration. "What does it take to contain him? He has a gut wound and you can't even take him into custody?"

"Good help is hard to come by these days," Leopold spoke for the first time since entering the hall. "I'd listen to my brother if I were you. I think he's serious."

"He won't shoot," Daniel said. "He's too afraid of hitting the baroness."

His taunt turned to a blood curdling scream of pain as he slumped back in the throne while Maria scurried down the steps. He pulled a dagger from his side and hurled it toward The Shadow. It bounced twice and skittered across the floor to stop at Leopold's feet. It was one of Midas's, no doubt given to Maria as a gift. At the attack, Maria's guards and The Shadow turned on Daniel's men, subduing them with little resistance.

"You idiots!" Daniel yelled. "Someone blow the wall!"

"Raven!" Leopold yelled, pointing to one of Daniel's men running from the hall. He wrestled a bow and quiver of arrows from a downed soldier and tossed them to her. She caught them and slung the quiver over her shoulder as she sprinted to the door of the hall. Drawing an arrow, she placed it on her bow string and pulled to full draw. Out of the corner of her eye, she saw Leopold dash past her as she released the arrow. It was high, sailing harmlessly over the fleeing man's head. In a moment, she had another on the string and was aiming again. This one was low, but it caught him in the calf, tripping him up and throwing him to the ground.

Leopold was on top of the fallen man before he could react, laying him dead with a slash of his knife. After the deed was done, he rose slowly to his feet, shaking his head at what had almost happened. When Daniel had said to blow the wall, he had obviously been referring to the use of his black sand. The effect of such a weapon on Maria's wall would have been devastating.

A flash of light near the wall caught Leopold's attention and he looked long enough to recognize what was happening.

An oath burst from his lips as he threw his hands over his head just in time for the shockwave of the explosion to slam into his body, hurtling him through the air to land painfully on his side. Dust and stone rained down around him, so he kept his head tucked beneath his arms.

"On your feet, Leo!"

Midas pulled his brother up and pointed to a hole in the wall gaping at least ten feet wide. His claymore was already free of its sheath as he rushed across the ground to take up a defensive position in the hole. Leopold staggered forward to join his brother, aware his dagger was nowhere to be found. Drawing his short sword, he took up a position on Midas's left and saw one of the worst sights of his entire life. An army, nowhere to be seen when The Shadow had arrived at the castle, was now rushing across the ground toward the newly opened entrance.

"Hold this position," Midas shouted to his brother over the sound of battle cries. "If we fall, the whole castle goes with us!"

Leopold didn't say anything but gripped his sword a little tighter in his fist. He looked sideways and noticed a dagger still on his brother's belt. Taking it with his left hand, he pulled both weapons in front of his body in a ready stance. The leading soldier took an arrow to the chest, and then the press was upon them. Leopold ducked and weaved, slashing and stabbing at any opening in the enemies' armor he could find while beside him, Midas swung his sword with a vengeance. Sometimes he found the opening in the armor, but sometimes he simply swung it into helmets and shields with such force as to cleave the metal in two.

With the pace and ferocity of the fighting, it was only a matter of time before the bodies began to pile up in the hole, creating a makeshift wall. By now, Maria's soldiers were arriving to fight alongside the brothers. They used polearms to stab at the enemies trying to climb over the pile of bodies while archers now posted on the walls poured arrows into the army outside. For another quarter hour, the frantic fighting continued, but now the tide was turned against the attackers. The element of surprise was gone, and they were not prepared for a long, drawn-out siege of Mountain Manor. It wasn't long before they realized their window of opportunity had vanished and retreated to the distant trees to hide themselves from the archers.

Leopold stood beside Midas and Raven in Maria's throne room. They had been stripped of their weapons and were constantly guarded by two armed soldiers, but their treatment otherwise had been remarkably civil. This was the moment of truth. As she stared down at them from her chair on the raised dais, Leopold could only wonder whether she believed their story or if they were all headed for a deep, dark dungeon someplace. There was a shuffling on the throne, and he looked up to see Maria adjust her dress before speaking.

"You lied to me," she said and waited for a response.

"You're right," Raven said after a long, drawn out silence. "It was a lie of omission because when we met for the first time, it was under less than favorable circumstances."

"Explain," Maria commanded.

"You're no one's fool," Raven said. "I know you've put two and two together and figured out we were the ones hired to kill the horse and start the war the first time we met." She paused, looking at Midas and Leopold before continuing. "If we had told you what we were really here for, I guarantee our first conversation would have gone very differently than it did. We would have ended up in a dungeon, the horse would have been killed one way or the other, and the war would have started anyway. We couldn't stop what was going to happen from inside a jail cell, so we didn't tell you who we were."

"And after?" Maria asked.

Raven said nothing, so Midas took over.

"We didn't even know how you'd react to the news afterwards. Once you thought we were good guys and then found out we weren't," he searched for the right words before continuing. "Let's just say I couldn't stand the idea of the look on your face. Kind of like the one you're giving us now."

"So you decided it was better to keep lying to me?" Maria asked. Choking back a sob, she added, "Even you, Midas?"

"Maria," Raven said. "Our slates are not clean, and our sins are many, but we're just kids. We didn't know any better and were led down a bad path. It's not an excuse for our actions, I just hope it counts for something."

"Besides which," Leopold spoke, stepping forward of the others, "ever since meeting you, everything we've done has been for you. We can't erase our pasts, but don't blame Raven and don't blame Midas. They're just trying to do the best they can with the hand they've been dealt."

"And you?" Maria asked.

"Don't worry about me," Leopold answered. "I'll be fine on my own, always have been, but they look up to you. A lot. I don't know what they'd do without someone like you for a role model. Don't condemn their lives for the sins of their youth."

"It was a very brave thing you did for me," Maria admitted. She sat in thought for several moments before speaking again. "I understand what you're saying, Leo, but I'm afraid I just can't do what you're asking."

"Please, I'm begging you," Leopold said, getting down on his knees. "Punish me but don't do this to them."

"What are you doing?" Midas whispered. "Get up off your knees."

"Shut up, brother," Leopold responded. "I'm doing this for you."

"Again, I understand the argument you've put forward, but I'm afraid I can't accept it," Maria said sadly.

"I understand," Leopold said, rising to his feet. "After what we've done, you have every right to hate us."

"I don't hate you," Maria said. "I owe you my life, but I'm just not crazy enough to trust a group of criminals."

Just not crazy.

The words bounced through Leopold's brain, landing smack in the middle of a scene he had played many times in his head. He was on the shore again, snow covered mountains behind and sparkling ocean in front.

"What's the matter? Are you chicken?" he asked, looking back at his sister. He could see her face this time, and it was definitely a younger version of Baroness Maria.

"Not chicken, just not crazy," young Maria answered. The shock of the sudden realization froze the image in place, burning it into Leopold's mind. Maria was his sister? He was nobility? It couldn't be, and yet, what else could the memories mean?

"I hereby banish you from my lands," Maria said, though her lips remained as frozen as the rest of the scene. Leopold shook his head, wiping away the image. He was back in the throne room again, and Maria had risen from her seat. "Do not show your faces in them again, or you will be punished."

"Understood," Raven said. Her voice was even but her countenance was downcast as was Midas's. Maria's castle was as close to a home as they had ever known, and it was killing them to know they could never come back. They turned and left quickly, but Leopold stayed where he was.

"Did you not hear me, Leopold?" Maria used his full name, something she hadn't done in a long time.

Rather than leave, Leopold moved toward the throne. The guards which had remained when Midas and Raven left, moved to restrain him, but Maria held up a hand to stop them. Leopold stopped mere feet from Maria, and as she looked into his eyes, she saw a sadness much greater than she had expected. What she witnessed was a pain so deep she could only remember feeling it once, when she had first learned of the deaths of her parents.

"I heard what you said, Baroness," he replied. His voice carried strength, but his words were rushed as if he didn't get them out now, he would never be able to say them. "Your pronouncement of banishment is just, so I will leave and never return; however, since this is the last time we'll ever see each other, I need..."

Leopold's words faltered, the power gone from his voice. He looked lost, like a young child, unsure of himself and unable to continue. He started to leave, but Maria stopped him.

"What do you need?" she asked. Leopold turned to back to her.

"Your crest, the flying Pegasus, I've seen it before," he replied. "I remember it from before I first met you."

"It's been the crest of my family for generations. You could have seen it anywhere," Maria replied. It was a reasonable explanation of the sudden revelation, but somehow it didn't ring true. Leopold was clever enough that he would not have assigned a mere memory such importance without due cause.

"Yes, I'm sure I've seen it a hundred other places, but the first time it was on a rattle," Leopold revealed. "A rattle I had as a baby."

"What are you saying?" Maria asked. Though her brain knew what he was implying, the shock of it rendered her incapable of connecting the dots. She could feel nothing but a numb detachedness from reality.

"You had a brother once," Leopold explained, driving the point home. "He was stolen from you and your parents while he was still very young." When Maria remained silent, he continued. "I know that time, the ways I've changed, my scars probably make it difficult for you to see the resemblance of who I used to be, but it's true, and I can prove it. Your brother's name, my name, used to be Jacob."

The revelation did not bring the reaction Leopold had expected.

"My brother's name was well known when he was still alive," Maria declared, her voice hard. "Unless you produce any proof, something only my brother would know, I have no choice but to disregard what you are saying."

Leopold said nothing, and Maria continued.

"I'm disappointed that you would try and lie to me again," she said. "Criminal though you be, I thought I had earned more of your respect than that."

"Until this moment, my memories have been inaccessible to me, but now that they flood my mind, it's difficult to determine which I should use as proof of my identity," Leopold explained his silence. "Is it mother's favorite broach, a swan, or was that public knowledge as well? How about riding lessons with father, or how scratchy his beard was when he hugged me. Or that your favorite food as a child was fresh bread, or that you hated blueberries. Or perhaps you would believe me if I mentioned the beach we visited every year. You'd tell me it was too cold because I always wanted to go swimming, even when the melting snow was running off into the lake. And one time, you pushed me into the water. Of course, that's all information I could have probably gotten one way or another, but there's one thing only you and I would know. The hollow wall between our rooms as children. We used to tap messages back and forth at night when we should have been asleep."

Leopold waited to see if his words would have an effect, but Maria remained motionless. Though her face was as stoic as ever, she seemed to avoid Leopold's eyes.

"I see you've made up your mind to not believe me," he finally said sadly. "I guess this is it. Goodbye, Maria."

Midas and Raven left Maria's keep and headed for the stables located across the courtyard. The sun was in the last few minutes before it would dip below the horizon and threw its final rays on the castle. As if attuned to the situation at hand, the dying light cast long shadows ominously across the courtyard. Everywhere, Maria's soldiers stood at the ready, manning the walls, the towers, and the grounds. Daniel had vanished along with his army at the conclusion of the fighting, but whether they would return was uncertain. No matter the case, Maria's soldiers would not be caught unawares tonight.

The inside of the stables was protected as well, but this time Midas got the impression it was being guarded against them, not some external enemy. A small squad of soldiers barred their way to the interior of the structure while a young lad handed them the reins to their horses. Midas took his own as well as Leopold's.

"I'm sorry things turned out this way," the squad commander intoned sincerely. "We know you're the reason we were not overrun today and don't know why you've been banished."

If they didn't know, it could only mean one thing. Maria had spared them the indignity of being declared The Shadow, and the common soldiers knew nothing of it. Of course, those who had been in the throne room had heard, and word would spread quickly, but they could at least leave without the reproachful looks of those betrayed.

"You are lucky to have a ruler as good as Lady Maria," Midas answered the officer. "You may not understand her actions now, but trust that she has the good of her people at heart."

"Whatever you say, sir," the officer replied. "We have taken the liberty of stocking your saddlebags with supplies, and you will also find your weapons there. You may be banished from this land, but as far as I'm concerned, you deserve a good turn for the help you have given to us."

"Thank you," Raven said. "We won't forget it."

"Good luck," the officer replied and raised his hand in salute to the two exiles before him. To a man, his soldiers followed suit. Midas quickly returned the symbol of respect as did Raven a moment later.

"We should go now," Midas murmured, and without any more ado, they led the horses out of the stable.

"Where are we off to now?" Raven asked. "And where in heaven's name is Leo? I thought he was right behind us?"

"Just as well that he's missing because I don't want him here for this part," Midas said, turning to face Raven fully.

"What do you mean?" Raven asked.

252

"I don't think there can be any more 'we'," Midas answered. "At least, not one that includes you."

Raven was silent as her brain processed the comment. It wasn't unexpected per se, but it hurt more than she could express, and the pain impeded her uptake.

"You betrayed Leo and me, and I can't trust you anymore," Midas continued.

"Are you saying you don't want me around anymore?" Raven asked, her voice quavering ever so slightly.

"No," Midas replied, voice even but eyes full of sorrow. "I want you around more than ever, but I don't think it's the right decision, not for me and not for Leo."

"And what about him?" Raven asked, anger rising in her voice. "Shouldn't he get a choice in the matter? Why don't we wait until he arrives and ask him for his opinion?"

"He loves you more than life itself," Midas replied. "If we ask him, we both know what he'll say. But will that decision be what's best for him? You tell me. I won't make you go or stay."

Midas's words, simple yet full of insight, crashed down on her like a pile of bricks. In that moment she hated him, but only because she saw the truth of his words. Given the choice, Leopold would vote to keep her around, but what would that do to him? His faith in and love for her had already almost killed him once. For him, to be with her would mean ignoring what reason told him, something she knew he would do in a heartbeat but which would also destroy him. If he couldn't trust his mind over his heart, what would that mean for his future? She could never, would never, put him in a situation asking him to cast aside reason for her.

"It's better if I go, before he comes out," she told Midas as she wiped a single tear from her eye. "You're right. He won't make the right decision, so I need to make it for him."

Facing her horse so Midas wouldn't see the tears falling down her cheeks, she pulled herself into the saddle and urged the beast toward the gates. In a clatter of hooves across cobblestones, she was gone.

"Well, boy," Midas said to his horse, but he couldn't get the rest of the words out. Silent he could keep his emotions in check, but if he were to speak, he would become a blubbering mess. At the moment, he needed be strong for Leopold.

"Well, I guess all good things must come to an end, right brother?"

Leopold's voice brought Midas back to reality, and he shook his head, wondering how long he had been standing there, lost in thought. He gave his brother a thin smile, desperately hoping the sadness didn't show through too much.

"Things could be worse," Leopold said, taking the reins of his horse from Midas. His eyes betrayed the bravery of his words. "We survived before meeting Maria, and we'll figure out how to do it again."

"Yes, we will, little brother," Midas lied. "Just you and me versus the world."

"Where's Raven?" Leopold asked, finally noting her absence. His eyes quickly scanned the courtyard before coming to rest once again on Midas.

"She's gone," the older boy said simply.

"What?!" Leopold exclaimed. "Why?"

"Given the recent past, she thought it best to part ways with us," Midas answered woodenly.

"And you didn't stop her?" Leopold demanded. After a closer look at Midas he exclaimed, "You agreed with her!"

Midas shrugged helplessly and watched as Leopold scrambled onto his horse. With a look back at Midas, he urged his steed forward.

"Where are you going?" Midas called.

"To chase down Raven!" Leopold shouted back and with the noisy clatter of galloping horse's hooves, he was gone.

The statement was simple, but Midas had known Leopold long enough to be able to read the subtext. His younger brother was angry with him and while Leopold would eventually get over it, there was no telling how long it would take. And that was assuming Midas had been right in running Raven off, because in the pit of his stomach, he had a sinking feeling that however justified the act had been, it was not what he should have done. He began to shake uncontrollably and was forced to cling to his horse for support. Uncertainty and failure were not new emotions for him, but the hopelessness which accompanied them was nerve-wracking.

With time, the pain slowly receded to numbness, and the shaking stopped. The sadness was replaced by an empty, aching void and the feeling of being lost, of not knowing what to do next. One thing was for certain; he couldn't remain at Maria's castle, so he mounted his horse. As he was situating himself in the saddle, a guard rushed out of the castle, casting his eyes quickly around the courtyard. Seeing Midas, he made straight for him, panting when he arrived.

"The younger boy, Leopold, where is he?" he asked. "The baroness wishes him brought back to the throne room."

"Good luck with that," Midas said. "He's already got a head start on you and was moving pretty quickly when he left."

"What about you, sir?" the guard asked. "Surely you know where he's heading."

"I don't know where he's going," Midas answered emotionlessly. "I don't even know what I'm going to do, but I know I can't stay here."

He tapped his heels against his horse's sides and cantered away, slowly leaving first the guard and then the castle behind. A hundred yards past the gates, he turned around and looked back at Maria's castle. He remembered arriving here the first time and how different things were back then. He'd had his friends, they still believed in Daniel, and The Shadow had been at the height of its power. But now, The Shadow was truly broken. Scratch that. It had always been broken, but now it was demolished, disbanded forever, no more to plague the realm or to help those who needed it most.

With a heavy heart, Midas continued on his way, allowing his horse to choose its own pace. Speed wasn't of the essence because it was a waiting game now. Leopold would look for Raven, but since she didn't want to be found, he wouldn't find her. And when he was finished looking, Midas would be there to look after him. Just the two of them against the world as it was always meant to be.

Note from the Author

Thank you for investing your time to read my story. It is a great honor for you to share in my creative visions, and I hope you enjoyed reading as much as I did creating! If you enjoyed this book, I would greatly appreciate it if you would look up the ISBN 9781949711028 on Amazon and Goodreads and leave an honest review. Even if you were not a fan, I would love to get your feedback so that I can make the next book better. Thank you for providing me the reason and means to improve my writing each and every time. Thanks. Peter M. Last.

About the Author

Peter Last was very nearly born in an elevator and has continued to be unconventional ever since. He is the sixth child in a large family but, despite having been homeschooled from kindergarten until twelfth grade, has an expansive social life and has never been locked in a closet. He began writing his first novel, *Guardians of Magessa*, at the age of eleven, receiving great encouragement from his family in the form of compliments such as "Your book is actually not that bad!"

After earning his degree in Civil Engineering and commission in the United States military, he is now serving in the US Air Force, protecting the nation from its enemies, termites, and HVAC outages. In the little spare time he has, Peter writes a blog (peterlast.blogspot.com) where he posts short stories, reviews books and movies, and addresses a mixture of serious and absurd topics, from global warming to pencil sharpeners. Peter's other hobbies include drawing, dabbling in amateur film directing, and discharging powerful firearms at shooting ranges. At present, he is busy finishing up *In the Service of the King*, the third and final book in his *Shadow for Hire* series.

Follow Peter Last:

- bwpublications.com/authors/peter-last/
- Facebook: on.fb.me/1JMJXsY
- Twitter: twitter.com/PeterMLast

Follow Bluewater Publications:

- bwpublications.com
- Facebook: bit.ly/2Tx7wDA
- Twitter: twitter.com/bwpublications

Read more from *Shadow for Hire*

Wages of Death
Shadow for Hire Book I
ISBN 9781934610183

In the Service of the King
Shadow for Hire Book III
ISBN 9781949711103
Coming Spring 2020

Also by Peter Last

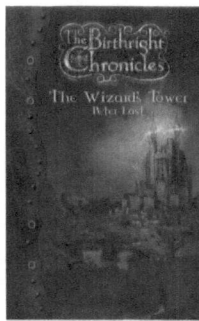

Guardians of Magessa
The Birthright Chronicles
Book I
ISBN 978-1-934610-88-6

The Wizard's Tower
The Birthright Chronicles
Book II
ISBN 978-1-934610-89-3

The Dragon Warrior
The Birthright Chronicles
Book III
ISBN 978-1-934610-90-9